WEREWOLVES OF BRISTOL MANOR

WEREWOLVES OF MANOR
BRISTOL

BOOK ONE IN THE CHRONICLES OF CRISPIN LIPTON

ADAM ZAYNE WHITENER

ISBN: 978-1-7368183-1-2 (Paperback)
ISBN: 978-1-7368183-2-9 (Hardcover)

Library of Congress Control Number: 2021939706

Any references to historical events, real people, or real places are used fictitiously. Names, characters, and places are products of the author's imagination.

Book design by Allison Chernutan.

Printed in the United States of America.

First printing edition 2021.

emily@fracturedmirrorpublishing.com
Fractured Mirror Publishing
Knoxville, Tennessee

www.fracturedmirrorpublishing.com

To Chris Colfer.
You've inspired me more than words can describe, and have helped me through everything from writer's block to heartache. This book wouldn't exist without you and the magical world you created.

CHAPTER ONE

I didn't want to die. Being only fifteen, I knew I hadn't experienced much. My life was dull and sometimes just plain miserable, but I didn't want to die. Though, it looked like I was going to anyway.

I was lying in the grass, in a puddle of my own my blood, waiting for death. Then I heard a voice, which startled me out of my thoughts. "Get up," he said. I couldn't see him in the darkness. Just his silhouette standing between the trees. I forced myself to sit up and winced. Searing pain shot through my stomach, and I placed a shaky hand over the wound. "It will heal," said the stranger. "Just apply pressure."

"Who are you?" I asked, my voice quivering. The air was freezing. I couldn't stop myself from shivering, though it was partly out of fear and pain. Was the man going to help me? Hurt me? Leave me for dead? "Who are you?!" I repeated, louder this time.

The man didn't respond. He simply turned and walked away, his footsteps hardly making a sound.

Still trembling, I collapsed back onto the ground where I waited for the pain to subside. The grass was damp, and sent a shiver down my spine. *It will heal,* the stranger had said. "Not if I die first," I muttered to myself. Blood trickled out of the open wound, but I forced myself to apply more pressure, grimacing as I did so. I exhaled a long, heavy sigh as a thought entered my mind.

I shouldn't have gone to that fucking gas station.

It all happened when I got home from school...Well, "home" isn't the best word for a *homeless* person to use, I suppose. I just got back to the alley my friend Kaiden and I lived in when he asked if I'd go with him to the gas station down the street.

"I'd feel better if you went with me," he said with pleading eyes. "Please, Crispin?" There had been a lot of vicious animal attacks and random killings lately, so I couldn't blame him for not wanting to go alone. It was way too dangerous.

I groaned, knowing I wasn't going to make my best friend go alone. "All right, I'll go." I grabbed my back-pack—never went anywhere without it—and zipped up my faded black jacket. We crossed the busy street. I shoved my hands into my pockets as we narrowly missed getting hit by a speeding car.

My friend yelled at the car, waving his fists in the air like a madman. "What a dick."

Kaiden Davis-Smith had been my best friend for a long time, ever since he moved to my alley a few years ago. He and his mother were the only people I knew personally who were also homeless. It wasn't a great thing to have in common, but it certainly brought us closer together.

His skin was dark, and his hair was short and brown. He was my age, fifteen, but was much taller and skinnier. He had dark circles under his brown eyes, and two of his fingers—pointer and middle—were fused together on his right hand.

Like me, Kaiden had some battle wounds from our fights with the other kids. On the bridge of his nose was a small scar from a fight with a couple of older kids with class rings, and we had similar scars near our eyes. Also like me, his clothes were faded and worn, falling apart at the seams. However, Kaiden's had far fewer holes in them.

Of course, I was a lot rougher than Kaiden. I was always climbing into or out of something. I had an excessive amount of energy, even after a full day of exercise, and always felt like doing something. I was always itching to go on an adventure while Kaiden was happy just sitting around doing nothing. It kind of drove me crazy.

"You okay?" Kaiden asked as we walked.

"I'm fine," I said miserably.

He raised his eyebrows. "No, you're not. What's wrong?"

Sometimes I hated how persistent he was, but I couldn't blame him. I was the same way. "I'm just sick of everyone at school. The things they say. . ."

I didn't need to finish my sentence; I knew he understood.

We continued our walk in silence, which was fine by me. When we reached our destination, Kaiden opened the door and held it for me. "You coming in?"

I shook my head. "No, I'll wait out here." I just needed to be alone for a bit.

He shrugged. "All right. I'll only be two seconds."

I decided to take a seat on the bench at the very back of the store by the dumpster. I leaned back and gazed up at the stars twinkling above. The sky was clear, though the smell of rain still lingered in the air. I took a deep breath and closed my eyes.

I found myself imagining what my life would've been like if my mom were still alive, if my dad had never walked out on us when I was a baby, or if anyone found out I was an orphan living on the street.

I imagined getting adopted and living in a house, having my own room and a bed. Not having to sleep in the backseat of a car anymore, and having a family, even if it were just a foster family. I knew I could probably have some of that if I just told someone my situation, but I never did. I guess you can say I'm kind of cynical. Trust never came easy to me, and rather than having people betray me,

WEREWOLVES OF BRISTOL MANOR

I preferred to keep to myself. You can't be betrayed if you don't trust anyone.

Besides, Kaiden and his mom were like family to me. I couldn't just abandon them. That was one thing my dad and I didn't have in common….

I inhaled the moist air, remembering the many times Kaiden and I had gone walking in the rain just for something to do. The memory sent a warm feeling throughout my body.

Then I heard a growl.

I turned toward the sound and saw big red eyes glowing in the darkness. I hopped to my feet and inched away with my arm outstretched, hoping to keep the creature at a safe distance. It took a few steps closer, and the lights from the front of the store finally illuminated it. My blood went cold. It looked like an extremely large wolf, though I hadn't heard of one being so big.

"Nice dog." My voice was shaky, and my throat went dry. "Goooood dog. You don't wanna hurt anyone, do ya?" As I went to take another step back, the wolf lunged at me, and I ran as fast as I could.

My legs felt like jelly, but I didn't dare slow down. I could hear the creature behind me, and practically felt its hot breath on my skin. Beads of sweat ran down my neck, and I shivered. I was gasping for air by the time I finally came to our alley. Every breath sent a jolt of pain throughout my chest, but Kaiden's car was only fifty yards away. *I can make it.*

Panting heavily, I rushed toward the car, dodging the wolf's outstretched claws. I risked a glance over my shoulder and shuddered. It wasn't far behind. I grabbed the handle of the broken-down car and yanked, but nothing happened. Kaiden must've locked it. "Shit!" After darting around the corner, I went for the forest across the street, hoping to climb a tree before the creature ripped me to shreds. That was my only hope for survival; there was no way I could outrun it.

He was closing in on me, and I was rapidly losing speed. I pushed myself to run faster, wondering how much more my heart could take. Black spots danced in my vision. The creature caught up to me, and pounced, knocking me down. I hit the ground hard, scraping my arm along the side of a tree root. Mud splashed in my eyes as I staggered to my feet.

But it was too late.

The wolf was only inches away, drool falling from its open mouth. It let out a low, terrifying growl and leapt forward, knocking me back down. I rolled on to my back, clutching my chest as I struggled to breathe.

The wolf met my gaze. Its eyes were wild but not filled with rage as I'd expected. Something about the wolf seemed familiar. I couldn't shake the feeling.

It growled once more and sank its sharp teeth into the side of my stomach, ripping away a huge chunk of flesh.

Blood gushed from the wound as I screamed in agony. I pushed the wolf's head away. My heart was racing so fast

I feared it would explode. I squeezed my eyes shut, expecting the wolf to kill me, finish me off. But several seconds passed, and I was still alive.

When I opened my eyes, I saw nothing. The wolf was gone. Bewildered, I let out a quivering sigh of relief, and my body relaxed. It actually let me live. When I looked down at my stomach, I saw blood was still spilling from the bite, and suddenly felt dizzy. It wanted me to bleed to death, I thought. How cruel.

Then a million questions seemed to enter my mind at once. Why was the wolf so big? Was it actually a wolf? Why didn't it kill me? Was it alone? Were others nearby? I couldn't understand why it wanted me to bleed to death. That didn't strike me as typical wolf behavior, but I was no expert.

My whole body shook with exhaustion. I felt feverish and nauseated, my muscles tense and sore. The world spun around me, and I was sure I was going to puke. I didn't get up for a long while. Instead, I closed my eyes, trying my best to calm down.

My head was throbbing, and my eyes were heavier than they'd ever felt before. Cold sweat slid down the sides of my warm face. I did my best to keep my lunch from coming up, but that task proved to be rather difficult.

That was when the stranger appeared and told me to get up. That my wound would heal. But he'd also told me to apply pressure. Did that mean he cared? Surely if he did, he would have done more to help me. Was it his wolf that attacked me? Did he plan this? Could he be one of the killers everyone was so worried about?

The pain was starting to subside, but only slightly. It was enough to convince me that maybe I wasn't going to die after all. Then everything went black.

CHAPTER TWO

The next day, I awoke to the sound of Kaiden's alarm. I didn't get up immediately, however. Instead, I covered my face with my pillow, and wondered how I got to the car. I was in the backseat, my usual spot, but couldn't remember walking back. The last thing I could remember was falling asleep—or passing out—in the forest after being attacked by the wolf. Was that all just a dream? I started to sit up, but found myself wincing at the sharp pain in my stomach.

Nope, definitely not a dream.

Kaiden, who'd been asleep in the front seat, turned his alarm off. "Come on, man. We can't be late again, or we'll get detention."

"Ugh," I groaned, wishing this day were already over. The pain in my side was excruciating, but I couldn't miss any more school. I'd already missed a lot to avoid the bullies. And on top of all that, I had to suffer through a day of work after school. This is so unfair, I thought as I placed a hand over the wolf bite. Maybe one more day wouldn't hurt…

No. I knew I couldn't miss another day, no matter how badly I felt I needed to.

Reluctantly, I dragged myself out of the car and hurriedly searched my backpack—which contained everything I owned—for something to wear. I grabbed the cleanest shirt I could find, which was a black ADTR tee with some holes near the collar, and threw it on. I then stood behind the car so passers-by couldn't see as I changed into a clean pair of faded black jeans.

Once Kaiden and I were dressed, we ran to the gas station we'd visited the previous night to finish getting ready. I kept a hand on my stomach, putting pressure on the bite, and tried my best to keep up with my friend.

When we got there, we dashed to the bathroom. I looked in the mirror and sighed at the sight of my messy, dark brown hair, and attempted to pat it down. Unfortunately, I failed miserably.

I hated the way I looked. My mother had always told me I looked like my dad, whom I never met. Or at least, I couldn't remember him. When she was alive, she never liked to talk about him, and I rarely ever asked. It really hurt her when he left.

Anyway, according to my mom, he too had dark brown hair and big green eyes. Well, one of my eyes was green.

WEREWOLVES OF BRISTOL MANOR

The left one was brown. There wasn't anything wrong with my eyes. I was just born that way. Heterochromia iridum, I believe it's called.

I could definitely see a resemblance between my mom and me, though. She was Korean, and I had her skin tone and features. We were both kinda on the short side, too. Now that she was gone, it was like there was a hole in my heart. She was the only family I ever had. I wondered if I'd ever feel whole again.

Glancing down at my hands, I noticed they were a little dirty from my encounter with the wolf, and washed them in the sink along with my face and arms. The blood stains on my fingers were the hardest to wash away, but the mud slid right off. When everything was as clean as it was going to get, I turned to Kaiden, who looked ready to go. "How much time do we have?"

He looked down at his old, beat-up watch. "About seven minutes. You ready?"

"Not really," I said, but I trudged out the door anyway.

The two of us hated going to school. Not a day went by where I wasn't shoved around, beaten up, or made fun of, despite the fact the school had an anti-bullying policy. It clearly wasn't enforced, and I was sick of it.

Teachers told me to stand up to the bullies. The one time I *did,* I went home with a broken nose, a black eye, and tons of bruises covering my entire body. Excellent advice.

Marcus Jones decided from day one of first grade that I was going to be his personal punching bag. Lucky for me,

Marcus followed me all the way to high school—I honestly didn't think he'd pass eighth grade—and he gained some bigger and meaner friends. One of my teachers told me that I couldn't let bullies like him get away with beating up on me. She told me to do something about it, so I did.

After lunch, one of the first days of freshman year, I ran into Marcus and his goons. Without saying a word, he came up to me, snatched my backpack from my hands, and started emptying everything out onto the hallway floor. I snatched my backpack from his grasp and glared up at him. "Pick it up," I said, trying to sound tough and unafraid, but secretly feeling terrified. I clenched my jaw and didn't back down.

Marcus came closer until his face was only an inch or two away from mine. His foul breath made my eyes water. "Or what, Lipton?" He sneered. "You won't do shit."

So I did the only thing I could think of: I shoved him backward and leapt onto him, screaming maniacally as I did so. Marcus and I tumbled to the floor, but my bravery ended there. By the time my head hit the floor, he was already on top of me, punching and kicking every inch of my body. I rolled to my stomach, hoping I could then get to my feet and run away. But Marcus's weight held me down, pinning me to the cold tile floor. He grabbed my hair and pulled until I raised my head. Several students recorded everything on their phones, laughing the whole time.

"Stop!" I shouted, desperately wanting to go back in time and erase the last few minutes. "Stop!" I tried to call for help, but no one came.

Marcus just laughed as he slammed my face into the floor, mocking my pleas. My nose made a painful *crack* and blood poured out of it. But Marcus didn't stop until a few teachers finally made their way over. Our school's head of security pulled him off me, and sent him to the principal's office, where he was suspended for a week.

I was sent to the emergency room via ambulance, but I also got suspended.

Several videos of the incident were posted online, and no one who recorded them was ever punished. There were hundreds of comments on them, laughing at me and cheering for Marcus. I looked it up once in the library a few days after it happened, and practically melted into a puddle of embarrassment.

Since then, I tried to stay as invisible as possible, never saying a word unless absolutely necessary. Sometimes not even then.

CHAPTER THREE

It took Kaiden and me five minutes to walk to school, leaving us two minutes to get to our first class. I tried my best to hide my injuries from Kaiden, but it was obvious he knew something was up. He asked if I was okay, and wrinkled his nose when I said I was fine, but didn't press on.

Kaiden and I had most classes together, which was great. Neither of us was very good at making friends.

We climbed the stairs to the second floor, and took our seats in the Algebra 2 class we both hated. However, we didn't hate it just because it was hard. Our teacher, Mr. B, made the hour-long class drag on and on with his sinfully dull voice. He spoke so slowly and with no enthusiasm whatsoever, which made it hard to concentrate on what he was saying. More often than not, I'd get lost in my thoughts and completely tune him out.

I couldn't have been the only one.

The bell rang right as a boy with dark brown, curly hair strolled in. I averted my eyes, and suppressed the urge to groan. "Ah, Marcus," Mr. B said as he looked up from his desk. "To be early is to be on time, but to be on time is to be...?"

"Also on time." Marcus nodded smugly. He took a seat at the only empty desk, which was next to me, and sweat rolled down the side of my head. One class without an incident with Marcus was all I was hoping for. Just one.

But I knew that wasn't going to happen.

"No," Mr. B said, and shook his head impatiently. "You're supposed to be at your desk with your homework, a piece of paper, and a pencil out on your desk by the time the bell rings. By coming in right as it rang, you, Marcus, are unprepared." He then spoke to the rest of the class, and rose from his desk. "Did everyone study for today's test?"

Oh no, I thought, and leaned forward. I forgot about the stupid test. After the incident with the wolf, I blacked out and couldn't even remember walking back to Kaiden's car. Yesterday had been so crazy it never crossed my mind.

Mr. B began passing out the test. I shifted nervously in my seat.

"Hey," Marcus whispered, and leaned toward me. "Did you study for this?"

"No," I said flatly, hoping he would leave it at that.

He stared at me a moment, a blank expression on his face. "Well, you're smart. Let me copy you."

I stared straight ahead, refusing to look at him. "No."

Anger flashed across his face. "If you let me copy, I won't beat the shit out of you in gym later."

Ignoring Marcus probably wasn't the smartest thing to do, but I *hated* letting people copy my work. It wasn't right, and it wasn't fair to me. Other students would snatch my paper from me, copy the answers and then throw my work in the trash when they went to hand theirs in. One time, a teacher actually saw someone do it. But did that teacher do anything about it? OF COURSE NOT! I'd had enough of that.

Marcus had been making my life a living hell for years, and always got away with it. Even if I decided to let him copy my test, he would find another reason to attack me later. Maybe I'll raise my hand at an angle that doesn't please him or simply look in his direction. Marcus never needed a *good* reason. Neither did any of the other assholes I went to school with. They enjoyed picking on those of us who were different.

And I was pretty damn different.

I never felt like I belonged anywhere, or seemed to fit in with anyone. It was like I was on the outside looking in, wondering why the other kids wouldn't talk to me. No matter how nice I was, I was never good enough for them. Before my mother and I lost our home, it didn't bother me so much. I guess because I could just lock myself in my room and read. Reading was the best way to escape the horrors of reality.

22

It became unbearable when I started high school, though. We lost our house and a lot of our things when my mom was fired. I had almost nothing in common with the other students at Valley Park High, which meant I had almost no friends.

Since I didn't have a television, computer, phone, or tablet, I felt pretty alienated. The other kids would mention movies, apps, or songs I'd never heard of. They'd talk about what they did online the previous day, and I couldn't relate. I felt so alone. It was one of the worst feelings in the world.

A feeling Kaiden knew just as well.

Our appearances also fueled the bullies' hatred of us. Our old, worn-out clothes, Kaiden's fused-together fingers, and my two different colored eyes were the punch lines of many jokes. A few kids picked on me for being half Korean, wearing too much black, and for being so quiet.

Sometimes I just felt so worthless that it literally hurt. The thought of suffering through another day of being bullied at school, and not having anyone to talk to about it made me want to cry. I constantly wondered if I'd ever belong somewhere, if I would go through my entire life always feeling like an outsider. Surely there were others like me out there somewhere.

Rolling my eyes at Marcus's stupidity, I glanced over the test and was relieved to find that I actually remembered how to do everything. I finished before anyone else, but waited for a few others before handing in my test. Mr. B flashed me an awkward grin, and went back to reading something on his laptop.

When I returned to my seat, Marcus leaned in again. "What's the answer for number three?"

I shrugged and stared down at my hands, hoping he wouldn't keep asking.

"What's the answer?" Marcus repeated, a hint of anger in his voice.

Tension swelled in my stomach, but I forced myself to remain quiet. Don't give in, I thought to myself, repeating the words over and over in my head. He wasn't going to get to me. Not today. Don't give in. Don't give in. Don't give—

Grabbing the sleeve of my jacket, Marcus pulled me closer, almost yanking me out of my seat. My eyes doubled in size. He looked down at my sleeves and wrinkled his nose. I silently begged for him not to notice the old grass and mud stains that just wouldn't come out, no matter how many times I washed the damn jacket. "Tell me the answer, ya dirty little bitch," he said, his jaw clenched tightly.

I exhaled a quivering breath. "Leave me alone." My voice was quiet but firm. I jerked free of his grasp and chewed my lip.

Marcus was wearing new shoes and a spiffy leather jacket. He probably got new clothes at the beginning of every school year. Even when my mom was alive, we couldn't afford that. My "new" clothes would usually come from secondhand stores. Nothing wrong with that, but my

24

peers certainly thought there was.

Marcus stared at me with an odd look on his face for a long while. I wondered what was going through his head, but my face turned red when he finally spoke. "Dude, why don't you ever wash your clothes?!" His voice was loud so the entire class could hear.

Several kids laughed at his remark, and I sunk down in my chair. My face was hot, and my body shook from either anger or embarrassment. I wasn't sure which. I looked up at the clock and my heart sank. Forty-five minutes to go.

Everyone gawked at me and continued snickering as Marcus made rude gestures behind my back. I pulled my hood up over my head, silently begging the universe to make me invisible.

Mr. B did absolutely nothing to stop Marcus, happy to ignore everything that didn't relate to Algebra 2. Teacher of the year, if you ask me.

After what felt like an eternity, the bell finally rang. I shot up and ran to my second class, nearly knocking over my desk with the abrupt movement. Second period was on the third floor, and the staircase was right next to Mr. B's classroom, so it didn't take long to get there. My normal spot in the back corner was empty, and I sighed with relief as I plopped my backpack on top of the wobbly desk.

Kaiden took the seat next to mine. "I looked up and you were gone."

"Sorry," I muttered, not meeting his gaze. "I just had to get out of there."

"I get it." He nodded sympathetically. "Marcus is a dick. One day he'll get what he deserves."

"I highly doubt that," I said flatly. "He's been doing this for years. Since I was six or seven. Nothing even remotely bad has happened to him."

"I know, I know. Calm down." Kaiden unzipped his backpack, rummaging through it. "It'll happen, Crispin." He pulled out the book our class was reading together, and skimmed over the previous day's pages to refresh his memory.

"And why do you think that?"

"I don't know." He put the book down, and placed his bag on the floor by his feet. "I just do."

"All right class," our English teacher, Ms. Watson said. "Phones off and books out."

The bell rang for third period, and I groaned. Gym was next, and it gave Marcus another opportunity to spread his cheer.

For the first ten minutes of class, we were supposed to change into our gym clothes, but Kaiden and I never did. We always sat by the bleachers, waiting for the announcement of what we would be doing.

Some days we'd go to the archery room, which I enjoyed because I was very good at it. I was even asked to join the archery team. Unfortunately, I had to decline the invitation, as the fee was too expensive and my only

26

source of income was a part-time job, for which I got paid minimum wage.

On other days we'd play basketball, soccer, or dodgeball on the basketball court. I rarely participated though. Team sports just weren't my thing.

When the weather was nice, we'd go outside and play football. I *hated* those days. I was much smaller than the other guys, so when they tackled, it hurt. Plus, I always bruised kind of easily. I'd walk away from the field with ten or fifteen new bruises on my body just from a few tackles.

Our gym teacher Coach Chang, the coach of the boys' basketball team, finally waddled onto the court. He was short and chubby, particularly in the stomach region, and had a large birthmark on his neck. Coach Chang wore a blue Kentucky Wildcats cap to cover his bald spot, and a whistle around his neck.

The man blew his whistle, and placed his hands on his hips. "Today, we'll be playing dodgeball." He pointed to the balls on the floor in front of him. "Let's keep it clean, kids." He made his way to the chair he'd been sitting in a few moments earlier, and propped his feet up on the table in front of it.

I groaned as Marcus anxiously ran to the balls and snatched one up. "Why did he have to pick dodgeball?" I asked as I shoved my hands into my jacket pockets. "You know Marcus is only gonna aim for me."

Kaiden shook his head. "Maybe Chang won't notice if we sneak—"

"Hey, Lipton!" Marcus shouted, showing off the dodgeball in his hands. "This one's got your name on it." He threw it at me, and I ducked just in time. I glanced over at Coach Chang, whose eyes were now closed. "Dodge *this!*" Marcus yelled. I turned toward him, but it was too late. The ball slammed into my face, and I stumbled back as a bunch of other kids snickered and sneered.

The blow to my face stung and rattled my brain. I blinked, trying to steady myself.

"Coach!" Kaiden called as he threw his arms up in the air. "Don't you think you should do something?!"

Coach Chang's eyes remained closed, and he waved his hand dismissively. "Play nice." He never had been very helpful. I wondered if he was like this with every class, or if I was just lucky enough to be in the one period he liked to doze off in.

Typical.

My stomach still hurt from the wolf bite, and I was pretty sure a fight with Marcus would cause it to start bleeding again.

I rubbed my reddened cheek and stared daggers at our useless coach, imagining his head exploding and the blood splashing all over the other students. Whoa, I thought. Where did that come from? I certainly didn't want something like that to happen. But when I pictured his head blowing up, it kinda soothed me, which made me a little afraid of myself.

Marcus strode over to us, flashing a smug grin. He

grabbed my shirt collar and shoved me against the wall. Kaiden inserted himself between us, trying to look tough.

But Marcus shoved past him and pinned me against the wall. "Guess you should've let me copy that test, huh?"

"Get off me!" I shouted. Not the most clever of comebacks, but I wasn't thinking clearly. I was angry and embarrassed and, though I hated to admit it, I was scared.

Marcus grabbed a fistful of my hair and dragged me onto the court, where a crowd encircled us. My best friend weaved through the onlookers, but couldn't come any closer. The bully raised his fist, preparing to launch it at my face, but something came over me.

It was like I was suddenly overcome with rage. I threw the first punch. Marcus stumbled back and raised a hand to his busted lip. I shoved him back as he grabbed hold of my arm, and we both tumbled to the floor, knocking several kids off their feet in the process. My sudden burst of anger and bravery—or stupidity—vanished as quickly as it had come.

Still recovering from the fall, I realized too late that Marcus was already coming at me. He pinned me down as the crowd around us happily chanted, "Fight! Fight! Fight!"

How did this happen? I was never one to attack. Especially not since Marcus broke my nose the last time I attempted to stand up to the guy. Rage I didn't know I was capable of seemingly took over my body for that short moment and vanished when I needed it most.

29

I felt a stabbing pain in the wound on my side, and hoped it wasn't bleeding again. That was the last thing I needed.

Marcus slammed my head into the hard, wooden floor of the basketball court, snapping me out of my thoughts. His hands held a firm grasp on my wrists as my legs flailed about under him, desperately trying to knock him off. Marcus forced my hands together so that one of his was clenched around both of mine.

Damn, he's strong.

I flinched as his fist came at my face. Again, and again, and again. I could feel my eye swelling and blood pouring from my nose. The crowd cheered for Marcus, and I stopped fighting back, ready to give up.

Kaiden attempted to pull Marcus away from me, but the bully was much too strong for my friend. He shoved him away, and Coach Chang finally realized what was going on.

"All right, all right, break it up," he said, making his way through the sea of students. "Come on, Marcus, that's enough. Leave him alone."

By then my face was already blue and purple. I carefully placed a hand over my nose and winced. Broken again. My hand came away bloody, and I was surprised Marcus hadn't knocked some of my teeth out.

Kaiden looked down at his feet. "I'm so sorry, Crispin. I tried."

"I know you did," I said weakly, stumbling to the

30

bleachers. "It's okay."

After talking to Marcus for a couple minutes, Coach Chang approached me, a stern look on his face. "You need to go to the principal's office." He pointed toward the door and I stared in disbelief. "Now."

"What?" I asked, bewildered. "Marcus was beating the shit out of me! Was I supposed to just let him do it?"

"I've sent him there as well." Coach Chang flicked his wrist at me. "Go on."

"It was self-defense," I protested again. "He should be expelled for everything he's done to me!" Rage boiled deep within my body, but I did my best to suppress it. What's coming over me?

Coach Chang frowned. "Do you need to go to the hospital?"

"No."

"Then go to the principal's office." He scratched his belly and glanced around the room, avoiding my gaze. "Off you go, Crispin."

I shook my head. "Whatever." Reluctantly, I trudged to the school's main office—taking my sweet time, of course—and hoped I wouldn't see Marcus there. Thankfully, he was already with the principal when I eventually moseyed in.

The receptionist looked up at me and frowned. "Back again, Crispin?" Her dark brown hair was in two pigtails, and she tilted her head when she saw me.

"Yeah," I murmured. I was no stranger to the staff

in the main office. The teachers didn't care if it was self-defense. A fight is a fight, and most wouldn't even try to break it up. They let it continue until security got there, which sometimes took a really long time.

Since I threw the first punch this time, I wondered if I technically started the fight. Marcus dragged me around the gym, pushed me against the wall, and threw a ball at my face before I fought back. How could I be in the wrong here? But I shrugged, figuring it wouldn't matter either way. Like I said, a fight is a fight to the teachers at Valley Park High.

"Have a seat," the receptionist said softly. "She'll be right with you."

There were only three chairs in the office, and a kid I didn't know was sitting in the middle. I didn't want to sit next to anyone, but I obviously had no choice. So I took the seat closest to the principal's door.

One of the office walls was made entirely of windows. I looked out at students in the hallway as they walked to their fourth class of the day. My stomach growled, and I licked my lips as the kid next to me pulled out a bag of chips.

He opened the bag and held it out to me. "You want some?"

I wanted to decline because talking to people I didn't know made me uncomfortable. Most of them turned out to be just like Marcus anyway. But I was really hungry, and he looked friendly enough, so I took a handful. "Thanks."

It didn't take long for the chips in my hand to disappear, and I licked my fingers.

"Hungry?" he asked.

My cheeks turned pink. "A little." That was one hell of an understatement.

"You can have more, if you want."

Right when I was about to take another handful, the principal opened her door. Her hands were on her hips, and she shot me a look of disapproval. "Crispin Lipton, follow me."

I sighed and did as instructed, hoping this would be a quick chat, but fearing the worst.

CHAPTER FOUR

"I'm really getting tired of seeing you in here, Crispin," the principal said. "If it happens again, I'm going to have to suspend you." She sat down behind her desk and flipped her long, red hair behind her shoulder. She gestured for me to take a seat, and clasped her hands together in her lap.

Her office had several inspirational posters decorating the walls, and a few photos of her children were placed on the sides of her desk. The room smelled like dying flowers, and when I looked around, I saw a few discolored petals on the floor by the trashcan.

"Suspend me for defending myself? Yeah, that makes sense," I said, my words dripping with sarcasm. I leaned back in the chair, folding my arms across my chest.

"Violence is never the answer, Crispin. You know that." There wasn't an ounce of sympathy in her voice.

"You should have told one of the teachers so *we* could deal with the situation. You can't fight everyone who disagrees with you."

"Yeah," I said, preparing for a rant. I balled my fists and clenched my teeth, trying hard to keep from bursting into a fit of screaming. "I should stand there while Marcus bashes my face in for fifteen minutes straight. And when he decides he's finished, I should tell an adult who will do absolutely nothing but tell me to stand up for myself. Maybe one of them will remind Marcus of the no bullying policy. But that won't do any good, because he's very much aware of that policy. He just chooses to ignore it. Everyone here ignores what he and his friends do."

She narrowed her eyes, and I met her angry gaze, refusing to back down. "You think you can run this school better? How old are you? Fourteen?" Her face was hard, and her eyes seemed to pierce through me.

"I'm *fifteen*," I corrected her. "What is the point of having an anti-bullying policy if it isn't enforced?"

Of course, she ignored my question, and went on to ask one of her own. "What is the deal with you and Marcus? How did all this start?"

I stared at her, desperately wanting to say, *does it matter?* I figured that remark would get me into even more, trouble. So, I shrugged. "I've never done anything to him," I said, bouncing my leg nervously as I spoke. "Not one thing. He came into class on the first day of school, and started shit with me. He hasn't stopped since! Maybe he continues because he knows he can get away with it. He knows no one will ever do anything to stop him, and that I'm too little to actually defend myself."

She sighed heavily, and looked up at the clock. "Maybe you should find another school if this one isn't up to your standards," she said sarcastically. "Or perhaps you'd like to try running it?"

"Or you could do your job and punish the assailant, not the victim."

My comment seemed to piss her off more than I'd expected, though honestly, I had no idea where this was coming from. I wasn't the confrontational type. I was the sit-there-quietly-as-you're-being-yelled-at type. Something came over me, made me speak the thoughts I'd been holding in for so long.

This! Isn't! Me! Why am I saying all these things?! They weren't untrue, but they didn't need to be said...did they?

The woman thought a minute before responding. "I'll punish the person I find to be in the wrong, Crispin. Marcus seems more friendly and polite than you, so I feel you probably instigate the fights."

WHAT?!

I felt like my eyes were about to pop right out of my head. "Okay, I don't know where you're getting your information from, but it is *way* off." Seriously? She's taking Marcus's side? "Yes, I threw the first punch today, and that was a mistake. But that doesn't mean I'm the one to blame for *every* fight. I guess I knew what was going to happen, and didn't want him to have the satisfaction of hitting me first. But I don't know what started it all. He and his friends just like to torment me, and that most certainly isn't my fault."

When I finished my rant, I inhaled a deep, quivering breath, trying to calm myself. I suddenly wished I hadn't told her I threw the first punch today. Another strike against me, I thought.

The principal studied my face. "Have you ever thought that maybe Marcus might be doing all this to you because he's getting bullied at home? If he is, doesn't he deserve some compassion?"

"That doesn't give him the right to go around terrorizing people," I shot back. "Look at me. I'm always getting bullied by him, but you don't see me taking it out on someone smaller."

"Crispin, I suggest trying to be a little more likeable when you're in here with me." Her voice was sickeningly sweet. It made me cringe. "We'll be more eager to help you if you're respectful."

I laughed out loud. Not the best reaction, but I'd had enough of this school's bullshit. "Shouldn't respect be earned? What have any of you done to earn my respect? Nothing. You punish me for being bullied. Great job! That's not getting respect from me." I gave her a double thumbs up, then crossed my arms, waiting to be expelled.

What has gotten into me?!

She shook her head with disappointment. "I don't know what to do with you, Crispin. I really don't. Adults don't need to earn the respect of children. It should be given without question."

Part of me wanted to tell her I wasn't normally like this. I had no idea what was going on, but this wasn't me. But I couldn't bring myself to say it. I stood by my statement: respect should be earned, not demanded.

She looked up at the clock again, clearly wanting this meeting to be over with as badly as I did. "Have you had lunch yet?"

I shook my head.

"Go to lunch, then. You'll be late for fourth period, so I'll write you a note." She grabbed a blue sticky note from her desk and began writing.

"So, am I getting detention or...?"

The principal met my gaze. "Not today. I think detention would serve you well, and give you time to reflect on your behavior. But I have a son a bit older than you, and I know he needs to be given a break every now and then. So this is it. Don't expect me to be so understanding next time you mouth off to me."

As soon as I had the note in my hand, I started out of her office, but she stopped me before I opened her door. "Crispin?" she said. Her tone wasn't as annoyed now.

I turned to face her.

"You need to work on that attitude."

I resisted the urge to roll my eyes. After closing the

office door, I dashed up to the second floor where the sophomores' lockers were located. There was no way I was going to my usual lunch spot alone, just to eat a bag of chips, so I pulled them out of my locker and scarfed them down as I ran to Biology. I may or may not have choked on the chips.

Biology was the only class Kaiden and I didn't have together. He had the fun Biology teacher for fourth period. My teacher wasn't the worst, but she wasn't fun at all.

When I got there, I plopped down in the only available seat, which was next to a cheerleader who was dressed in her uniform and staring at her phone. Some kids who were also in Algebra 2 with me snickered when they saw me. I sank down in my chair and put my hood up over my head.

"How nice of you to join us, Crispin," Ms. Kathy said. "Do you have a note?" She walked over to my desk, her hand on her hip. Her long, blonde hair was pulled back in a ponytail, as it was every day, and she wore an ugly dress that looked like something an elderly woman might wear.

"Yeah." I reached in my pocket for the note, which was now crinkled and barely legible.

She took a minute to look it over before frowning down at me. "Okay." She returned to the front of the class. "All right everyone, get in your groups. The project is due on Monday."

In the middle of class, a deep voice boomed into the intercom, announcing that it was time for all freshmen and sophomores to report to the gym. Apparently, police officers came to talk about safety precautions we should be taking outside of school. The upperclassmen had the seminar earlier in the day, and now it was our turn. I didn't like the idea of sitting in a hot, overcrowded gym for an hour and a half, but if it got me out of class, I wasn't going to complain.

The officer talked about the recent murders happening in our town. He explained that no pattern in victimology had been identified, whoever was killing seemed to be killing at random, so we needed to be extremely careful until they were apprehended. He also said there'd been several wild animal attacks, and recommended not being out too late until something could be done. Not many of the students seemed to be paying attention to the officer, though I wasn't sure he noticed. He awkwardly stood there, staring hard at his note cards as he spoke into a microphone. By the time he finished, the school day was over.

I couldn't have been more relieved.

CHAPTER FIVE

Kaiden and I met up outside the gym. We made our way through the sea of people, trying to get to the sidewalk in front of the school. Most of the other kids were headed for the parking lot, where they liked to hang out, which was in the opposite direction.

"So," Kaiden said casually, staring straight ahead. "How was your chat with the principal? Did you get in trouble?"

My stomach twisted. My face suddenly felt hot. "Why?" I snapped, my tone harsher than I intended.

My best friend looked at me, clearly surprised by my tone. "Jeez, you don't have to bite my head off. If you don't want to talk about it—"

"I don't," I muttered angrily.

Why am I acting like this? Why am I so angry? Kaiden didn't do anything to me; he was just trying to show concern, and for some reason unbeknownst to me, I was pushing my best friend—my *only* friend—away.

We walked in silence for a bit. I couldn't believe how I'd treated Kaiden. I wanted to tell him I didn't mean to snap at him, that I wasn't angry or anything, but I couldn't force the words out of my mouth.

I took a deep breath, trying to clear my head.

"How was Biology?" I asked, shoving my hands into my jacket pockets. The wind was blowing hard, and the cold air stung my swollen face. My nose wasn't hurting anymore, which was shocking considering I thought it was broken earlier.

Kaiden frowned at me. "Fine."

I rolled my eyes, annoyed with his simple response. "Whatever."

When I started to take a different route home, Kaiden grabbed my arm. "Crispin," he said, and yanked me back. "Dude, what's with you today?"

"Nothing!" I jerked free and started to walk off again, but stopped myself. *I'm not angry,* I thought. *Stop being such a dick!* I turned back toward my friend, staring down at the sidewalk. "I'm sorry," I whispered. "I don't— I don't know why I'm acting like this." Kaiden tilted his head but said nothing. "It's like everything is pissing me off, and I don't know why."

Kaiden nodded. "One of those days, I guess."

But it was more than that. I just couldn't figure out what it was.

We began walking again, the anger I felt only moments before now fading, almost completely subsided. I wondered if I should tell him about what happened at the gas station. I never offered an explanation as to why I ditched him.

Secretly, I wondered if maybe the bite could have transmitted some sort of disease to me, and that was why I had so much trouble controlling my anger today. Mad Wolf Disease? Was that a thing?

"Listen," I said as we turned down our alley. "Remember when we went to the gas station yesterday?"

"Yeah," Kaiden said, gripping the straps of his backpack. "I've been meaning to ask you about that. Where did you go? When I got out, you were gone. I almost got mugged on my way home."

Shit.

I told him about the wolf-like creature, about the man in the woods, and how I had no memory of walking back to the car that night. I also told him that when I got angry, it wasn't my normal, I'm-going-to-ignore-you-until-I-get-over-this kind of anger. It was like my blood was boiling. With each beat of my heart I got angrier and angrier, no longer feeling in control of myself, no longer feeling like myself at all. Then I told him I thought the bite was to blame for everything. He listened intently and didn't interrupt once.

That's how I knew he didn't believe me.

"So, you were chased by a big dog?"

"It wasn't a *dog*," I said impatiently. When we reached the car, Kaiden unlocked the doors and I threw my backpack into the back seat. I hurriedly searched for my work clothes. After school and on weekends, I worked at a grocery store called Greeny's to help us buy food and clothes and stuff. Kaiden's mom could only provide so much.

When I found my uniform, I threw it on over my T-shirt and groaned. "I have to go." I threw my backpack over my shoulder and stormed off.

"Oh, no." Kaiden jogged after me. "First you say you were chased by a giant dog, and then you say it wasn't actually a dog." He stopped in front of me and crossed his arms. "What was it then?"

"I never said it was a dog, Kaiden!" I shouted, anger filling my body once again. "It looked like a wolf. I should have known you wouldn't believe me." I tried to walk around him, but he wouldn't let me pass.

"I never said I don't believe you," he said skeptically. "I just haven't seen a wolf around here before."

"Well, I *have*," I yelled. "And it could have killed me!"

"You said it only bit you once," Kaiden replied dully, his brow furrowed.

"I know what I said!" He took a step back but still wouldn't let me by. "It bit me once, but how often does a wolf come up to someone, bite them, and leave? It must have heard that man or something; otherwise, it probably would have killed me."

Kaiden narrowed his eyes. "I don't think the mere presence of one man would stop a wolf from killing you. It couldn't have been a wolf."

"You wouldn't know!" I threw my arms up in the air. "You weren't there. I know what I saw, and what I saw was a huge wolf!"

"A minute ago you said it *looked* like a wolf," he argued, and shifted his weight to his other foot, a judgmental look on his face.

I didn't want to yell at Kaiden anymore. I tried once again to shove past him. This time, he let me go. "I'm gonna be late for work. I'll see you later."

He didn't follow me.

Greeny's was a mile away from the alley, and I only had five minutes to get there, so I ran the whole way. As I made my way to the break room, I ran my fingers through my messy hair in attempt to tame it. I tossed my things into my assigned locker before heading over to the employee check-in.

"Lipton," a man's voice boomed from behind me. "The watermelons are in the back. I want you to put 'em out front." My boss, Aaron Cooper, towered over me, arms crossed. He glared down at me, almost daring me to say something. His bright red button down shirt—that matched his cowboy boots perfectly—made him look like a giant cherry.

"But that's Micah's job," I said. "I'm not a stocker."

Aaron raised his bushy grey-brown eyebrows. "You are

today, boy." He turned on his heel, and walked away with his head held high, as if he'd just won a mighty victory.

You're making me set out the watermelons, I thought as I watched him saunter away. Some victory.

I rolled my eyes and wheeled the crate of melons to the front of the store where the fruits and vegetables were. Several shoppers eyed me, probably staring at the bruises on my face. As I grabbed a watermelon, a sudden burst of pain shot through my arms. I dropped it, staring in horror as it splattered across the floor. Juice and seeds and chunks of watermelon were everywhere.

A man, probably in his early fifties, slipped in the juice and almost fell on top of a small dog. I could feel the eyes of many confused customers staring at me, but I didn't care; the pain in my arms was getting worse by the second.

My face contorted in agony as I bent down to pick up the chunks of fruit at my feet. The burning pain shot through my legs. "Aaaaagh!" I fell to the floor and clutched my left thigh, as it was in the most pain. What's going on?! The burning increased with every breath I took.

A small crowd gathered around me, and Aaron made his way through the onlookers. "What's the meaning of this, Lipton? Just look at this mess! You're gonna have to clean every bit of this up." Realizing that customers were staring at him, he quickly softened his tone, and tried for a look of sympathy. To me, however, he just looked consti-pated. "For now, though, you can go sit in the break room until you feel better."

46

I waited a moment for the pain to subside. When I realized it wasn't going to, I struggled to my feet and trudged to the break room, clutching my stomach in hopes of keeping myself from throwing up. As soon as I got to the break room, I collapsed in a chair. I rested my head on the table as the pain crept up to my chest. My breath was now coming in short gasps. The room spun around me.

Oh, my god. What's happening? This can't be happening. WHAT THE HELL IS WRONG WITH ME?!

I clutched my chest and squeezed my eyes shut. The dizziness grew in intensity. The pain spread to my head and I crashed to the floor, unable to hold myself up anymore. My entire body was trembling.

Am I dying? Did I catch an infection from the wolf?

I rolled onto my back as panic rose in my chest. Concentrating on breathing was all I could do.

My insides were burning. Every organ in my body felt as if it were being twisted around by a giant pitchfork. My hands were shaking uncontrollably, and I screamed as I forced myself to sit up. I'd never felt pain this intense in my entire life.

Then, just as suddenly as it came, the pain was gone, but my muscles ached.

My eyes flew open. I gripped the edge of the table next to me, and pulled myself up into the chair. My skin was hot. My body was sweaty—and probably a little smelly. I pressed my face against the cool surface of the table, grateful but terrified.

I still felt like I was going to throw up, though now it was because I was afraid there was something wrong with me. First, the unexplained fits of rage, and now, extreme pain throughout my entire body. That didn't sound too healthy to me.

Mad Wolf Disease....

The door to the break room swung open. I sucked in a deep breath, desperately trying to steady my breathing. My poor heart was still racing.

"You okay, Crispin?" It was Micah. The older boy took a seat in front of me, his eyes full of concern. His short brown hair was messy and curly. Micah Coleman, who just turned seventeen, was one of those guys who could pull off the messy hair look. He always had tons of girls—and even a few guys—crushing on him, yet he remained a kind, down-to-earth guy. His puke-green Greeny's uniform shirt was half tucked into his faded blue jeans. "Aaron said you collapsed after picking up a watermelon." He arched an eyebrow. "That true?"

"Pretty much." I exhaled a long, heavy breath and winced at the sharp pain in my chest. "I don't know what happened. All of a sudden, I got these shooting pains all over. I don't...I can't explain it."

Our boss pushed the break room door open, and stood at the edge of our table, an annoyed, unsympathetic look on his face. "You might want to get to cleaning up that mess you made, Lipton," he said with a snarl. "Them melon chunks ain't gonna clean up themselves."

48

"Don't you think Crispin should take the rest of the day off?" Micah asked. "This sounds serious."

"Oh, he's all right." Aaron eyed me suspiciously. "Aren't ya, Lipton?"

I shrugged. "A day off sounds like a good idea. I'm still in a lot of pain." I wasn't lying per se. My muscles ached, but it was a dull pain that just felt the need to linger. It was tolerable.

Micah stared up at him, and I could tell Aaron felt defeated. He glanced down at his shoes, probably thinking how hideous his bright red cowboy boots were. "Fine. Go on home, Lipton." Then he turned his glare to the older boy. "Clean up his mess, Coleman."

I got to my feet and started over to my locker when Aaron grabbed my upper arm. Shocked, I looked up at him with wide eyes and tried to jerk free. "This better not happen again, boy." He tightened his grip and sneered. "Or your ass is fired."

When he released me, I opened my locker, grabbed my stuff, and slowly made my way back to the alley. In front of another grocery store, there was a group of people selling grilled hotdogs and steaks. I bit down hard on my lip until I tasted blood. It smelled so good. My stomach growled, but I kept walking until I came to Kaiden's car.

If only I'd had just a few dollars. But I shook my head, knowing I wouldn't have bought myself something if I didn't have enough for Kaiden as well.

I opened the car door and threw my backpack inside.

I then plopped down in the back, preparing for a nap and trying not to worry too much about what happened.

Random muscular pains as severe as what I experienced couldn't be a good sign, but there was no way I could afford to go to the doctor. Even if I somehow managed to go, what if I found out I had some sort of muscular disease and only had a few weeks to live? My stomach knotted up, and I forced all thoughts from my mind. Scaring myself wouldn't do me any good. In fact, it would just make things worse.

Images of the wolf flashed before my eyes, and I shuddered. I tried to picture nothing at all, but the blackness was the backdrop to the horrifying beast that haunted my mind. I felt as if I were back in that moment. The wolf's hot breath on my face, its piercing red eyes glaring down at me, a low growl erupting from deep within its throat.

I rolled on to my stomach. "Don't think about it," I told myself. "Just don't think about it." I squeezed my eyes shut and finally drifted off to sleep, despite the nagging feeling of hunger.

CHAPTER SIX

The next morning I woke in a cold sweat. It dripped down the sides of my face and back. The cool morning air was refreshing against my warm skin. The only pain I felt was a slight burning sensation in my stomach where I was bitten.

Last night, I dreamt about the wolf. My hands were still a little shaky from the nightmare that felt way too real, and I decided to go for a walk to clear my head. After grabbing my jacket and backpack, I began walking along the side of the road to no place in particular.

Staring at the ground, I saw dozens of empty cigarette cartons, discarded bottles, and cans of soda, along with the occasional used condom.

I could still smell rain in the air. Other scents then filled my nose, suddenly much stronger than ever before. Burning rubber, dog shit, and freshly cut grass. I could smell coffee from the empty cups that littered the ground, though they looked as if they'd been there several days. But the scent was so strong.

How is that possible?

I made my way down a rarely traveled road, and found myself standing in front of a large house I'd seen only a few times before. It was massive and old-looking. It was a beautiful house, but sort of gave me the creeps. The leafless trees in the yard only added to the creepiness. It was four stories high with an enormous backyard surrounded by a privacy fence. On the fence was a sign that read, **Private Property, Trespassers Beware.**

They seem friendly, I thought.

The front yard was equally uninviting. The yard itself was nicely cared for, but humongous shrubs acted as a fence, surrounding the entire perimeter of the yard. To the side, the garage door was open, and it housed three cars. A black school bus was parked in the long driveway.

The few times I'd seen the house, I never saw anyone on the property, but I assumed it wasn't vacant because fresh flowers bloomed in a well-cared for garden near the garage.

I noticed movement in one of the upper level's windows. The curtains fluttered, and I got the feeling I was being watched.

I averted my eyes and kept walking.

I strolled through the woods, sort of close to where the wolf attacked me. The forest was massive, and extended for miles, so I stayed close to the edge, where the streets were still visible.

The only thing I could hear was the distant footsteps of a couple out for an early morning jog. The two girls' matching shirts read "she's mine" inside a big heart, and an arrow under it pointed toward the other girl. They waved as they jogged past me.

I wandered a bit deeper into the forest, and eventually came across two men kneeling next to a large paw print that undoubtedly belonged to the wolf I'd encountered. I was instantly rattled at the sight of the print.

One of the men looked to be about mid-twenties, the other late thirties. They both had short brown hair, and appeared to have gone several days without shaving. The men wore khaki cargo pants, white t-shirts, and combat boots. A plain black jacket lay at the feet of the younger one. Both had bulging muscles and tattoos, but the older man looked stronger and more terrifying.

As I passed them, the older man jumped to his feet, and stared at me, tilting his head to the side. He came toward me and I halted, unsure what to do.

Part of me wanted to shout *"What the fuck are you doing?!"* but a bigger part of me just wanted to run away screaming. Brave, I know. Something about these guys just seemed...off.

The younger one followed his lead, and rose. "Is he one of them, Wes?"

The older man, Wes, nodded slowly. "Oh, yeah. He's

one of them." He had guns strapped around his leg the way I figured an FBI agent might, and I couldn't tear my eyes away from the weapons.

"One of what?" I asked, my voice quivering.

"Oh, come on, kid. You can't fool us," the younger one said as he took a single step closer. "We know what you are."

"What do you mean?" I inched backwards, my gaze fixed on Wes. "I don't know what you're talking about." And I didn't care. All I wanted to do was run, but my feet wouldn't obey.

"He's a pup, Tom." Wes grinned. "He doesn't know what he is yet." The man came closer, his eyes glued to mine. "Hmm," he said, and his expression changed. "I know you."

"What?" I backed away and my throat tightened. "I've never seen you before."

But neither of them were listening to me. "Go get the car," Wes said to Tom. "I'll take care of the boy."

My eyes widened. "Stay away from me!"

The man came forward, his hand extended as if he were afraid of frightening off a wild animal. "It's okay, pup. Just calm down. It'll all be over soon."

"Leave me alone!" My legs wobbled. My stomach was in knots, and my vision blurred. It wasn't long before I collapsed on the ground, my body convulsing. Not again, I thought. This couldn't be happening. Not now. Not when I needed to run for my life. I had a feeling *"take care of"* didn't mean invite me over for milk and cookies, and I didn't want to stick around to find out. I struggled and squirmed on the ground, trying to get to my feet, but I couldn't. My arms were weak and unable to hold me up. Eventually, they gave out, and I hit my head on a rock. Everything seemed to be moving in slow motion.

"Just hold still, pup," Wes said as he knelt over me.

Blackness crept into my vision. I moaned as my limbs became too heavy to move. The world was fuzzy, growing darker and darker. Out of the corner of my eye, I saw several humanoid figures heading our way. Their shapes blurred together. Their shouts echoed around me. My head was throbbing, and I felt sick. I closed my eyes, and my body relaxed.

CHAPTER SEVEN

I awoke with a start. My eyes flew open, and my heart pounded painfully. I sat up, gawking at my unfamiliar surroundings. Nervous tension built in the pit of my stomach. Where am I? How did I get here? Am I dreaming?

I was in a large bed with blue sheets, and a big black comforter was draped on top of me. The room was warm and cozy, and I was comfier at that moment than I'd ever been in my entire life. I never wanted to move...even though I hadn't the slightest idea where I could be. That was a little unnerving, but I was too comfortable to be overly concerned.

The walls were blue, like the sheets, and the curtains were black. Along the edges of the curtain were long vines, stitched in white. To my right, there was a small desk, and my backpack was on the chair in front of it, with my shoes just below.

I looked down at the wound on my stomach. There was a large gauze pad taped over it. Wonder who did that? It wasn't something Kaiden or his mother would do. Even if it hadn't been bandaged up, I knew they had nothing to do with where I was.

Kaiden's mom, who lived with us in the broken-down car, had two jobs to pay off all her credit card debt, and was hardly ever home. She'd been like a mother to me ever since mine was killed, and was trying to save up for an apartment the three of us could live in. She worked so hard for so little, and deserved better.

The door creaked as it opened, and a girl about my age flipped the light switch. I squinted at her. "You're finally awake," she said, a little rudely. She glided over to the bed, and sat cross-legged on the side. "What's your name?"

The girl had long, dark brown hair with a hint of blonde near the bottom, and her eyes were golden-brown. She was very tan, and wore a dark blue hoodie, tight jeans, and unmatching socks on her small feet.

Is this her house? If so, why am I here?

"Umm." My voice shook, and I looked away anxiously. I was nervous and awkward around new people, but there were things I needed to find out, questions I needed answering.

Still, I knew nothing about this girl. For all I knew, she could be a cannibal about to devour her next victim.

Stay calm, I told myself. Now you're just being crazy.

"What is this place?" I asked finally. "Who are you? How did I get here? Why am I here?" The questions spilled from my mouth, one after the other.

"Shhh." The girl folded her arms across her chest, annoyed. "Dude, all your questions will be answered soon. Can you tell me your name?"

I swallowed hard. "Crispin Lipton. H-how long have I been out?"

"Two days," she said with a shrug.

"Two days?!" My eyes grew wide. I couldn't believe I'd been asleep that long. The fact she was acting as if it were no big deal, and that this sort of thing happened all the time, made me even more uneasy. I tried to wipe the flabbergasted expression from my face.

She stared at me, her expression unreadable. Why is she looking at me like that?

I chewed my lip anxiously. "What is...um, what's your name?"

She opened her mouth to speak right as the bedroom door opened again.

A boy strolled inside, and our eyes darted over to him. He smiled sweetly and blood rushed to my cheeks.

He had black, messy hair that fell into his bright blue eyes. He looked a year or so older than me, and a few inches taller. The boy was a little chubby and super-pale, with freckles splashed across his face, and I noticed something on his left wrist. A tattoo, perhaps? He wore a purple beaded bracelet, and flicked it nervously as he approached. The girl waved cheerfully at him, and left without another word. "You'd better get dressed," he said, not unkindly. He pointed toward a door on the right side of the room. "That's your bathroom. You can take a shower and change your clothes, if you want." He took a second to look me over. "I'm gonna assume you want to."

"That was kind of rude, don't ya think?" I said, eyeing him. I noticed his nails were painted black, and the paint was badly chipped. "I don't have any other clothes here, anyway. I couldn't change even if I wanted to."

He was right, though. I desperately wanted to take a shower. And I actually had clothes in my backpack, but they didn't look any better than the ones I had on. I didn't want him to know I looked this crappy all the time.

"I'm sorry! I didn't mean it that way." He averted his eyes, his cheeks turning bright pink. "We have some that should fit you, if you want." He walked over to the dresser next to the bed, and pulled out a change of clothes that looked pretty close to my size.

On the night stand, he placed a pair of black jeans and a black T-shirt with a design in the middle I couldn't quite make out. A wolf? Maybe this was a private school and a wolf was their mascot? Under the symbol were the words Bristol Manor, and I suddenly knew where I was.

The creepy house near the woods. But why?

"I think these will fit," he said quietly. "I'll be back in a bit. And I'm sorry about before. I just get a little nervous around…umm…" He stopped himself, unable to meet my gaze. "I'm really sorry."

"It's okay," I said shyly. I was nervous too.

The boy closed the door as he left the room, and I stared sightlessly at the wall in front of me. Who are all these people, and why am I here?! I wanted to shout those words, to scream them at the top of my lungs because I hated to be so clueless. But I knew I needed to control the new fits of rage I'd developed, especially if I wanted some answers.

I had to assume someone would tell me everything eventually.

Suddenly, memories of the men in the woods flashed before my eyes. I wondered what happened to them. Why were they so interested in me? Why did the older one call me a pup? Would they have killed me if no one came to my rescue?

The man had said, *It'll all be over soon.* He was definitely going to kill me. But why? What if those kids were my rescuers? Could two teenagers have taken on two fully armed men? Did they have help? If so, how many others were there? Dozens of questions were swimming around in my brain. It hurt to think.

Not wanting to miss an opportunity to take a hot shower, I grabbed the clothes from on top of the nightstand and ran toward the bathroom.

The water was refreshing. Kaiden and I usually washed up as best we could in the bathrooms of gas stations, so it had been a while since I'd taken an actual shower. The soap slid under the bandages and into my wound. I winced as I ripped the bandages off. I let the water fall over the bite, washing it out, and tried to ignore the stinging pain.

The skin around it was discolored and stained with blood. It was disgusting to look at.

When I got out, I threw on the Bristol Manor shirt—which fit perfectly, by the way—and the pair of black jeans that looked brand new. Part of me wondered if I could keep them, or if they'd ask for them back before I left.

My thoughts drifted to the boy I'd met earlier. He seemed shy but kind. I wondered what he was going to say before he cut himself off.

After I got dressed, I stared in the mirror at my stomach, and my eyes doubled in size. The bite was almost healed! How is that possible?! A few moments ago, it looked just as bad as the day it happened. But the discoloration of the skin was gone, and the scar was fading right before my eyes.

I furrowed my brow, trying not to think about it. There had to be a logical explanation for this.

As I reentered the bedroom, the door swung open. The blue-eyed boy from earlier stuck his head inside. "Are you ready?" he asked, a hint of excitement in his voice.

I blinked in confusion. "For what?"

A smile tugged at his lips. "The tour." He motioned for me to follow as I tied my shoes. I joined him in the hallway, grabbing my backpack on the way. "Your name is Christian, right?"

I resisted the urge to groan. "Crispin, actually." Teachers—and practically everyone else—were always getting my name wrong. I'd usually have to spell it three or four times before it finally sunk in.

"Oh, my bad." He blushed. "I'm Eden."

Eden's Bristol Manor shirt was splattered with old paint. His clothes looked almost as old and worn as my real clothes. There were paint stains on his fingers, hands, and arms (more on his left than right), and a little on his cheek. Eden must have noticed me staring, because he chuckled and said, "I like to paint."

"Yeah, I noticed," I said with a nod. "What kinds of stuff do you paint?"

"Mostly things I make out of clay, but I also paint on canvases sometimes. That's what I was doing earlier. Had an image I couldn't get out of my head, so I decided to paint it."

"That's cool."

"What kinds of things do you like to do?" He tilted his head, genuine curiosity in his voice. "Are you artsy at all?"

I shrugged. "Yeah, kind of."

"Kind of?" Eden arched an eyebrow.

"I like to write. Short stories, mostly." I gripped the strap of my backpack.

"That's awesome!" he said enthusiastically.

"I'd love to write a book someday, but I don't know

what it would be about."

"Can you expand your short stories?"

I ran a hand through my hair. "I don't know. I feel like they're pretty much as long as they're gonna get."

He nodded. "So, is there a reason why you brought your backpack? We're just going on a tour of the house."

I shrugged again. "I feel more comfortable when I have it with me. Call me paranoid, but I'm afraid if I leave it out of sight, it will get stolen. I mean, there isn't anything valuable in here, but it was taken before, and I have no intention of letting that happen again." I decided to leave out the fact everything I owned was inside.

And while everything I told him was true, it wasn't the only reason. I felt uncomfortable being in a house full of strangers—even if they were friendly—and needed to be ready to make a run for it at any moment. People are crazy. You never know their true intentions.

"You seem a little cynical," he said. "No one here is gonna to steal your stuff." When I didn't respond, he smiled. "I can understand, though. This is a new place, and you don't really know anyone here. I would probably do the same thing."

Somehow, I got the feeling Eden knew exactly what it was like to be in this situation. Being in a new place, meeting all kinds of new people, even having a pretty crappy past. I made a mental note to ask him about that, though I knew I'd probably forget.

We climbed down the stairs, and made our way to

the enormous living room where we came to a halt. Eden and I stood by the front door of the house so I could see everything.

There were four comfy-looking dark purple couches surrounding a large black coffee table. A dark grey rectangular rug covered most of the light grey hardwood floor. To the left were several floor-to-ceiling black shelves filled with tons and tons of books. On the wall to the right were about a dozen framed pictures. Most of the people in the photos appeared to be between fourteen and twenty.

"Wow" was all I managed to say. I wondered who the people in the photos were, but if Eden wasn't going to offer up the information, I wasn't going to ask.

"This is, obviously, the living room," Eden said, gesturing around.

When the older boy wasn't paying attention, I glanced over my shoulder at the front door. Could I make it out? Would he stop me if I tried? He seemed nice, but I needed to get back; I don't belong here.

Although part of me didn't want to leave…

Eden started walking again, and called over his shoulder, "Come on. I'll show you the kitchen."

I wondered why he bothered to show me around. Why was it so important that I see everything? But Eden was intriguing, and it wasn't often that I had the opportunity to make a new friend. So, I followed him to the kitchen, pushing my concerns aside.

Compared to the living room, the kitchen was rather

small. It had all the cabinet space one would need, I suppose, and a decent sized refrigerator. But in the middle of the room, there was a small circular table with four mismatching chairs surrounding it. "How many people live here?" I asked him.

"About thirty," he said, casually. "Not including the adults."

My eyes widened. "Thirty?!"

"Yup." Eden nodded. "Why is that so surprising? This is a big house, ya know?"

"What's with the ridiculously small table, then?"

He giggled. "No one eats in here, bonehead." He took me past the kitchen, and through a short hallway. It was dimly lit by two purple lamps on each side, and white vines were painted along the light grey walls. "This," he began as he opened the double doors, "is where we eat."

We entered the room, and my mouth dropped open. There were ten large circular tables spread throughout the gigantic dining room. Each table had a purple tablecloth, four placemats, and four big black chairs tucked into it. In the center of each table was a vase of blue flowers surrounded by four white candles. At the far end of the room was a big fireplace. A long rectangular table with three massive black chairs was directly in front of it.

I knit my eyebrows. The single rectangular table seemed a bit out of place. "Who sits there?"

"The Elders," he said quietly. "Perinious, Tealios and Lusious. You'll meet them later." Eden turned to leave, and held the doors open for me, but I didn't move.

I gawked at the Elders' table a moment longer. Who were the Elders? What was so special about them? I'm not gonna lie, I was just picturing people in their nineties clutching bibles to their chests.

"Crispin?"

"Sorry," I murmured before following the older boy out of the room.

We climbed the first flight of stairs. On that floor were several rooms, but all of the doors were closed. "These are the classrooms," he said, pointing at random doors throughout the hall, "for those of us who are still in school."

"Wait a minute," I interrupted, holding a finger up. "So, this is just a school?"

He hesitated. "Um, not exactly." Eden shifted on his feet, and looked like he was having a hard time figuring out what to say. "Most of us are runaways. We choose to live here, and take our classes here. It's better for us than public school."

I crossed my arms. "So this is a private school for runaway teenagers?"

Eden's mouth was a thin line as he thought of how to respond. "You could say that."

"What do you mean?" I asked. "That's what it *is*."

"It's been a while since I've had to explain this to anyone." Eden sighed heavily, exasperated. "Do you know what you are?"

I stared blankly at him. "A pancake."

"That thing that bit you the other day," he said, ignoring my sarcasm. "Do you know what it was?"

A heavy feeling crept into my stomach. "It was a wolf," I said after a while, and swallowed hard. "I-I think it was a wolf." How could he know about that?

"Close," the boy said. "It was a *werewolf*."

"Yeah," I scoffed. "It was a werewolf. And it bit me, so I'm gonna turn into a werewolf too, right?" I couldn't stop myself from laughing.

But the older boy's eyes were dead serious. "I'm not kidding. It *was* a werewolf. And yeah, you are one too."

"Do you seriously expect me to believe this shit? I mean, come on. Werewolves? Nice try, but I'm not buying it." I turned to head back down the stairs, but Eden grabbed my upper arm, his grip so painfully tight I couldn't pull free.

"Just listen for a minute," he said. "Werewolves are real. I didn't believe at first either, but I swear to you they're real."

"You're hurting me!" He loosened his grip, and I jerked free. "This is not funny."

"I'm not trying to be! I didn't believe it until I shifted for the first time, and it was utterly terrifying. You need to be prepared. It could happen any time now."

I took a small step away from him, my eyes glued to his face.

"All those tales you hear about werewolves only

67

changing on full moons," he began, "that's not true. We change when we're angry or afraid if we don't learn to control it. If you *can* control it, then you can shift whenever you want. For most of us, though, it's really hard, and if you're not careful, you could end up hurting someone you love."

"Us? You're a 'werewolf' too?" I used air-quotes around the word werewolf, and Eden was not amused. This kid was actually trying to convince me that werewolves were real. Maybe going through with the tour hadn't been the best idea.

The older boy's eyes were wide and full of fear. "Do you want to kill your friends? Your family? It'll happen if you don't learn to control it, and you can't learn on your own. You *need* us. I'm not trying to freak you out, and I know I sound nuts, but I promise you, this is real." He took a moment to calm down, exhaling a huge breath. "No wolf could possibly be that big. But werewolves are much bigger than normal. You were bitten, and you need to open your mind for a second and think about what your next move is. You shouldn't have to go through this alone."

My throat tightened. What scared me wasn't the fact this boy truly believed that what he was telling me was true, but that I was starting to believe him. The bite disappeared right before my eyes, I could smell things I shouldn't have been able to smell, and it all started with that damn wolf.

Was Eden telling the truth? Could werewolves have been around all this time? All the stories I grew up reading about, could they be based on real events? Or, perhaps, written by a werewolf to shed some light on their secretive existence? Was I really going to believe him about this?

Eden wasn't laughing, and didn't look like he was trying to keep himself from it. He looked dead serious. "Like I said, I didn't believe any of this until I saw proof. Unfortunately, the proof was my first transformation, which sucked, by the way. Have fun with that."

"So, this school is really for...werewolves?" I asked, trying to sound more skeptical than I was now. I hated myself for starting to believe. Was I really that gullible?

The older boy nodded. "And Bristol Manor isn't a school. It's a Wolf House. Werewolves of all ages can live here."

I thought for a moment. If I was going to believe everything he was telling me, I needed to start asking some real questions. I needed to know that what I went through could be explained by the existence of werewolves. "We heal right?" I asked, thinking about the bite.

"What?" Eden asked, befuddled.

"Like, if I were to bite you right now and draw blood, it would heal rather quickly, right?"

He nodded. "You're not gonna bite me, are ya?" His face turned bright red, and he averted his eyes. "Did yours heal yet?"

"Yeah," I said, my voice low. "But I got it few days ago. Why didn't it heal more quickly?"

"You were just a regular human when you were bitten.

69

It took a while for your new abilities to kick in, and for the virus to spread. You're good now, though. Any wound— well, almost any wound—will heal really fast."

I looked up at Eden, deciding to buy into the premise. "So, why is it so hard to control?"

His face brightened a little. "Apparently, it's because we aren't *supposed* to be werewolves. There are some people out there who are meant to become one, and they are the ones who can control the change and the wolf almost effortlessly. I don't know who is meant to be one, or why they're meant to. I asked a teacher once, but he didn't know."

Eden leaned his shoulder against the wall. "So, when the rest of us get angry, we lose control, and innocent people get hurt. It's safer for everyone if we stay here." He looked down at his feet, and I wondered if perhaps he'd hurt someone before. Eden looked so ashamed.

"We also learn what regular humans learn," he continued. "Math and science, that sort of thing. But we learn techniques for controlling the wolf, turning back to human, and the history of our kind. Oh, and there's a course on famous werewolves throughout history. That one isn't mandatory."

"Famous?" I asked, intrigued.

"Yup."

"Who?" I tried to keep the excitement from my voice.

"You'll learn about them if you stay," he grinned. "Some actors, authors, dancers, a president, few astronauts—"

"Astronauts? That's really cool!"

Eden nodded excitedly. "I know, right?"

We resumed the tour, and Eden continued pointing out which classes were held in which rooms. "Can you control it?" I asked after a while.

He looked at me, clearly bemused. "What?"

"The change. The wolf." I shifted awkwardly on my feet. "You said it's hard for *most* of us to control, not everyone. Can you?"

"No," he said, lowering his head. "I can't."

"So, when you get angry, you turn into a big—"

"Yup. Just like everyone else here."

Staring down at the floor, I felt a dull pain in the pit of my stomach. The idea of turning into the scary creature that bit me made me sick. Would it hurt? How would I go back to being human again? What exactly would I do when I lose control? I still wasn't completely sure I believed anything Eden was telling me; he looked serious the whole time he spoke, but part of me thought maybe he was just crazy.

Maybe Bristol Manor is really a hospital for delusional kids.

I gazed up at Eden, who was studying me with curious eyes. I could tell he knew I wasn't completely convinced, but the fact he wasn't doing everything he could to make me believe, actually made me want to believe him. If werewolves *are* real, and I am one of them, would I ever be able to control myself?

"Don't worry about it," Eden said, as if reading my

71

thoughts. "We also learn how to fight here. If you change and we need to defend ourselves, we'll be able to."

"Somehow, that doesn't make me feel any better."

I decided to ask the questions that had been gnawing at me since I woke up. "So, um, those guys in the woods... what did you do to them?"

Eden shrugged. "We chased them off. There were ten of us and just the two hunters. They knew they couldn't take us all, especially since they were running low on bullets. When they left, we brought you here."

"Oh." I frowned. "Well, why did they call me a pup?"

"That's just what the hunters call the ones who are new to everything. After about a year or so they stop, usually. I don't know how they can tell. Maybe the rest of us exude confidence or something."

"They were *werewolf* hunters?" I asked him.

"Yup," Eden said with a nod. "They've been hunting us for years. They're everywhere, but I've only had few encounters with them around here. They like to be where the werewolf population is high, and there aren't enough of us here for hunters to take up residence. Mostly the ones we deal with are traveling hunters."

Just when I thought my life couldn't get any more nightmarish. I brought a hand up to my face, and wondered how I was going to survive with a terrifying group of hunters after me now.

"They can't get us here," Eden said after a while. "They're smart enough to know not to go after the Elders'

Wolf Houses."

"Are you sure about that?" I asked as I wiped my sweaty palms on my pants.

He struggled to answer, his brow furrowed. "I'm sure," he said, although it seemed more like he was trying to convince himself.

I nodded slowly as one more question came to mind. "When am I going to, you know, transform? Is it gonna be next time I get angry or what?"

Eden looked thankful for the change of subject. "It will come soon. You were bitten three or four days ago, right?"

I nodded again.

"Have you had any weird pains lately?"

Before I could answer, two girls came running down the hall, screaming at each other. Eden and I hurried out of their way as they came storming by.

"Yeah, I have," I said once the girls disappeared into one of the rooms. "Twice, actually. The first time was after I picked up a watermelon at work, and then again in the woods with those guys. Both times it felt like my body was on fire."

"That's your body's way of preparing for the change." He shoved his hands into his pockets as he spoke. "Adjusting to your new form would be a lot more painful if you hadn't experienced something like that. You'll probably transform any day now. Next time you get a little worked up, that's when it will happen."

"Great," I said unenthusiastically, and wrinkled my nose. "What about—" I stopped myself, unsure if I should bring up my recent rage issues. What if it meant something bad? I couldn't meet his gaze. "I've been getting really angry for no reason lately. Is that normal?"

But Eden nodded, and I sighed with relief. "That is perfectly normal. That's the wolf taking control of your emotions, and trying to get used to them. The wolf is pretty hotheaded, though some calm down after a while. I'm nowhere near as bad as I used to be."

"Some? That wasn't exactly the answer I was hoping for." I nervously bit my lip.

"I'm sure you'll be okay," he said softly, and placed a comforting hand on my shoulder. "Just don't worry so much. You'll have plenty of people here to help you through everything." When I met his eyes, he looked away, a bashful look on his face.

I tilted my head, eyeing him. "Since I had those pains earlier, it won't hurt?"

"Oh, it'll still hurt, but not as much."

On that cheery note, I decided to drop my line of questioning, and we continued on with the tour of the Wolf House known as Bristol Manor.

We then went up another flight of stairs. Eden made his way down the hall, and pointed to the room next to the one I'd slept in. "This is my room," he said as I peeked inside. The room looked chaotic. There were easels and canvases everywhere, and the furniture had dozens of paint bottles scattered about on top. There was a Famous Last Words poster hanging above the bed closest to the paint bottles, and I assumed it was Eden's. "If you ever need anything, just come get me. I share it with Rex, so if I'm not in here, you can also talk to him. He's cool too."

My eyebrows drew together in confusion. "You know I don't live here, right?"

He stopped walking, and shot me a puzzled look. "I thought you'd want to stay. I mean, if the Elders invite you to, why wouldn't you want to move in? It's dangerous out there for us, especially when you're new at this." He approached me, his shoulders slightly slumped now. "You don't want to be around others like you?"

"Like me?" I asked. "I'm pretty sure the only thing I'd have in common with anyone here would be the fact that we were all bitten by a wolf. No one gets the struggles I have, but my best friend does. I'm not going to abandon him."

"A lot of us have had hard lives. We may not know exactly what you're going through, but I'm pretty sure there's someone who will understand. There will be someone here you can relate to. I just—I don't want you to be alone."

I looked in his big blue eyes, and saw pain. What was his secret? What struggles has he had to face? I was dying to know.

Eden folded his arms across his chest, staring down at his shoes. "Wouldn't it be nice to live in a real house?

When was the last time—?"

"Wait, what?" I blinked. "How did you...?"

Eden's mouth was a thin line. "Don't look so surprised."

Maybe he would understand after all.

Neither of us spoke after that. I followed the older boy down the hall, and when we got to the end, I saw another flight of stairs. This one had a red rope across it, denying entry to the final floor. "What's up there?" I asked, curiously.

"The Elders' bedrooms," he said. "They are the only ones allowed to go up there."

"Why?"

Eden shrugged. "I guess they don't like to be disturbed. I wouldn't want to visit them anyway. Haven't spoken to them in a few years, and I never want to again."

I knit my eyebrows. *Years?* "How long have you lived here?"

He thought a moment before responding. "Three years. I came to live here when I was thirteen, though I was turned when I was a bit younger." He raised his hand to wave at a guy walking past, and I was reminded of the symbol on his wrist. The other guy had one too.

"What does that symbol mean?" I asked, taking his wrist in my hand. His skin was warm and smooth.

Eden's breath caught in his throat, probably surprised by my sudden movement. "You sure ask a lot of questions," he said as I studied the tattoo on his wrist. "It's the pack symbol. Every member needs the tattoo because it's a way of showing that you belong to the Elders. While this can be a great place to live, the Elders aren't exactly the friendliest bunch. You'll get the same tattoo after they meet with you…if they decide you can stay, and if you want to stay. Not gonna lie, kinda hope you do."

I tried my best to hide a smile. "Does it hurt?" The idea of "belonging" to the Elders was kind of creepy, but I chose to ignore that for now. What could that mean, anyway? How bad could it be?

I wasn't sure if I'd stay, though. Kaiden was like my brother, and I couldn't just leave him. But there was something about Eden….

"It didn't hurt me," he said. "But you? Yeah, it'll probably hurt you." He chuckled.

"Hey! I can handle pain. Pain is my middle name! Well, it would be if it wasn't Lee."

Eden shook his head, a big smile lighting up his face. "You're crazy, Cris."

No one ever called me Cris before. Not even Kaiden, whom I'd known for years. It felt nice; it made me feel like we could actually be friends. And there was something kinda special about him. "When you said if they decide I can stay—"

"The Elders don't accept everyone," he said slowly. When he saw the look on my face, he quickly added, "But I'm sure you'll get in! They'd be crazy to turn you away." Eden paused a moment, looking at me. "Do you think you'd want to live here?"

I shrugged. "I'm not sure yet." Then I thought about all the murders and animal attacks, and asked if they had anything to do with werewolves.

He nodded. "They have *everything* to do with werewolves."

"What do you mean?"

"The animal attacks are done by werewolves," he said. "The victims are either hunters or innocent people that were in the wrong place at the wrong time." He sighed. "They're done by werewolves from other packs."

I arched an eyebrow. "How do you know?"

"We aren't allowed out at night, which was when the killings took place. And the murders..."

I waited for him to finish, but when he didn't, I asked, "Werewolves killed by hunters, I'm guessing?"

He nodded.

I couldn't imagine being on the run from people like the men from the forest. Maybe the Wolf House was the answer. It could not only keep me safe, but it could prevent me from hurting Kaiden as well. I thought back to how easily I'd gone off on him before.

Just then, a man dressed in the same clothes Eden and I were wearing approached, a friendly look in his eyes. "Eden Lambert."

Eden turned to face the man, who was probably in his late thirties. "Ian!" The older boy seemed very excited and full of life. I liked that about him.

"Why don't you go get our new friend here some more clothes? He'll need more than just the one set, won't he?" His voice was loud and full of authority. I figured he must be a teacher.

"Yes, sir." The boy turned to me, a hopeful look on his face. "I'll see you later. Hope you decide to stay."

As Eden strolled off, I looked up at the tall, muscular, dark-skinned man in front of me.

"I am Ian Campbell." He held out his hand, grasping mine firmly. "I guess Eden has been showing you around?"

I nodded, unsure what to say. I sort of wished Eden hadn't left me.

Ian looked down at me with kind, light brown eyes as I crossed my arms. My stomach growled and the man said, "I'm sorry, you must be starving! Come with me. We'll get you something to eat."

We descended the stairs, heading down toward the kitchen.

That was the first time since waking up that I'd thought about food. I *was* hungry, but I was unsure if I'd be able to keep anything down. Ever get so hungry that eating more than a few bites made you sick? That happened to me quite often.

But I followed the man downstairs, and kept my thoughts to myself. If I didn't eat, it would only make things worse. I had to have a little something.

When we entered the kitchen, Ian motioned for me to sit down at the small table. "I thought we weren't supposed to eat in here," I said.

"It's all right to have snacks in here," he replied. "That's what it's for. Meals are eaten together in the dining room. Dinner is at 7PM, and it's only a little after 3PM now."

I nodded, thinking about all the information I'd been given throughout my tour of the Wolf House. "So, is everything Eden told me true? Are you guys...?"

"Werewolves?" Ian asked. "Yes, we are. Just like you. Eden is a very honest, trustworthy boy. Everything he told you was the truth, I'm sure." He searched through the cabinets as he spoke. "Did you think Eden was out of his mind?"

My face turned pink, and I stared down at the table. "Kind of. I never met anyone who believed in werewolves before. The way he explained everything though...it was hard not to believe him."

The man chuckled lightly. "Well, if you have any un-answered questions, feel free to come to Eden or myself. We will be more than happy to answer anything. Everyone is confused and hesitant to believe at first."

I nodded and a tall boy joined us in the kitchen.

He flipped his blond hair—which was slightly dark-er near the roots—out of his small brown eyes. He had long muscular arms. When he opened the refrigerator, he asked, "Who's the kid?"

"This is Crispin Lipton," Ian said as he prepared something for me to eat. "Hopefully he will be joining us."

The boy held an apple between his teeth and extended

his hand. "I'm Rex," he said and I shook his hand. He then pulled out the chair next to mine, chewing loudly. "You meet the Elders yet?"

I shook my head.

"Oh." He took a large bite out of his apple. "Well, if you don't go crazy after meeting them, I—"

"Rex," Ian said, his voice firm. "Don't scare him."

Ian placed a large plate of food in front of me. It was meatloaf, which I loved. Normally, I'd be thrilled to have the chance to eat so much at one meal, but I knew my body well enough to know that if I ate more than a few bites, I'd throw up. I forced down a bite or two of the meatloaf— which was the best I'd ever had—but couldn't eat any more. I scattered a few bites around on my plate, hoping it would appear as though I'd eaten more than I had.

Rex said, "I still have an occasional nightmare about the Elders."

I placed my fork down on the plate. "Why? Are they really that bad?"

"They're not like us." He stared down at the table with a vacant look in his eyes. "They try to make you as uncomfortable as possible so you're easier to read. And their faces…." His voice trailed off. After a moment he shook his head, as if he were coming out of a trance. "They were the very first werewolves, and the only immortal ones. Needless to say, they're really old. Hence their name: the Elders." He chuckled.

"What's wrong with their faces?" I asked as Rex took

another bite.

"You'll see," he said, shivering at the thought. "Don't stare too long. Trust me."

I glanced nervously up at Ian as Rex retreated to the living room, having finished his apple. "Oh, it'll be okay, Crispin. Rex is just exaggerating. The Elders aren't that bad." Ian's tone wasn't very convincing, but I decided not to say anything about it. He glanced down at my plate and frowned. "You didn't eat very much. Are you feeling okay?"

I nodded. "I'm fine."

He nodded, seeming to understand. "I can't eat much on a nervous stomach either. Are you ready to meet them, then?"

I swallowed the lump in my throat. "As ready as I'll ever be."

Ian led me down into the darkness of the basement. The steps were concrete, as were the walls. When we reached a wooden door with a rounded top, Ian knocked three times, and waited in silence.

Did I want to stay there? I didn't know. Yeah, I had a little trouble making decisions, and it was frustrating. Before anything could be decided, though, I needed to at least find out if they'd let me stay. If not, there was no decision for me to make.

My heart pounded and beads of sweat rolled down my face. A shiver ran down my spine. I didn't know what to expect. What would they look like? What's wrong with their faces? How could they make me uncomfortable? My palms were sweaty, and I wiped them on my pants just as the door opened. Cold, musty air rushed to my face, and I took a deep, quivering breath before stepping into the darkness.

The door slammed shut behind me, trapping me inside.

CHAPTER EIGHT

Dim lights flickered on as I approached the middle of the room. The air turned icy, and a shiver ran down my spine. I saw my breath when I exhaled. The air smelled musty, and it made my eyes water as I tried not to sneeze. Cobwebs hung loosely from a dusty chandelier above my head. Several cockroaches skittered across the dirty floor, and I wrinkled my nose.

Three old men, who looked as though they'd died about a hundred years ago, sat in tall, throne-like chairs near the back wall. The men gawked at me in complete silence as I scanned the room.

There was an old door off to one side. The wood was dark, and covered with strange markings. It looked like it might break apart any moment. There was nothing in the room other than the thrones, and I wondered why the Elders chose to stay down in the basement when the rest of the house was so nice and clean.

I met the milky eyes of the man in the middle. His face was emotionless, and looked hard as stone. He had sunken features that were hidden behind long black, greasy hair. His cold eyes glared down at me. I took a step backward as he opened his mouth, revealing sharp, rotted teeth. There was a jagged scar along his cheek. His face, like the other Elders', was long with loose grey skin. His lips were thin and chapped.

That horrifying face would be burned into my brain for the rest of my life.

I stood there in awkward silence for a long time. Rex said the Elders wanted to make you uncomfortable so they could read you. What exactly were they trying to read? My thoughts? My personality? What could they be getting from me right now?

I opened my mouth to speak, but the man in the middle raised his hand, signaling me to stay quiet. This was, by far, the most unsettling experience of my life.

My gaze lowered to the floor, and flickered over the men's shoes. Much like their ancient and decrepit-looking bodies, their clothes were old, worn, and dirty. The Elders appeared to be wearing old tablecloths made to look like clothes, though I was pretty sure that wasn't actually the case.

They looked so frail, but still filled me with dread. How long were they going to keep me down here? Should

I leave? Would they let me? I thought about how nice it'd been to sleep in a house for a change. Then I thought about Eden, and decided not to run. At least not yet.

After what felt like an eternity of deafening silence, the man in the middle stood, raising his thin eyebrows. "Do I frighten you, little one?" The old man's voice was deep and raspy, and it boomed in my head. I noticed the letter P stitched in purple on his tablecloth outfit. P for Perinious, perhaps?

Perinious's milky eyes pierced through mine, but I didn't know what to say. I felt as if he were inside my head. I could practically feel him digging around in my brain, though I had no idea what he was searching for. "I—"

"Do not fret, Crispin Lipton, for I have already come to a decision about you." His voice was revolting, like nails on a chalkboard. It took every ounce of willpower in my body to keep from covering my ears when he spoke.

The man arched an eyebrow. Time was dragging on and on, and I wondered just how long I'd been down there. My legs were a bit shaky, and my hands were sweating profusely. I tried to keep my breathing calm and steady, but failed.

Perinious cleared his throat and, startled by the sudden noise, I jumped. The Elder slowly glided toward me. When he was just a few inches from my face, he stopped, and placed his frail hand on my shoulder. "You wish to stay here." His voice sent another set of shivers down my spine.

"I-I'm not sure," I said, my voice embarrassingly squeaky.

"That wasn't a question, young one. I know you want to stay. And I know *why* you want to stay." He placed his fingertips on my forehead, and closed his eyes. "I know every single thought that has ever entered your mind since the day you were born."

Oh, great, I thought. Does this mean he knows what I thought of his appearance? His expression was hard to read. That couldn't be a good sign.

He was sickly thin. The man towered over me, making me feel small, and I got the feeling that's what he was aiming for. Perinious tilted his head, examining me. "Hmm," he said after a while, and furrowed his brow. "Another one."

I wanted to ask what he meant by that, but he suddenly grabbed my wrist, and turned my hand palm up. His skin was numbingly cold. The Elder placed his index finger in the middle of my wrist, and closed his eyes again. He mumbled a few words I couldn't understand before my wrist began to burn.

"Aaaaaaggh!" I shouted, my eyes practically bugging out of my skull.

I staggered backward. The old man yanked me closer, and I held my breath until he was finished. It felt like a knife was digging into my wrist, pressing down harder and harder. I tried to pull away, but his grip only tightened.

When he finally let go, I looked down and saw that

a crescent moon had been branded on to my skin. I felt a little lightheaded, but forced myself to remain upright. Obviously, I'd been accepted by Perinious, but I still hadn't made up my mind.

Was Bristol Manor going to be my new home?

As soon as the basement door creaked open, I rushed out, almost knocking over the man who was standing guard. I made my way up the stairs and planned on going to my room—well, the room I was staying in—but as I turned the corner, I slammed into Eden. We both fell to the floor.

He got to his feet, and offered me his hand to help me up. As I took it, I glanced at the crescent moon tattoo. Unlike me, Eden's was on his left wrist. After he helped me up, he grabbed my other hand and turned it over to check for a symbol. "They accepted you!" he shouted happily. "That's awesome!"

I stared at the floor. "Yeah."

His smile faded, and he looked at me with sympathetic eyes. "They're creepy, aren't they?"

Nodding, I managed a small, humorless laugh. "Creepy. That is quite an understatement."

"Yeah, but now that you got it over with, you never have to speak to them again. You see them occasionally, like at meal times, but if you avoid looking at them, it's not so bad." Eden fidgeted with his bracelet as he spoke.

"Good," I said, trying to sound somewhat cheerful.

Then I lowered my head. "Every time I close my eyes, I can still see them."

The older boy paused before responding. "Same." His shoulders slumped. "But maybe other horrors will take their place in your mind's eye."

I made a face. "Well that's a lovely thought."

"I'm sorry," he said sheepishly. "That got a little dark."

"Rex said he still has nightmares about them."

Eden scrunched his nose in confusion. "You know Rex?"

I nodded. "Do you?"

"He's my roommate. Of course, I know him." Eden giggled, trying to lighten the mood.

"I mean, do you still have nightmares about them?"

"Oh." He stepped backward as he pushed his hair out of his face. He took a while to answer, and for a moment, I thought he wasn't going to. But he shoved his hands into his pockets, and finally said, "Yeah, every now and then. I think everyone here does. So, which one spoke to you?"

"Only one talks to each person?" I asked.

"Yup. I got Tealios."

I shrugged. "I think it was Perinious."

His eyes grew wide. "Perinious? Are you sure?"

"He had a P on his...um...shirt." It looked more like a tablecloth dress to me, but fine, we'll call it a shirt.

"Wow," Eden said incredulously.

"Is that a bad thing?" I asked. Things were finally starting to look up for me, but having the wrong Elder invite me to stay could be a step in the wrong direction.

Eden shook his head, and the unease I'd felt in my stomach dispelled. "No, it's not a *bad* thing. It's more of an uncommon thing."

"Huh?"

"Perinious never really speaks. Tealios and Lusious usually decide who gets to stay. The only other person I know of that he's spoken to was a guy named Pierce—"

"Ah, Crispin." The voice came from behind me. I turned around to see Ian standing with his hands on his hips. "I'm glad to see you will be joining our little family."

"Perinious is the one who accepted him!" Eden shouted.

"He is? Curious." The man looked me over. "Well, that certainly is interesting." He turned toward a room that must have been his classroom, and gestured for me to follow. "Come in here, Crispin. I'd like to speak with you a bit more, if you don't mind."

I did mind, but I wasn't going to tell that to him.

Eden gave me a reassuring nod before disappearing down the hall. A one-on-one conversation with someone I didn't know wasn't something I was in the mood for. I sighed heavily, and chewed my lip a moment before following him into the room.

"Could you close the door please?" he asked.

Oh, damn. Door closings were never good.

The man sat behind his desk at the front of the room, and I stood beside one of the student's desks in the first row. When I looked down, I noticed the letter P had been carved into the top of one of the desks. The carving actually said "penis" but the first letter was so much bigger than the rest that it took me a while to realize. I ran my fingers over the letter. Images of Perinious flashed before my eyes.

I wondered why he spoke to me, but was afraid I wouldn't like the answer. Who was that guy Eden mentioned, Pierce? And why did the Elder talk to him? Was there something wrong with us?

Ian cleared his throat, snapping me out of my thoughts. "Perinious must have high expectations of you, Crispin. He doesn't talk to just anyone, as Eden told you, I'm sure. So, why don't you tell me a little bit about yourself? I'd like to figure out what Perinious sees in you."

I know I don't look like much, but damn.

Ian waved his hands as if to erase his last sentence. "I'm sorry. I didn't mean for it to come out that way. I only meant that Perinious spoke to you for a reason, and I would just like to know what that reason is."

I shrugged and began my story. I told him that when I was younger, my mother and I lived in a tiny two-bedroom apartment, just the two of us. I told him we were forced out of it after she lost her job, and we'd been living on the street since I was ten years-old. I explained that she died shortly after my fourteenth birthday. She'd been hit by a car because the driver was texting behind the wheel.

He watched me closely as I talked about how my dad

left when I was so young that I couldn't remember anything about him. I didn't know anything about my dad except that, according to my mother, I looked a bit like him. He left without an explanation, leaving my mother alone, in debt, and with a baby to raise all by herself.

I told Ian about the fights Kaiden and I got into at school, about my job at Greeny's, and that I'd been living with Kaiden and his mother in their car since my mother died.

Normally, I didn't share such personal details with a complete stranger, but it'd been a long time since I opened up to someone, and I guess I kind of wanted to.

He listened quietly the entire time, nodding occasionally. When I finished, he rubbed his chin, scribbled something down on a piece of paper, and met my eyes. "Hmm. Tell me about the bite. Do you know who bit you?"

I stared at him blankly. Was he serious? Did he really expect me to recognize them? "You're kidding right? He was a big...wolf!" I shoved my hands into my pockets. "How could I possibly know who that was?"

"He didn't come to you afterwards?"

"No. Was he supposed to?"

Ian bit down on the top of his pen, confusion clear in his eyes. "Not *supposed* to, but most do. At least, most that I know. They come back to apologize and to explain what will happen. Becoming a werewolf can be unnerving if you're not sure what's going on. Some don't even survive the first transformation, although that's not the only thing

92

that could get you. The infection kills as well."

"Wait. What?" My heart thumped hard in my chest. "I could die?!"

"It is a painful transformation for one's body to make, and some just aren't strong enough to handle it." When he saw the fear in my eyes he said, "Eden was ten when he was bitten, Crispin. If a ten-year-old can survive—"

"Has anyone older than that died during the change?" I asked.

Ian sucked in a deep breath, and remained quiet for a moment, chewing on the tip of his pen again. "Yes," he said softly. "Many."

"Then how could a ten-year-old make it? How can *I?*" I suddenly felt as if I were about to throw up what little I'd managed to eat earlier. This is a nightmare, I thought.

Ian rose from his desk. "You'll be fine. I'm sure of it."

"How do you know? I'm not strong, not at all. I'm gonna die! There must be something I can do to keep from changing!"

"Crispin!" Ian shouted, and I flinched. He joined me in front of his desk, folding his arms across his chest. "If you think that way then no, you aren't going to survive. If you believe you'll die, then you will. And no, there isn't anything you can do. Your inevitable change will happen sooner or later and, if I were you, I'd stop working myself up so much. You may not be strong physically, but I'm sure there is a bit of strength somewhere inside you. I mean, take a look at Eden. He doesn't look very strong, does he?

Picture him six years younger. He found the strength to make it through that first change, and you will too."

I stared down at the floor, unsure what to say.

He returned to his seat, and shuffled through some papers on his desk, pretending to glance over a few. "Was it a large beast?"

I blinked. "What?" My mind was still taking in the fact I could die during the transformation. What am I gonna do?

"The wolf," Ian replied. "Was it very big?"

"Oh, yeah. Extremely."

"Hmm. Then it wasn't a teenager." He frowned down at the papers on his desk. "How many times did it bite you?"

"Just the one."

The man looked puzzled. "Are you absolutely positive that you don't know who bit you?"

"I'm positive." I remembered feeling as if I'd seen him before. I definitely recognized something about him. Could it really be someone I knew? A teacher at my school, perhaps? Or my boss at Greeny's?

No. There's no way it could be Aaron Cooper. That big goober was afraid of his own shadow.

"Teenagers and newly bitten werewolves can't control themselves," Ian said. "Once you've been one for ten, twenty years, you do learn to control it. It takes a long time for the wolf and the human to connect, since most of us weren't meant to become werewolves in the first place. But whoever bit you was an adult. Since he only bit you the one time, I believe he was in control of his actions, and bit you intentionally."

My breath caught in my throat. "But...why?"

Ian shrugged. "I wish I knew." The look on his face made it seem as if he knew a little more than he was telling me, but I didn't press on.

I couldn't imagine why anyone would intentionally turn me. I was useless; there was nothing I could do that someone else couldn't do better and faster.

What could Perinious have seen in me? Remembering that Eden had mentioned another guy the Elder had spoken to, I decided to ask about him.

"Ah, yes, I remember Pierce." Ian's tone was dark.

"Is he still here?" I asked, regretting the question as soon as the words left my mouth. His tone wouldn't have been so dark if he were still here. I felt like a moron.

But Ian was polite, and didn't make me feel worse about it. "No, Crispin. Pierce isn't at Bristol Manor anymore."

"What happened to him?" I took a seat in the front row of the classroom, gently placing my hands on top of the desk.

"He's still alive," the man said. "Pierce just left, much like your father left you and your mother, without an explanation." Ian shook his head, and brought his hand up to his chin. "He was great to have here, though he didn't stay long. Skilled fighter, good with the kids. He didn't like being unable to take action, though. That's probably why he left."

"What kind of action?"

Ian sat back in his chair, lightly tapping his foot on the floor. "He always thought we should kill the hunters. We at Bristol Manor never kill if we can help it. There are other packs out there that search for the hunters with the intent of hunting them to extinction, just like the hunters are doing with us. I wouldn't be surprised if Pierce was out there with them right now, leading the pack. Natural born leader, that one." Ian stared off into space, and I wondered if he and Pierce had once been close.

"Perinious expected great things from him," Ian continued. "Pierce became the best fighter Bristol Manor or any of the other Wolf Houses had ever seen. But he was constantly getting into trouble for disobeying the Elders' rules." The man smiled faintly at the memory. "Always the troublemaker. And unlike everyone else, he had the ability to control the wolf at a young age. Pierce could transform almost effortlessly, and everyone envied him. Like I said, it takes many years for one to develop these skills."

I ran my fingers over the giant P on the desk again. "How long did Pierce stay here?" I asked. "You said he wasn't here very long."

Ian's eyes rose to the ceiling as he tried to recall. "Oh, I'd say about three years. He moved in when he was around eighteen. Nowhere near old enough to possess the abilities he had."

My mind was racing. I thought about everything I'd just learned about Pierce, but couldn't make a connection. There must've been a reason Perinious, the Elder who rarely spoke, decided to personally accept Pierce and me. What was so special about us? Did we have anything in common?

Again, Ian rose from his chair, and I did the same, sensing our talk had come to an end. "Well, you'll start your classes Monday," he said. "For the next few days, I want you to just get to know everyone. Make some friends. I'm sure you'll like it here, once you get settled." He made his way over to the door and held it open for me. "The dinner bell will let you know when it's time to head to the dining room."

I wasn't completely sure I wanted to stay at Bristol Manor, but figured it couldn't hurt to get to know everyone before coming to a decision. I descended the stairs and walked down the hall until I came to my room.

I collapsed on the bed, trying unsuccessfully to get the images of Perinious out of my head. Everything that happened with the Elders replayed in my mind over and over.

My thoughts then turned to everything Ian had said, and unanswered questions swarmed through my brain. What did Perinious see in me? Why did he have high expectations of me? What exactly was he expecting me to accomplish? Did he foresee Pierce leaving? I wanted my questions answered, but I knew they wouldn't be any time soon.

My thoughts eventually drifted to Kaiden and his mother.

Part of me loved the idea of moving in. I'd have a bed, my own private bathroom, three meals a day, and I even had a friend here. But Kaiden was like a brother to me. We'd been through so much together. And if I moved in, Kaiden would be all alone. How could I do that to him?

A knock came at my door. I looked over as Eden entered. "Didn't you hear the dinner bell?" he asked, leaning against the doorframe.

"No." I got to my feet and shook my head. "Guess I was lost in thought."

"What were you thinking about?"

I shrugged. "You name it, I've probably thought about it. This is all just a lot to process, ya know?"

"Yeah, I know." We headed down the hall, and dashed down the stairs. "We're gonna be late, so we better hurry up. The Elders don't like to be kept waiting."

We quickened our pace and as we turned a corner, I slammed into a tall guy with thick muscles, and short brown hair. The boy's eyes were so dark they looked almost black.

"Sorry," I murmured.

He shoved me into a wall. "You *will* be sorry. Watch where you're going!" He put a rough hand on my shoulder, pinning me to the wall.

Eden knocked his arm away from me. "Leave him

alone, Zak. It was an accident, and he apologized, so let it go."

Zak turned to face Eden, an ugly scowl on his face. He was so much bigger than my new friend. "Stay outta this, Lambert! Nobody asked you." Zak returned his attention to me, and threw me to the floor with a flick of his wrist.

What a dick.

"Zak!" Eden shouted. "I said leave him alone!"

"Shut up, Eden! Don't you listen?" Zak launched his fist at Eden's face, and my friend stumbled back. Zak bent down and grabbed the collar of my shirt. I couldn't help but be reminded of Marcus, the bully from my high school.

Great, I thought. I finally escape one bully, only to have another one thrown at me. And this one is a were-wolf!

I tried to knock his hand away as Eden had, but failed miserably. Zak laughed at my attempt. "Watch your back, kid." His breath smelled foul and I cringed. "You've awakened the beast, and he's pissed."

Eden chuckled. "Really? The beast? Okay."

"I SAID STAY OUT OF THIS, LAMBERT!" Zak's face turned red as he yelled.

My friend started over to us, but a tingling sensation shot through my body, and I suddenly felt as if I'd been electrocuted. My muscles were burning. I was trembling all over. I squeezed my eyes shut, hoping I wasn't about to spontaneously combust. The voices of other kids who'd gathered around us slowly morphed together.

Panic rose in my chest, and my eyes flew open. After a few moments of agonizing pain, I realized with a jolt that everything was distorted. I couldn't tell one face from another. My clothes began tearing and ripping apart, and I knew what was coming.

My eyes darted down to my wobbly legs. Pants ripping off, shoes splitting open, at least half a dozen kids gawking at me. Could this be any more embarrassing?

My head throbbed. I felt nauseated and feverish. A couple of my ribs made a horrifying crack, and burning pain shot through my entire body. Why are my bones breaking?! My legs and arms snapped as well, and I fell to my knees, screaming in agony. My breath was coming in short gasps, and I felt dizzy. Is this normal? I frantically looked among the blurry shapes that surrounded me, trying to find Eden, but couldn't; everything was too distorted.

I remembered Ian telling me not everyone survived their first transformation. Panic rose in my chest when the taste of blood filled my mouth. Oh, no, I thought. I cried out as my broken bones began shifting. My poor heart felt as if it were about to burst; it was beating way too fast.

Part of me wanted to just lie down and die. I knew it was coming. There was no way I could survive this. The pain was unlike anything I'd ever experienced.

I closed my eyes, and inhaled deeply, holding my breath as long as I could. But my brain was throbbing, and I started to feel lightheaded. You can do this, you can do this. I exhaled when I knew I'd reached my limit.

The quivering of my limbs intensified, and so did the pain. Out of the countless voices that surrounded me, I was finally able to locate a familiar one. I heard Eden saying softly, "You got this, Cris." He believed I could, so I had to as well. When I opened my eyes, black fur sprouted all over my body. With one final *crack* of my bones, I exploded into a wolf.

CHAPTER NINE

One thing I wasn't aware of at the time of my transformation from human to wolf: everyone blacks out the first time. When I finally came to, I was lying in my bed with three claw marks on my arms, and a cold, wet rag draped across my forehead. With a start, I realized my clothes had been changed. The shredded ones from before were next to my backpack on the desk. I slowly sat up and clutched my stomach as a sharp pain forced me back down.

Eyes darting around the room, I found Eden and Ian talking quietly in the doorway. Eden looked over and giggled, which seemed a bit unnecessary considering what I'd just gone through. "Congratulations," he said happily. "You survived your first change. You are now officially one of us!"

Behind him, someone chanted, "One of us! One of

us!" as he walked by, and Eden grinned.

If I'd had doubts about the existence of werewolves, they were definitely gone now. "Great." I rubbed my head, wincing at the pain. "Wait. Did you think the transformation would kill me?"

Eden and Ian exchanged glances. "It has killed so many before," Ian said, his voice low. "I didn't want to say anything when we spoke of it earlier, but your lack of confidence, coupled with the fact you're so scrawny, I wasn't sure you'd survive."

"Honestly," Eden said, walking over to my bed, "for a minute there, I didn't think you were gonna make it. No offense."

"None taken," I said with a shrug.

"I'm really glad you did, though." I met his gaze, and he blushed.

I wanted to tell Eden that hearing his voice through all the chaos helped me through it, but I decided to keep that to myself. "What happened when I was out?" I looked up at Ian, who crossed his arms. "Did I hurt anyone?" Please say no, please say no.

Eden laughed. "You attacked Zak. He was so surprised and angered by it that he turned too. He got a couple good scratches in, but you really roughed him up."

I managed a weak smile. "I did?" At least I attacked a bully, and not some random kid.

"Yup." Eden plopped down on the side of my bed. "It was awesome, and everyone saw! Zak was so embarrassed."

103

I nodded. "Good. I think. So, how long was I, you know, a wolf?"

Ian joined Eden by my bed, and brought his hand up to his chin. "Twenty minutes," he said. "After your fight with Zak, you collapsed and reverted back to human. The rest of your wounds should be just about healed by now."

I could tell my body was healing at a much faster rate. I wasn't sore anymore, and I no longer felt sick. "Will I black out every time I turn?" I asked.

Ian shook his head. "No, that's just a first-time thing."

"Good." I wasn't sure I actually wanted to be aware of what was going on once I turned. The thought of being unable to control myself terrified me. What if I ended up hurting or even killing someone I really cared about? I could never live with myself if that happened.

And that's when I knew what I needed to do. I couldn't return to Kaiden and his mom if I was like this. It's way too dangerous. Looks like I'll be staying at Bristol Manor.

I looked up at Eden, who still seemed excited about my transformation. His blue eyes sparkled when he smiled, and his enthusiasm was refreshing. We'll get along just fine, I thought, a warm feeling spreading through my chest.

"I saved you some dinner," he said. "But someone got hungry. It's gone now. I'm sorry."

"Did you eat it?" I asked.

His face reddened a bit. "It's possible."

I laughed. "It's okay. I'll find something else."

As I got to my feet, Ian looked me hard in the eyes.

He stepped in front of the door before we could walk out. "I want you to stay away from Zak," he said. "He's terrible at controlling his temper, and I know he likes to torment those who are smaller. I don't want you getting into another fight with him."

"He can take him!" Eden shouted. "You should've seen him. He was awesome back there!"

Ian's eyes flicked over the older boy. "You know how first times are, Eden. Next time, he might not be so lucky." He returned his attention to me. "And I do believe it was just *luck*, Crispin."

"I'll try to avoid him," I said as Ian stepped out of the way. "I don't want to change again anytime soon. That was the most painful and embarrassing experience of my life." Satisfied with my answer, Ian left the room with a nod. "No one took pictures or anything, right?"

Eden shook his head. "We're not allowed to use our phones in the house."

I breathed a sigh of relief. "Good. I'd hate to have that moment memorialized in a meme."

"You're fine. Nothing to worry about."

Eden and I left the room, and made our way down to the kitchen, where I fixed myself a turkey sandwich. Eden made one that consisted of several layers of turkey, bologna, ham, chicken, salami, and several other types of meat. I gawked at his enormous sandwich and cringed.

Eden grinned goofily. "You'll eat like this someday. We all do." The older boy paused, and tilted his head.

105

"You're not a vegetarian, are you?"

"Nope."

"That's good." He took a huge bite of his sandwich. "You wouldn't be able to keep that up after this."

I pulled out the chair next to him and started eating as the girl I met in my room earlier joined us in the kitchen. She glided to the cabinet beside the sink, retrieved a cup, and poured herself some lemonade.

"Hey, Summer," Eden said, his mouth full of the oversized sandwich.

"Hey," the girl, Summer, said quietly. She searched through another cabinet until she found a bag of barbecue chips and, after emptying the bag into a bowl, the girl sat down across from him. "Who do you think is gonna fight tonight?" Summer asked. She brushed her long dark hair out of her face, and shoved a handful of chips into her mouth.

"I don't know." He licked his lips before continuing. "Hopefully they don't put him up against Zak. I heard he's pissed about getting his ass kicked."

"Wait, what?" I asked.

Eden turned to me, and dropped his sandwich on a plate. "When the pack gets a new addition, they go into this big fenced-off area in the basement and fight another kid in wolf form. The Elders choose who you're up against. They say it's to help us better our fighting and transformation skills, but I think the Elders just enjoy watching us tear each other apart."

A look came over his face that I couldn't quite place. Was it fear? Sadness?

Not only did I not *want* to fight, but I was worried I wouldn't be able to change on command. How would one even do that? The one time I turned, it wasn't intentional. I voiced my concerns, and placed my sandwich back on a plate, no longer feeling hungry. "What if the other kid turns before I can? What if I just can't do it?"

"You'll turn. Trust me." He spoke slowly, his voice full of dread. "The first couple times you see a huge, angry wolf lunging toward you, you'll change whether you want to or not." Eden licked some Miracle Whip off his fingers and stole a sip of Summer's lemonade.

"Eden!" she shouted, and pursed her lips. "Well, Zak hasn't fought in a long time, so I think they'll make him fight tonight." She turned to me, her expression hard as stone. "You're a goner."

I stared blankly at her. "You don't know that."

"Yes, I do."

"No," I said, appalled. "I could turn out to be a lot stronger than Zak. What if I just happened to be the strongest of them all? I could tear him limb from limb!" I was kidding...for the most part, but Summer was having none of it.

"I hope he rips your throat out!" she screamed at me.

I blinked. "Well that escalated quickly."

"Geez, psychopath," Eden said to Summer. Then he whispered to me, "Zak is her boyfriend."

"Oh," I said. "I'm sorry."

"Me too," Eden laughed. "It must suck being his girlfriend. Man, is he *ugly!*"

Summer punched his arm and rose to her feet. Her hip bumped into the table, knocking over the cup of lemonade. She didn't even stop to clean it up. "I really hate you sometimes, you know that, Eden?"

She then left the kitchen without another word.

"That girl can't take a joke," Eden said as he cleaned up her mess. His tone turned more serious when he spoke to me. "Are you nervous? About the fight tonight?"

I stared sightlessly down at my hands. Of course I was nervous. I had no idea what I was doing, and knew I'd probably lose. If others were going to watch the fight, it would be extra embarrassing. "Yeah," I said when I finally found my voice. "Fighting isn't something I particularly enjoy. Plus, I haven't had any training, so I know I'll get my ass kicked."

Eden avoided eye contact, his eyes shifting around nervously. "The fight will be pretty good training. Your wolf will learn what to do pretty quickly."

"You've fought, right?" I asked.

He nodded. "Everyone fights when they're accepted. It's awful, but there isn't anything I can do about it. The street packs are too wild for kids like me, and it's too dangerous to abandon the Elders, so I had no choice but to participate." His eyes were full of sadness, and tears welled in his eyes. When he spoke again, his voice was strained.

"I feel like bits of my soul are destroyed every time I fight."

Although I didn't know exactly what to expect out of these fights, they sure seemed to be soul-crushing. My heart sank. I couldn't imagine feeling the way Eden just described. "You've gotta get out of here then."

Eden met my gaze. He was hunched over the kitchen table, resting his head on his hand. "Where am I supposed to go? I told you, there aren't any other options, and the Elders would have me killed for deserting them."

Killed?! The Elders were crazier than I thought.

"Would the street packs be as dangerous if you joined one with friends at your side?" I asked. There must be something he could do to get out of these fights, I thought. They were destroying him.

He shook his head. "Who? I think you'll find that no one is crazy enough to willingly leave this place. And are you choosing to ignore the fact the Elders have deserters *killed?*"

I definitely wasn't ignoring it. That thought weighed heavily on my mind as I wondered what I'd gotten myself into, but I was more focused on finding somewhere safe for Eden to go. Though I didn't know him well, he seemed to be such a happy and enthusiastic guy. It saddened me to see him so frightened and sad when talking about these fights. How was no one else willing to leave with him?

"I'm sure we could find someone who'd be willing to leave with us," I said.

"Us?" He tilted his head. "You're new, and don't know

109

anything about this. Trust me, leaving Bristol Manor would be suicide, and everyone here knows it."

I bit my lip as I pondered the predicament. "If we found a pack, couldn't they offer us protection from the Elders?"

Eden looked thoughtfully at me for a moment. "Honestly, I'm not sure how powerful the Elders are anymore. I know they're getting weaker." He sat up straight in his chair, his hand resting in his lap. "But what would we do if we found a pack that decides to accept one of us, and not the others?"

"Um...." That thought hadn't crossed my mind. "We could start our own pack?"

A small smile tugged at his lips. "I appreciate how hard you're trying to get me away from these lunatics, but starting a pack is not that simple." With my new wolf hearing, I knew that his heart was pounding heavily. His cheeks flushed a bit.

"You're afraid to leave, but I know you're afraid of staying too." I placed my hand on his arm. His skin was warm to the touch. "There must be something we could do."

"Just accept that this is where we have to be, okay? Trust me; I wouldn't last five minutes without the protection of the Elders. You don't know what it's like out there."

I nodded silently, and decided to drop the issue...for now. I didn't want to push my new friend away.

The two of us made our way into the living room,

where three other kids were hanging out. We sat on the couch, which was as comfy as a cloud. Two boys sat cross legged on the floor around the coffee table, and the other kid was stretched out on the other couch across from us. One of the boys on the floor eyed me before turning his attention to Eden. "Who's he?"

"His name is Crispin," Eden said. "He's the one who fought Zak earlier."

"Oh." The boy looked me up and down, and pursed his lips. "I can't believe that was *him!* He doesn't look very—"

I cleared my throat rather loudly, and shifted uncomfortably in my seat.

"Ha-ha, sorry, dude. I'm Rylan." He waved. Rylan had short brown hair and big green eyes. He looked to be about fourteen years old and, like everyone else, he wore a Bristol Manor shirt and jeans. He also wore a dark purple jacket that looked to be three sizes too big. "You meet the Elders yet?"

I nodded. "Do they ever turn anyone down?"

Eden put his feet up on the coffee table, eyes glued to his shoes.

"Yes," the boy next to Rylan muttered, his tone filled with anger. "They rejected a guy I went to school with."

Rylan rolled his eyes. "Dexter is *still* upset about that."

"Of course I'm still upset!" Dexter shouted as he shot to his feet. "He deserved to be here just as much as anyone they *did* accept."

"It's been six years," Eden chimed in. "They denied him, and there's nothing you can do about it."

"Six years?!" I looked up at Dexter. "You've been here six years?"

He nodded and folded his arms.

Dexter had blond hair and light brown eyes. He looked to be a year or so older than Eden, which would put him at seventeen. He was tall and wiry. The skin around his eye was slightly discolored, and he had bloodstains on his bottom lip. I wondered who he'd gotten into a fight with, but didn't ask. Maybe it was Zak, I thought. "I've been here since I was eleven." He sat on the arm of the other couch, and glared down at the table. "Vik should have been accepted as well. He was a good kid. Because of the Elders, I haven't seen him in years. He was my best friend!"

"I've only been here three months!" The kid on the couch bolted upright. "I was the newbie. Now it's you!" He bounced up and down excitedly. "Just so you know, it really sucks being the newbie. Have fun with that!"

I sank back in my seat.

"You need to lay off the sugar, Max," Eden said and turned to me. "Ignore him. He's crazy."

Max seemed as if he'd had a few too many energy drinks. He laughed sort of maniacally before he spoke. "No, I'm good. I loooove sugar! Can't get enough, man. Cannot! Get! Enough!" Max, like Rylan, appeared to be about fourteen. He had brown hair and eyes, and very dark skin. He spoke with an accent I couldn't quite place.

Unlike the others, he was very short (even shorter than me!), and kind of pudgy. There was a trans pride pin on his shirt collar, and he had doughnut crumbs all over his shirt, mouth, and fingers.

Rylan laughed. "If you don't like Max, he will understand. He annoys me too, and he's my best friend."

"Oh, yeah? I annoy you?" Max happily yanked on Rylan's arm, and Rylan swatted at him, giggling.

I shifted my gaze to the floor. *Kids.*

"So," I said to no one in particular, "what is it that the Elders do to decide who is worthy of staying here? When I was down there, they didn't do anything except stare at me."

Dexter and Rylan exchanged glances. Rylan was the one who spoke up. "They can see things."

I arched an eyebrow. "Like the future?"

"Kinda." He pulled his knees up to his chest. "Sometimes they can get a glimpse into your future. If they think having you here will endanger the pack, they reject you."

Dexter rolled his eyes.

"Which one rejected your friend?" I asked him.

"Tealios," Dexter spat. "Same bastard who accepted me! Vik and I were so much alike. There isn't one damn reason that kid shouldn't have been accepted."

"Maybe they figured having one hothead here was enough," Eden said, dodging a shoe Dexter launched at him.

"Eden, I swear to god!"

Suddenly, a bell rang, nearly giving me a heart attack, and everyone shot up. "Time for the fight!" Max shouted. "Good luck, dude."

"Uh, thanks." I looked uncomfortably at Eden as blood roared in my ears. "I don't think I can do this."

He looked worried too, though I could tell he was trying hard not to show it. He placed a gentle hand on my shoulder. "Relax. I'm sure you'll be fine. You can do this."

I exhaled a quivering breath and nodded. Was I really going through with this? Would the Elders really kill me if I chose to leave instead? "So, where do we go for the fight?" My knees were shaking uncontrollably.

"You know the room you went in to visit the Elders?" Eden asked.

"Yeah."

"Did you happen to notice another door in there?"

"Yeah," I said with a gulp. "I wondered where it led to."

"Well, you're about to find out."

CHAPTER TEN

When we reached the basement, someone pushed the dilapidated door open, and I was a bit surprised when it didn't swing right off its hinges. Eden walked inside and I followed, looking around in amazement. The room was enormous. The floor was white tile, and a coat of grey paint covered the walls. In the center of the room was a circular cage made out of chain-link fence. In the middle of it was a drain, and the tiles inside the cage were stained blood red.

Bristol Manor inhabitants gathered around, and anxiously awaited the announcement of who I'd be fighting. Some seemed nervous, but most seemed oddly excited. What the hell was wrong with these people?!

Ian stepped inside the fighting pit. "Crispin Lipton," he said as he motioned for me to join him inside.

I swallowed hard and turned to Eden, who gave me a

reassuring nod. He seemed sad and scared. "Good luck," he whispered.

I stood by Ian's side, and the crowd began to whisper.

"That's the new kid," one kid said.

"He's the one who beat up Zak," said another.

"Zak is gonna kill him," a third voice muttered.

My stomach was in knots as I looked around at the many faces ogling me. All this attention made me uncomfortable, and wished I could go back to being invisible.

Ian raised his hand, and the crowd fell silent. All I could hear was the hammering of my heart, and my unsteady breaths.

Could I get out of this? Eden said the Elders killed those who left. I felt trapped and claustrophobic. My body was heavy and tingly.

Ian leaned closer to me, his eyes full of sorrow. "This is a fight to the death, Crispin."

"WHAT?!" I shouted.

"I'm so sorry you had to find out this way. The Elders forbid us from telling anyone before they participate." He lowered his head. "I really am sorry."

How could they be okay with this? How could the Elders make us go through with something like this? There was no way I could kill someone. Especially not a kid my age. What am I going to do?

It was getting harder and harder to breathe. I could feel my throat closing up. Unshed tears burned my eyes. This cannot be happening. Someone was going to die today. Could I really kill a kid for the amusement of the Elders? Well, if I didn't, I would be one who was killed.

Panic rose in my chest as reality set in. This is happening. This is *actually* happening. I'm a werewolf, and I'm about to fight another to the death! What if the other person killed me as soon as the fight began? They could snap my neck before I even knew what was happening. What if my wolf wouldn't do anything? What if I just sat there while the other kid ripped me apart?

If I ran now, how far would I get? How long would it be before the Elders had me killed? How would they do it?

The Elders were sitting in thrones behind the cage, across from the onlookers. Perinious was leering at me, and I did my best to avoid his gaze.

I searched the crowd for a friendly face. To the left was Summer, and standing next to her was Zak. Rylan, Dexter, and Max were to the right, though they were closer to the back, which made them harder to see. I kept scanning the crowd until I found Eden.

He met my eyes and mouthed, *you got this.*

Perinious's face was expressionless, and I wondered if he'd been staring at me this whole time. Was he reading my thoughts? I couldn't tell. To be safe, I cleared my mind, and just concentrated on breathing.

My legs were weak and shaky.

Tealios handed Ian a small, wrinkled piece of paper. Ian glanced at it briefly before crumpling it up in his hands. "Rylan—"

But he was cut off.

Perinious was shaking his head as he handed him another small piece of paper. Tealios glared at the other Elder as he reclaimed his seat. Ian then looked at me with sympathetic eyes, and I knew that meant I'd be fighting Zak or someone equally as big and terrifying. I didn't stand a chance tonight and Ian knew it.

Please don't say Zak, please don't say Zak. Anyone but Zak.

Blood roared so loudly in my ears I was sure everyone else could hear it too. I could feel my pulse throughout my entire body. Holding my breath, I forced myself to stare straight ahead, my face as expressionless as I could make it.

Ian sighed, shaking his head slowly. "Eden James Lambert."

My throat went dry as Eden, the person I was closest to at Bristol Manor, forced himself to step inside the fighting pit. I had to remind myself to breathe when he met me in the middle of the cage. I shouldn't have wished so hard not to fight Zak. If I'd known it would be Eden...

There was no way I could hurt him. How did Perinious expect me to kill the only person I really connected with at this place? Was this some kind of sick joke? Did he get off on shit like this?

Ian motioned for my friend to go to the other side of the cage. He led me to the opposite side, and placed his hand on my shoulder. "I'm very sorry, Crispin. I know the two of you have become good friends. But this is how it has to be."

I felt like I was sort of on autopilot. I was going through the motions of what I needed to do, but wasn't really there. Not mentally. Otherwise, I would have been fighting back. Kicking and screaming and punching until this was all over.

"Are you okay?" he asked. He sounded genuinely concerned.

But I didn't respond. No, I wasn't okay. And I wasn't going to lie to make Ian feel better about the whole thing. I didn't want to hurt Eden.

Without another word, the man exited the cage, and locked us inside. The ceiling lights dimmed. I took several deep breaths, trying desperately to calm my nerves. Eden looked equally frightened and horrified. He seemed to be on the verge of tears.

How was I supposed to do this? I *can't* do this.

The crowd actually seemed excited, which baffled me. Who would want to watch two of their classmates, their friends, fight each other with no control over their actions? Did they enjoy participating as much as they enjoyed watching? Or was it all an act?

This isn't happening, I thought. I'm going to wake up in the back seat of Kaiden's car or maybe even upstairs in the bedroom, but none of this fighting stuff is actually happening. It couldn't be happening.

Seconds dragged on for hours.

I snuck a glance at Eden, who looked equally terrified, and it made me sick. He removed the purple bracelet from his left wrist, and squeezed it tightly before dropping it to the floor. He was eyeing the bloodstained drain in the middle of the cage, refusing to look at me.

What would happen if the two of us refused to fight? Could we do that? Would they kill us both if we did? Probably.

Out of the corner of my eye, I spotted Ian standing next to a small group of adults. "Let the fight begin!" he shouted.

My heart felt as if it were going to pound right out of my chest. I didn't know what to do; I knew they wanted me to turn, but wasn't sure how to trigger it. When my eyes landed on Eden, I was surprised to find an enormous grey wolf in his place. His eyes were now glowing bright red. I staggered backward as he leapt toward me, snarling.

Suddenly, my stomach tightened, and my muscles burned. My head throbbed as my bones started breaking, and my clothes began to rip. My scream became a howl as my body covered itself in the thick black fur of my wolf.

Eden was right. I turned at the sight of him without even trying.

I watched helplessly as Eden came toward me. I was unable to move out of his way; my wolf and I were petrified. *Move, dammit!* But my legs wouldn't obey.

Eden landed hard on my back, and bit down on my ear. I yelped and threw him off. He tried to scratch me with his claws, but my wolf took Eden's paw, and chomped down. Blood dripped into my mouth as he winced, and retreated to the other side of the cage, growling.

I couldn't believe what I was doing. This had to be some sort of nightmare. Unfortunately, it was all too real. I was hurting Eden, and my heart broke a little each time.

I lunged forward and slammed his face into the fence. He yelped, and bit the side of my neck, rising up on his hind legs. I dug my claws into his belly. His teeth sank deeper into my throat, and I feared I'd bleed out in seconds.

I couldn't stand hurting him. But I just couldn't stop. Controlling the wolf was impossible.

I tried to shut my eyes so I wouldn't have to see the horrific events that transpired around me. Unfortunately, my wolf wanted to see everything he was doing. It was torture.

Please stop, please stop, please stop, please stop. I repeated the words over and over in my head. I didn't know who or what I was praying to, but I hoped someone would hear me.

The crowd cheered loudly. Some cheered for me, some for Eden. One kid shouted, "Bite his tail!"

Another yelled, "Yeah, bite the tail! Bite the tail!"

Eden raised his paw, and slashed his razor-sharp claws across my furry forelegs before digging them into my lower back. I tried to shout, "Ouch!" but it came out "Woof!" I couldn't believe I had just barked. No one laughed, and then I remembered that I was a wolf. Not quite as embarrassing.

After Eden removed his claws from my back, I spun around and sliced mine across his face. I wanted to scream at myself when the blood trickled down his face. Did he feel the same way? Was he panicking and hating himself every time he hurt me?

I bit down into his shoulder. My heart skipped a beat when blood gushed out, but my teeth sank deeper and deeper. Blood spilled down to the drain in the floor, and my paw slipped in the warm red liquid.

I knocked his feet out from under him, and he landed on his belly. I had Eden pinned to the floor. I twisted his fur with my teeth until he howled in pain, and attempted to throw me off him. He rolled to his back, and I bared my teeth, staring into Eden's bright red wolf eyes. He whimpered and my heart sank. He looked so frightened.

Don't do this to him, I begged silently. Please don't hurt him. Please don't hurt Eden.

But my wolf wouldn't listen.

I dragged Eden around by the nape of his neck, and ripped away a chunk of flesh and fur. He tried pouncing on me, but I was too fast. I dodged his outstretched claws, and threw myself behind him. Eden halted and turned to me, unsure what to do. A low growl erupted from my throat as I flung toward him, scratching and biting everything I could.

The teachers scattered throughout the crowd had

nervous expressions on their faces. Teens killing each other obviously didn't sit well with everyone at Bristol Manor, so why not stop the fight? If everyone fought against the Elders, could they really come out on top?

The fight went on, though, and no one attempted to stop us.

I stood over Eden as he howled in pain. He was lying on his side, struggling to breathe, but my wolf wasn't going to let up. I knew I was going in for the kill now. Eden stared up at me, a fearful look in his eyes. He knew it too.

The look on his face hurt my soul.

I felt hopeless, full of despair. Stop, I begged. Don't do this!

I won't do it! I WON'T DO IT!!

My body trembled as I fought against my wolf. My heart pounded even faster, which didn't seem possible. I knew it was pointless to fight against the wolf; I hadn't had enough experience to control what it did yet. But I had to try.

Eden was clearly in so much pain. I couldn't bear the thought of killing him, and losing the one person I truly cared about at Bristol Manor.

My muscles burned as I fought for control. Refusing to give up, my body shook more violently. Beads of sweat rolled down my neck (or was it drool?), and I wondered how much longer I'd be able to fight. My limbs ached. Blood oozed from several wounds, pooling around my feet. I was rapidly growing weaker and weaker, my entire

123

body felt as if it were on fire, and I was sure my heart was about to explode.

Eden's eyes never left mine. I don't want to hurt him, I thought. I can't let myself do this to him!

Then I felt something inside of me change.

All the tension between the wolf and me was gone; it was as if it had been lifted away by a giant pair of invisible hands. I forced my wolf to retreat. I collapsed on the floor next to Eden, who could barely move. At least he was alive.

I couldn't believe I actually did it! I didn't understand how, but at the moment, I didn't care. I was so relieved that I beat my wolf and wasn't hurting Eden anymore.

Though, I couldn't celebrate my victory. He was lying still on the floor, breathing heavily. How could I have done this? Why did I participate in this fight? I shouldn't have gone inside the cage. I shouldn't have let him get hurt.

The Elders must've been angry, since the fights were supposed to be to the death. I didn't bother looking up at them to find out.

Everyone in the crowd gasped, and whispered amongst themselves.

My body painfully shrank back to its normal size. I bit my tongue to keep from screaming. When the two of us were human again, some of the teachers tossed some clothes at us, though I was too weak to put anything on at the moment.

The older boy sat up, pulling his knees up to his chest. He brought a quivering hand up to his face, and I saw that it was scratched and bloody. His whole body was covered in battle wounds.

I wanted to apologize; I felt terrible for hurting him, but I couldn't bring myself to talk yet. Would Eden ever forgive me? Blood slid down my face from a cut on the side of my forehead, and I shivered.

Ian made his way to the middle of the circle. His expression was a mixture shocked and happy. "For the first time in many, *many* years, the fight will not end with the death of a pack mate!" He shouted excitedly. "Give it up for Crispin Lipton!"

The majority of the crowd cheered. There were a couple scattered boos that I tried to ignore, mainly coming from Zak and his friends. The Elders didn't look pleased at all, though Perinious's expression was different. Unreadable.

Ian looked down at me, his smile reaching his eyes. "You did great, Crispin. We'll get you and Eden fixed up in just a few moments."

The crowd started heading up the stairs as Eden and I caught our breath. I hoped I wasn't about to lose the only friend I'd made at the Wolf House. "I'm really sorry, Eden," I said, wiping the blood from my face.

The smaller bruises and scratches on his body were already starting to fade, but the bigger ones still had blood oozing out of them. How could I have done that to him?

He managed a weak smile. "It's okay. This is what we were supposed to do."

"I didn't want to."

He met my gaze, his cheeks flushing. "Well, you didn't kill me, so I'm not complaining." We put our clothes on, but remained sitting on the bloody tile floor. He ran a hand through his hair, and retrieved his bracelet from the floor. "Can I ask you something?"

"What?" I asked as I struggled to tie my shoes. My hands and arms were still shaking.

"How did you, you know..."

I shrugged. "I'm not sure. I just knew I couldn't let myself kill you."

Our eyes met. "What you did was amazing. No one else has managed to control their wolf with so little experience in a *long* time."

"So I've heard." I rubbed my eyes, suddenly very aware of how tired I was. My muscles ached and most of my wounds still burned, but I didn't care. All I wanted to do was go to my room and sleep for the next three or four days, though I'd settle for eight or nine hours.

Eden and I were the only ones left in the basement other than the Elders, who were eyeing us suspiciously. When Eden got to his feet, he extended a hand to help me up.

The two of us silently made our way up to our rooms, and were greeted by Ian standing by my door. "Would you like someone to take a look at your wounds?" he asked us.

"No," Eden and I said in unison. *Just let me sleep...*

"Are you sure?" Ian examined the cut on my forehead,

and the three claw marks on Eden's cheek. "Well, it looks like you boys are healing. I'll let you get some sleep."

"Are the Elders angry?" I asked him.

Ian shook his head. "I don't think so. They prefer when these fights end with a death, but Perinious chose Eden as your opponent for a reason. He probably knew you'd be able to control the wolf if you had the right motivation." His gaze shifted from me to Eden, and I swallowed hard.

With that, the man disappeared down the hall.

"You going to bed?" I asked Eden.

"Yup," the older boy murmured. "I feel like I could sleep for a week."

"I know, right?" I knew I'd probably fall asleep as soon as my head hit the pillow, but I couldn't let what happened downstairs go. I felt guilty every time I looked at my friend.

He must've sensed this, because he said, "I'm fine. I promise. All these cuts and bruises will be completely gone by morning. It'll be as if it never happened."

I nodded but said nothing. Now I knew why Eden was so afraid of the fights, and why they traumatized him so much. How many times had he been forced to fight? How many kids had Eden killed because of the Elders?

"You need to get some sleep," he said. "Good night, Cris. I'll see you tomorrow." Eden opened his bedroom door and trudged inside.

"Good night, Eden." My voice was barely audible when I spoke. I went into my room and threw myself on the comfortable bed that I could now officially call mine. Memories of the fight flashed before my eyes, and I groaned. This is gonna be a long night, I thought. But within seconds of lying down, I fell asleep.

CHAPTER ELEVEN

The next morning, I woke to the sound of Eden bursting into my room. He pulled back the curtains, letting in the bright morning light, and I shielded my eyes with my arms. "Dude, you're a *werewolf,* not a vampire!" He chuckled, and tossed a fresh change of clothes on the bed. "Hurry up and get dressed."

I rubbed my eyes. "Why? What's going on?"

"A few of us are going on a little outing, and you're coming too!" He brushed the hair out of his eyes, and nudged the clothes a bit closer to me. "You do want to come, right?"

"Yeah," I said.

It was a relief to see there were no remaining marks on his face from the previous night. Everything healed overnight, just like he'd said.

Eden grinned. "Good. But you better hurry, because we're leaving soon. Meet me downstairs!" He ran out of my room, and closed the door behind him.

I stayed in bed a moment longer, letting myself fully wake up. It was nine in the morning, which meant I'd slept a little over nine hours, yet I was still exhausted and sore. "Guess I should get up," I said to myself. It felt good to be included, so I pushed aside the aches and pains, and struggled out of bed.

Part of me was having a hard time adjusting to everything that was happening to me; I kept expecting to wake up inside Kaiden's car, and find that it was all a dream. Finding out I was a werewolf wasn't the only thing that was hard to accept. It was also the fact I had a place to stay and, for once in my life, more than one person I could call a friend.

However, there were also new horrors to get used to as well. Thoughts of werewolf hunters and the sadistic Elders weighed heavily on my mind. I imagined getting dragged into another fight down in the basement, being killed by the hunters, and accidentally killing one of my new friends.

Maybe I won't have to worry about that, I thought. Maybe controlling the wolf would be easier from now on.

After forcing the thoughts from my mind, I hurriedly got dressed, and prepared to go wherever we were going. My muscles screamed every time I tried to move too fast. Needless to say, getting dressed took a bit longer than expected.

I opened the door, my eyes lingering on my backpack. For the first time in years, I felt comfortable leaving it out of sight. I left it on the desk, and zipped up my old black jacket.

As I made my way down to the living room, I wondered who would be joining us. I hadn't met very many people at Bristol Manor yet. The few I'd met seemed pretty cool. Except for Zak, of course. He was a dick.

When I entered the living room, I was greeted by a very happy Rylan, who was sitting on the couch. He was playing a game on his phone, despite the fact phones weren't allowed to be used in the house. "You're coming?" he asked. His hair was crazy and stuck out wildly, but he didn't seem to mind.

"Yeah," I said, shoving my hands into my jacket pockets.

Max came running in. "Crispy's coming!" He threw himself on the couch next to his best friend, and bounced up and down. "Awesome!"

"It's Crispin," I corrected him.

"Oh, sorry." Max giggled, hiding his face with his hand. "Can I call you Crispy?"

I shook my head. "Absolutely not."

"Oh, come on," the younger boy protested. "It'll be a cool nickname!"

"No."

Rylan stifled a laugh, but didn't look up from his phone. "Crispy. That's so funny."

I chose to ignore the Crispy comments being made. "So, where's Eden?"

"Getting Summer," Rylan replied. "Crispy."

I rolled my eyes. Definitely not cool with that nickname.

I groaned, and plopped down on the couch next to Rylan. If Summer was going with us, her boyfriend would probably tag along as well.

As if reading my thoughts, Rylan said, "Zak isn't coming."

"He isn't?"

Rylan shook his head. "Nope. Looks like you get to live another day." I glared at him. "Kidding. Anyway, Ian gave him some extra credit work that has to be turned in today." He snickered. "He's failing."

Dexter and Eden joined us in the living room, and Dexter folded his arms across his chest. "Hey," he said angrily. "Someone failing is *not* funny! I was failing, and only just got my grade up."

Rylan shrugged. "It's funny when the person failing is Zak. I can't stand him."

"Yeah," Max said, and shoved a doughnut in his mouth. "He's an ass."

Rylan made a face, and shoved his phone into his pocket. "Looks like one, too."

Eden grabbed a set of keys from on top of the coffee table, and Max snatched them from his hand. The younger boy made his way to the front door. "Can I drive?"

Eden shook his head as he took the keys back. "Hell no! You're only fourteen."

Summer finally sauntered in. "Gentlemen, I'll be driving today."

Dexter's eyes widened. "Pah! *I'm* driving. I'm the oldest, remember?" He grinned and straightened his back, obviously quite pleased with himself.

"Congrats on being closer to the grave than the rest of us," Summer said, and flipped her hair over her shoulder.

Dexter frowned. "Damn."

The six of us then made our way out to a grey SUV that was just barely sticking out of the garage. Dexter and Eden took the front seats, Summer and I sat in the second row together, and Rylan was in the very back with Max. I still didn't know where we were going, but honestly, I didn't care. It was just nice to go out with friends.

On the drive, everyone was laughing and talking about random things going on in their lives. I was trying to listen, to learn more about them, but my mind wandered, and I found myself thinking about my encounter with the Elders. Their eyes seemed soulless, and their hideous faces still haunted me. I understood why Rex had nightmares about them.

The sound of Rylan's voice shouting my name eventually caught my attention. "What?" I asked, blinking in confusion.

He leaned forward in his seat. "I said I'm surprised you weren't rougher with Eden at the end of the fight."

His eyebrows drew together. "You actually pulled away. Did you do that on purpose?"

I stared out the window, watching a few birds as they flew around. "Yeah, I did."

"How?" Rylan asked. "It's all anyone could talk about."

"I'm not sure," I said with a shrug. "I just—I didn't want to hurt Eden anymore."

Eden looked back at me, his expression unreadable, but there was a look in his eyes... Then he turned to look at Dexter, who ran a red light, but Eden didn't notice. "We should be coming up on it soon."

I shifted in my seat. "Where are we going?"

"We're going to this little strip of stores in the next county," Eden said as he fidgeted with the bracelet on his wrist. "Ian asked me to go to a sporting good's store, and pick up some fishing gear for a trip he's taking with his siblings. He said to bring some friends, so I figured we'd just look around, grab something to eat, and just have fun for a while."

"Maybe we could go exploring in the woods too?" Rylan asked, a hint of eagerness in his voice.

Eden shrugged. "Sure. We have to be careful, though. First sign of hunters, and we're gone. Everyone understand?"

"Yes," we all said in unison.

"Good." He clapped his hands together. "We can be out all day as long as we're back in time for dinner."

"Awesome!" Max shouted happily. "Are we there yet?"

The kid shouted almost everything he said. It was giving me a headache.

"Not yet."

I knew Rylan and Max were best friends, but I didn't see how Rylan could stand to be around him so much. He was too energetic and loud. I could barely tolerate one class sitting next to Kaylee Wright from my old high school. She was just as bad as Max. I won't miss seeing her every day, I thought. I wouldn't miss anyone from my old school except...Oh, no! Kaiden!

Was he looking for me? Did he think I'd been killed or kidnapped? Would he or his mother have gone to the police by now? Then I wondered how long I'd been missing.

I had to see Kaiden, and explain what was going on. He deserved to know the truth. I leaned forward, and lowered my voice a bit. "Before we head back, do you guys mind if we swing by an alley that's not too far from Bristol Manor?" Kaiden needed to know that I was okay, and why I wouldn't be coming back. At least not for a while.

But then I wondered...would he feel like I'm abandoning him? Technically, I was. I didn't know when I would see him again. How would I feel if the roles were reversed? If he were the one leaving, going off to live in some big-ass mansion with new friends, dropping out of Valley Park High. I'd be hurt and furious. I can't do that to him, I thought.

Maybe he should become a—

"I guess so," Eden said, snapping me out of my

thoughts. Probably for the best. "Can I ask why?"

I paused, clearing my head before responding. "I need to talk someone."

"In an alley?" Max asked, tilting his head. "Why?"

"Because he lives there."

Max's eyes widened. "You know someone who lives in an alley?"

"Yeah," I said, my tone harsh. I didn't want to explain to him that I'd been homeless, and that Kaiden still was. That kind of information was really personal, and too embarrassing to admit to just anyone. Eden found out on his own, and I was okay with that, but I had no intention of telling anyone else.

"How did you even meet someone like that?" Max wrinkled his nose in disgust. I seriously considered punching him. "Yuck."

"Homeless people aren't disgusting!" I glared hard at the kid, but he didn't seem to notice.

"Yes, they are," Max replied. "They're dirty bums who don't have a place to live because they're too lazy to get off their butts and get a job."

"Or they're drug addicts," Dexter interjected. Eden whacked the side of his head. "Ow! What was that for?"

"None of that is true!" I shouted, turning back to look at Max. "Some people have jobs, but still can't afford even a crappy little apartment. Some people lose their jobs, and can't find another. And some are teenagers who were kicked out of their home by their parents for whatever reason. Shit happens. Yeah, there are people who basically do it to themselves. But not everyone who lives on the street is lazy." I balled my fists, and felt my claws come out. I dug them deep into my hand, trying to keep calm. "When you live on the street, you start to see the hatred in people's hearts. Very few offer any help, and too many think like you guys do, that they're lazy and had it coming. That kind of thinking is just wrong." My heart hammered in my chest as I sank back in my seat. My face turned red, and I brought my hands up, running them through my hair.

"Why does this bother you so much?" Max asked. His voice sounded small now.

"Max," Eden said. "Drop it, okay?"

"But—"

"I said drop it." Eden's tone was full of authority without being harsh. I liked that about him.

He looked over his shoulder, and I smiled at him appreciatively.

The rest of the drive was awkwardly silent. I felt bad for snapping, but I couldn't let Dexter and Max think like that.

Eventually, we pulled into the parking lot of a small white building. The sign read, Tom's Sporting Goods, and it made me think of the werewolf hunter I'd met named Tom. I shuddered at the thought as I climbed out of the car.

Tom's Sporting Goods was by itself on the right side of the road. On the other side were four or five clothing stores, a dollar store, couple restaurants, and a movie theater. Kaiden and I never visited this area before, so it was all new to me.

Tom's Sporting Goods was dirty on the outside, and the paint was chipping badly. The welcome mat was crooked, and the L was missing. Max and Rylan laughed at the 'we come' mat. There was an old, beat-up pickup truck in the parking lot, the only other car there, and I figured it belonged to the store owner.

"I'm gonna check out the stores across the street," Dexter said, eyeing the welcome mat. "All of us don't need to go into that dump." Max and Summer crossed the street with him.

Rylan and I joined Eden in the sporting goods store, but it didn't take long to retrieve the fishing equipment. After rejoining the others, we ate at a 50s styled diner. Most of them complained that the food wasn't very good, but I was happy to have something in my stomach other than chips and bread.

After we returned to the van Max asked, "Are we visiting Crispy's homeless friend now?"

"Don't call me Crispy," I muttered. "The alley I need to go to is right across from the woods by Bristol Manor," I said.

"All right," Eden said, and buckled his seatbelt. "We'll go there next."

I was a little nervous to see my best friend again. I didn't know if he would be upset, or if he'd just be relieved to see that I was okay. I felt terrible for leaving him, but I couldn't stay there anymore. If I got too angry and lost control, he could get hurt. I couldn't have that.

CHAPTER TWELVE

When we turned down the familiar alley, my stomach filled with dread. I wished Kaiden could join us at Bristol Manor, but I wouldn't do this to him. If he couldn't survive the bite, I wouldn't be able to live with myself. If he could though, he wouldn't have to be homeless anymore...unless the Elders turned him down, that is. But with so many uncertainties, there was no way I could turn my best friend.

I got out of the SUV, and made my way over to the car we'd called home for the past few years. When I peeked through the window, I saw nothing. No backpack, no blankets, and no Kaiden. Perplexed, I scratched my head and circled the car, silently taking in the scene. I trudged back to my friends as knots formed in my stomach.

Where could he be? Kaiden obviously wasn't planning on returning. Unlike me, he always left everything he owned in the car. When going to school, he'd bring his backpack, but left his clothes, comforter, and everything else.

Did he move? Was it because I disappeared, or did something happen to him? Kaiden wouldn't leave without telling me, and making sure that I was all right. The thought of being abandoned by my best friend made my head throb. How could he do this to me? Didn't he care that I was missing? Was he not worried?

With a heavy sigh, I climbed back into the car, staring down at my feet. I'd never felt so empty in my entire life… with the exception of when I found out my mother had been killed.

Max turned to me, and asked about a million questions: Where'd you grow up? How old are you? How do you know a homeless kid? Were you homeless too? Does your friend live in that car? Where is he? I didn't see you talk to him. Was he there?

I did my best to answer Max's questions, but after a while, I ignored him. He was asking so many, and I couldn't stop thinking about Kaiden leaving me. It felt like he didn't care. Part of me was starting to wonder if he ever did.

When we got to the forest, I jumped out of the car and casually strolled away from Max.

Eden arched an eyebrow. "Max getting on your nerves?" he asked.

I shrugged. "Kinda."

"Kinda? Yeah, right. You look like you're about two seconds away from strangling him." He playfully shoved me.

I laughed nervously. "Yeah, I guess he is a little annoying."

"Tell him to leave you alone."

I shook my head. "I don't want to hurt his feelings."

"Oh, he'll be all right," Eden said. "He knows he's a lot to take."

"Nah, I'm good."

"You're too nice."

"Not always," I said, and stuffed my hands into my jacket pockets. "I have my moments."

I looked over at Max and Rylan, who started walking away from the group. It was nice being outdoors and with friends, even though it was a little chilly. Sunlight shone through the leaves, and birds happily chirped as a slight breeze caused the trees' limbs to sway. I took a deep breath, enjoying the fresh air.

Eden sat on the hood of the car, talking to Dexter.

"Hey," Summer said to me. She was standing in front of me, waving a hand in front of my face.

"Uh, hi," I stammered.

She began walking further into the woods, motioning for me to follow. When I caught up to her, she asked, "So, I wanted to ask you something." She spoke quietly until we were far enough away from the others to avoid being overheard. "How did you and your family lose your home?"

I blinked. "Ummmm—"

"It's pretty obvious, Crispo." Summer stared down at the leaves on the ground. "But you don't have to be embarrassed."

"It's *Crispin*."

"Whatever." She waved her hand, as if my name weren't important. "Anyway, you had three sets of clothes in your backpack, most of which were pretty worn out and faded. You ate like you hadn't had a decent meal in weeks, and you wouldn't let your backpack out of your sight. Plus, you got super defensive when Max and Dexter said that shit about homeless people. Need I go on?"

"Hey! We all ate like that," I protested.

Summer stared at me, eyes squinted. "Come on, dude."

My shoulders slumped. "My mom worked at this bakery a few streets down," I began. "She was having trouble making it there on time, as I was apparently difficult to get up and off to school when I was younger. I caused her to be late so many times; they had to let her go because of it." I sighed heavily, knowing that everything was my fault. "I was ten years old. My mom couldn't find another job, and eventually, we were forced to leave the apartment. We had to live on the street all because of me."

"What about her parents?" she asked. "Wouldn't they take you guys in?"

I shook my head. "I'm not sure why, but they never spoke to her. I've never met my grandparents."

Summer lowered her head. "Where is your mother now?"

I chewed my nails anxiously. "She, uh…She was killed last year."

"Oh shit. I'm sorry." Her hand flew up to cover her mouth, a sad look in her eyes. "What was she like?"

"She was…" I let my voice trail off, wondering how exactly to describe my mom. The wind blew a bit harder, and I sniffled from the cold. "She was all I ever had," I said finally. "We never had the best relationship, but it wasn't the worst. She and I always seemed to bring out the worst in each other. But she knew when something was really important to me, and would do her best to help."

"You brought out the worst in each other?" she asked. "How?"

"We couldn't really be around each other without arguing," I said with a shrug. "Everything had to be her way; there was no compromising. She was always right, and I was always wrong, no matter what. I found it easier to completely avoid her, which became a lot easier after we lost our apartment."

I hated talking about my mother that way.

Summer stared sightlessly off into the distance, her eyes seemingly vacant.

I cleared my throat, and took a step backwards. "I loved her, though. She was hard on me, but what parent isn't hard on their child when they're as bad as I was? Unlike some parents I've seen, she never hit me. Not that

144

I remember, at least." There was an awkward silence. "But she was a good mother."

"Are ya sure about that?" Summer asked, a funny look on her face.

"Yes!" I shouted, and she jumped. I swallowed the lump of sadness in my throat, and averted my eyes. "She was difficult to be around sometimes, but everyone has moments like that. There were times when I couldn't stand to be around Kaiden, and he was my best friend. My mom raised me all alone. I was happy, healthy, and for most of my life, I had a roof over my head. That was all because of her."

Summer tilted her head. "What about your dad? Was he not in the picture?"

I shrugged. "I think my dad left when I was just a baby, or maybe before I was born. I'm not sure. The few times I'd ask about him, my mother's story would sometimes change a bit. I rarely asked about him, though, because my mom hated talking about him." She probably wouldn't have answered my questions anyway. "Now, I don't care where he is, or if he's even alive. He's been gone too long for me to care, and he's obviously never cared about me."

Summer looked down at her shoes, a heartbroken look on her face. I wondered if one of her parents had abandoned her as well. When I was about to ask, she looked up at me, a tear sliding down her cheek. "I—I'm really—" She turned away, wiping her eyes. "I'm very sorry."

If the same thing had happened to her, she clearly

didn't want to talk about it.

We strolled a bit farther into the woods. The air was cooler, and the chirping of the birds was barely audible. Twigs snapped beneath our feet as we walked. Thunder boomed as a few drops of rain fell from the greying sky. It soon began to pour.

Summer shrieked. "Oh, no!" The girl dashed back to the car, her arms covering her head. "Is it locked?"

Eden hopped off the hood, rain sliding down his face. "Nope."

She jumped inside and slammed the door behind her.

Eden, Dexter, and I hopped in the SUV with Summer, and waited for the others to return. I wondered why they wandered off so far from the rest of us, and why no one seemed to be worried. After all, we were in the same part of the woods where I'd met the hunters.

Eden's phone beeped, and his eyes skimmed over the message. "Rylan said there is something we have to see."

Dexter groaned. "Tell him to take a pic and send it to you."

He typed out a reply. Moments later, his phone beeped again. "Can't. His camera is broken."

"Well, that sucks," Dexter said.

"He said they aren't far, though, and that it's really important that we see it. Does anyone wanna go with me?" Eden glanced from Summer to me, and then to Dexter, who was lying down in the back row. "Or am I going alone?"

"Yeah, that sounds good," Dexter said. "I'll keep an eye on the car."

Eden frowned. "Your eyes are closed."

"Well, you know what I mean."

Eden stuck out his bottom lip, and looked at Summer and me with big, sad eyes. "You guys are really gonna make me go out in the rain by myself?" His lip quivered. "All alone. . ."

Summer giggled. "Look at your cute little pouty face."

He tried to hide a smile. "Is it working?"

"I'll go with you," I said, and his face lit up.

"I would," Summer said as she looked up at the clouds. "But it's raining, and I'm cold."

"I'd make ya go alone," Dexter said with a chuckle. His long legs were bent awkwardly, pressed against the door.

Eden shot him a glare, but Dexter didn't see.

The two of us hopped out of the car, and hiked through the woods toward Rylan and Max. It wasn't raining quite as hard as it had been a few moments before.

When I glanced at Eden, he had a thoughtful look on his face.

"What are you thinking about?" I asked.

His mouth was a thin line when he looked away. "I'll tell you later."

A small part of me thought I already knew, but I didn't say anything. I didn't want to be wrong.

After a while, we saw Rylan and Max sitting on a fallen tree. The rain had only stopped a moment ago, so the four of us were now completely drenched. The two boys hopped down, and ran over to us. "Guys, you *have* to see this!" Max shouted.

Rylan grabbed the sleeve of my jacket, and dragged me over to a large paw print in the mud.

Eden stared at it, unimpressed. "Okay? So?" He folded his arms, and squinted at the younger boys. "You both know there are other werewolves around here."

"But look how big it is," Rylan said, glancing between the two of us. "Pierce is the only one I know whose wolf is that big."

A look of realization came over Eden's face. "He's here?" He knelt down by the paw print, and scowled. "That's not good."

"Why is that a bad thing?" I asked.

He turned to me. "Did Ian tell you anything about Pierce?"

I nodded. "A little bit. Why?"

"Pierce wanted to kill the hunters," Eden replied. "We, at Bristol Manor, do not kill."

"Unless it's in one of those fights you two participated in," Rylan added. "Where's the logic in that?"

"Although he didn't say why he left," Eden continued, "everyone knows it's because he couldn't sit around and do nothing. Several hunters have been killed recently, and in too great of numbers for one person to have done it. If he's here, his pack is with him, which makes him extremely dangerous."

"They'll even kill werewolves who stand in their way," Max said, eyes wide.

"That's never been proven," Rylan said, wrinkling his nose.

I shifted my weight to my other foot. "Killing the hunters doesn't sound like a bad thing," I admitted. "I mean, the hunters are killing us. So...?"

Eden shot to his feet and shoved me. "Don't even think like that! They kill the hunters, regardless of their age."

I threw my hands up in the air. "What does that even mean?"

"There are young hunters, Cris. Our age and younger." His tone was dark, and I could hear his heart pounding. "Guys like Pierce hunt them mercilessly. They're animals. Cold-hearted animals. As for the hunters...I know they're trying to exterminate us, but two wrongs don't make a right. Even if a kid is just being *trained* as a hunter, Pierce sees them as a threat, and kills them. Brutally." Eden shook his head. "It's not right."

The idea of kids being trained as werewolf hunters left a bitter taste in my mouth. I wondered how young they started.

Then I realized something. Pierce left the Elders, but wasn't killed. Eden said they'd kill anyone who abandoned the pack. Was he wrong? Did that mean I could leave? If I did, I'd have to take Eden with me. The fights the Elders made everyone participate in were barbaric, and I knew

Eden didn't want any part of it.

Thunder rumbled in the distance, and rain began to fall again. The clouds overhead grew darker, and the sound of a twig snapping made me jump.

I turned to Eden, whose eyes were darting in every direction. They were wide with fear. "What was that?" he whispered, and the rest of us exchanged glances.

Just then, a tall woman wearing jeans and a tight-fitting dark green tee appeared between the trees. A man was standing beside her, tranquilizer guns in their hands.

Eden swallowed hard, not taking his eyes off them. "I think it's time to go."

I locked eyes with the woman, and she aimed her weapon at me. "They're over here!" she shouted. Several others appeared, all with guns aimed at the four of us. "I want them all alive!"

Eden took a deep, quivering breath. "RUN!"

We didn't hesitate. I took off as fast as I could, the cold rain beating down on my shoulders. I stumbled blindly through the forest after my friends, my arm shielding my eyes from the rain. Eden and Max made it to the car first.

When I finally jumped in, Eden shouted, "Go, go, go!" to Dexter, who was now in the driver's seat. He drove off before I even closed the door.

We were panting heavily, and I coughed a few times as I tried to catch my breath.

"Anyone see how many there were?" Eden looked at me and I shook my head, needing a moment to think back.

I was scared out of my mind, and couldn't believe what just happened. "Max?" he asked. "Did you get a look at them?"

Max was squished in the middle seat with Summer and me. He tilted his head at Eden's question. "I saw at least four...I think."

When my brain finally started working again, I said, "There were six." How could they have known we were werewolves? Were they hunters? They must've been.

When I voiced my question aloud, Eden said, "I don't know. I've never seen hunters carry tranquilizer guns before. They shoot to kill, and that lady wanted us brought back alive." The car went silent for a moment. We were all jittery and on edge.

"You okay, Rylan?" Dexter asked. "You've been pretty quiet."

When there was no response, I looked over my shoulder to where he should have been, and what I saw terrified me to my very soul.

Rylan was not with us.

CHAPTER THIRTEEN

Dexter slammed on the brakes, and Max and Summer shot forward, landing on top of each other. They groaned as they reclaimed their seats. "What the fuck happened to Rylan?" Dexter shouted.

Eden's eyes were wide, and they darted around nervously. "He must still be out there!" He ran both hands through his hair. "We have to go back for him!"

Dexter glared at my friend. "How could you leave without making sure he was with you? He's just a kid, Eden!"

"We thought he was!" Eden replied, fidgeting with his bracelet. "We had to leave or we would have all been captured."

"Better him than you, right?" Dexter snapped.

Eden's face turned red from embarrassment. "No!" he

protested. "Let's go back and look for him. He might have gotten away." His voice was quiet and pleading.

"I can't believe you guys," Dexter muttered harshly. His angry gaze was fixed on the dashboard, refusing to look at the rest of us. "Especially you, Eden. You were the oldest one out there, so you were responsible for them. You should've thought to make sure they made it back safely. Put their needs before yours."

"I..." Eden brought his hands up to his face, and leaned his head against the window. "I panicked. I thought he was right behind us."

"Rylan's my best friend," Max said quietly, a sad look on his face. Summer put her arm around him, and I wondered if he blamed Eden too.

"I know he is." Dexter's voice was softer now. "We're gonna find him."

Without another word, he turned the car around and rushed back toward the woods. When we returned, everyone jumped out of the SUV, and began searching for our friend.

"Rylan!" the five of us shouted in unison. Summer and Max were walking together, and Eden was trudging behind the group, punishing himself for Rylan's disappearance.

"You need to be more responsible, Eden." Dexter wasn't looking at him, but he still had an angry, wild look on his face, like he might snap—or transform—any moment. I gulped when he stormed past me.

"I'm sorry!" Eden's face was twisted with frustration.

"We made a run for it when we saw the guns, but I swear I thought he was with us."

The oldest boy got in my friend's face, looking down at him. "That's no excuse. Only you would run away without making sure your friends were safe first. That's not what a real friend does." He turned on his heel and walked away. "You're a coward, and that's all you'll ever be."

Eden wiped his eyes with the sleeve of his jacket. He continued yelling the missing boy's name over and over again, refusing to meet anyone else's gaze.

Muffled screams caught my attention, and my breath caught in my throat. "Rylan?" I ventured deeper into the woods, hoping I wouldn't be spotted by anyone who might still be out there. When I got to the fallen tree we'd seen earlier, I scanned the trees for any sign of him, but found nothing.

I thought about the super-senses werewolves possessed in movies, and tried to tap into that. I knew I had a heightened sense of hearing, but when I tried to focus, all I could hear was blood roaring in my ears. I groaned and crossed my arms.

Eden sat on the fallen tree, and stared down at his feet, a look of sadness on his face. "I can't believe this," he said dejectedly, shaking his head. "How could I have let this happen?"

I sat next to him, and the wet bark made me shiver. "It's not your fault," I said.

"Isn't it? This wouldn't have happened if Dexter had

been out here instead of me." He pulled his knees up to his chest, and wrapped his arms around them. "He's right. I'm a fucking coward."

"No, you're not! We all panicked, not just you." He rested his chin on his knees. "We'll find him, Eden. You gotta stay positive."

Just then, we heard another muffled scream. Eden and I exchanged a look, and shot further into the woods. But the screams soon stopped, and the only sound I could hear was our heavy breathing, and frantic heart beats.

My head snapped in every direction until my eyes fell on a small sheet of paper. It was stuck to a tree and only slightly damp, which meant it couldn't have been there long. "Eden," I said as I snatched it from the tree. At the bottom of the note were the letters SFT. "Does that mean anything to you?"

He nodded and brought his hands up to his temples. "I'm not sure what it stands for, but I've seen them before. Those people, I'm not sure what their deal is exactly, but I know they're bad news." He looked over the note in my hand. "We hadn't seen them for a while. I thought they gave up or moved."

"They're not hunters?" I asked.

"Not exactly."

The others eventually caught up, and Eden handed Dexter the letter. It was written in cursive, and I kind of had trouble reading it. The others looked a combination of frightened and livid.

155

"Great," Dexter said as he balled up the note. "We have to tell the Elders now. Nice job, Eden."

I looked between the two of them, confused. "What's going on?" But no one was eager to answer the question. "Guys?"

Summer shook her head, and Max chewed his lip to keep from crying.

Trembling with frustration, Dexter launched a rock into the air, and screamed. Eden flinched. "SFT," Dexter muttered. "These assholes have been determined to expose us to the public for years. They're not as big a threat as the hunters, usually. The hunters kill us, and that's the end of it. What these people want to do is capture us, study us, and show us off to the world." He paced back and forth, and Eden made sure to steer clear of his path. "They're mostly random people who've seen things they shouldn't have, or parents of lost children. They're not trained and not well armed. But every now and then, you come across a group who really know what they're doing."

"Lost children?"

"Kids who were bitten and became werewolves, or kids who were killed by others like us," Dexter said dully. "This curse splits families apart."

"And now they have Rylan," Eden said in disbelief, his lip quivering. "And it's all my fault." Summer wrapped her arm around his shoulder, and whispered something in his ear.

"Damn right, it is," Dexter muttered, his jaw clenched.

"But the note says we can get him back for a price."

"Fifty dollars?" Max asked, sounding a little too hopeful.

"Not that kind of price." Dexter shoved the crumpled note into his pocket. "Come on, guys. We need to get this to the Elders."

My friend lowered his head, as we trudged back to the car. I could tell he was being even harder on himself than Dexter was. I wished there was something I could do to make him feel better, but couldn't think of anything. Comforting people was never my strong suit, and my mind was still processing everything that's been happening.

What would the Elders do to Eden when they found out?

The ride back was completely silent. No one spoke until we were back in the basement with the Elders. Dexter and Eden explained what happened, but the Elders' faces remained hard and expressionless.

My friend was trembling like a leaf. Dexter stood beside him, but he was of no comfort. Summer, Max, and I had been instructed to keep to the side during the meeting.

"Eden Lambert, it is because of you that Rylan was taken," Tealios said, his raspy voice like nails on a chalkboard. "We will organize a search party in the woods, but if he is not found, you must go to the SFT and find him."

"Wait a minute," Ian spoke up. He'd been so quiet I

hadn't realized he was in the room with us. "He's just a kid. Are you gonna send him alone? The SFT will have two of us instead of just one."

Eden shot me a terrified look. There must be something I could do, I thought.

"He is a coward for putting himself first." The Elder rose from his throne, eyes practically piercing through Eden. I could smell the older boy's fear, and it made my stomach hurt. "He must find a way to bring Rylan home."

"And what if he's killed while making the journey?" Ian asked, and Eden's body tensed.

The Elder didn't say anything, but he smiled menacingly.

"If he doesn't go," I said, trying to keep my voice calm, "will he be kicked out?"

Tealios shook his head. "Eden will be put to death."

"WHAT?!" Eden and I shouted in unison.

Tealios clapped his hands together, his milky eyes scanning the small crowd before him. "The search for Rylan will begin immediately."

Eden took a small step forward. "D-do I have to go to the SFT alone?"

Tealios chuckled humorlessly. "Is anyone stupid enough to go with you?"

"I am!" I said, stepping into the middle of the room. "I mean, I'm not stupid, but I want to go with him." Eden looked both relieved and concerned. "I'm not letting you go alone."

"You don't have to do this, Cris," he said sadly.

"I know. I want to."

"Count me OUT!" Dexter crossed his arms, glaring at Eden. "It's your damn fault he's missing. It's you who should be punished for it." He turned his attention to me, and stepped between us. "The hunters will be on your asses the whole time, and you two will be killed before you make it anywhere near the SFT. Trust me. You don't want to go with him."

"I'm going," I said firmly.

"I'm going too," Summer said, and joined the rest of us in the middle of the room. "If there are three of us, we might actually have a chance of bringing Rylan home alive."

"And keeping them from taking Eden too," I said.

"Your funeral." Dexter scoffed. "You two are making a huge mistake. But by the time you realize that, it'll be too late."

"ENOUGH!" Tealios exclaimed, and the other two Elder rose from their thrones as well. "The search will begin immediately. Afterwards, you three are on your own. I don't want to hear another word about it from any of you." We all turned to leave, but as the door creaked opened, the Elder continued, "You may not ask any outsiders for help. Keep in mind, we can see everything. And if you return without Rylan, the *three* of you will be put to death."

Everyone who lived at Bristol Manor was in the forest searching for Rylan. But we knew we wouldn't find him there. The sun was setting, and it was getting colder and colder by the minute. Flashlights scanned the trees in all directions, and kids shouted the missing boy's name every time they took a step. Leaves crunched under feet and twigs snapped.

A cold wind blew Summer's hair across her face, and her teeth chattered. "They couldn't let us eat first," she complained. "I'm cold and hungry."

"Think about Rylan," I said, shining a flashlight straight ahead. "Think about what he could be going through right now."

Summer pushed her hair behind her ear. "I've heard some fucked up stories about the SFT. What they do to the people they take. . ."

I wanted her to elaborate, but Eden came to an abrupt halt. The two of us stopped as well.

"I can't believe this is happening," he said, his blue eyes full of fear. "Because of me, Rylan is gone. The three of us aren't going to make it on our own." He turned to face Summer and me. "You really don't have to go with me, guys. I want you to because I'm terrified of what will happen if I go alone, but I can't ask you to risk your lives."

"You didn't ask," I said softly, and clicked off my flashlight. "We volunteered. I'm going with you no matter what you say."

"We're not gonna let anything happen to you," Summer chimed in.

Tears slid down Eden's chubby cheeks. "You guys are the best." He wrapped his arms around the two of us, squeezing tightly.

After a couple hours of searching, the forest was completely dark. "All right everyone," Ian said to the others. "Let's head back." There were whoops and sighs of relief, but Max was on the verge of tears.

"He's my best friend!" the younger boy yelled. "How can we stop now?"

"He's not out here, dumbass!" Dexter snapped, his tone bitter. "We know where he is. The SFT has him, and this whole search was nothing but a waste of time."

"Looks like you'll be going to the SFT after all," Ian said to Eden. "Come here. I'll tell you where you need to go." I watched the two of them walk off, but they soon got lost in the crowd of kids starting their long hike back to the Wolf House.

"Are you sure you want to go with them, Summer?" Dexter asked. "You're basically throwing your life away. The hunters will kill you all, and you know it's true. No one here has enough experience to survive alone."

Summer didn't answer at first. She had a far off look in her eyes as if she were lost in thought. "I'm going with them. Eden is like a brother to me. Besides, I can't stand the thought of Rylan being another one of their lab rats."

Dexter shook his head as he walked away, muttering

something under his breath. Max trailed behind him, his eyes glued to the ground. The poor kid was lost without his best friend.

Eden returned, and we hiked toward the edge of the woods with the others. I was pretty sure he wasn't listening to the conversations going on around him. He looked worried and scared and lost in thought.

When we reached the road, Rex handed Eden, Summer, and me our backpacks. He hugged Eden before heading back to Bristol Manor. "Come back in one piece."

Eden nodded to his roommate. "I'll try."

Summer furrowed her brow. "Don't we get to eat before we leave?"

Ian shook his head. "I'm sorry. Tealios's orders." He sighed as Eden shouldered his bag. It was clear the man didn't think we were going to make it back. "Make sure not to tell anyone where you're going. You don't know who can be trusted out there." His gaze shifted between the three of us. "There's enough money for the bus in your bags, so unless you'd like to walk the whole way, don't spend it on anything else." He paused, a sad look on his face. "Good luck, kids."

Good luck, I thought. We're gonna need it.

CHAPTER FOURTEEN

"We're gonna get lost," Summer muttered, wrinkling her nose. She was shivering and her ears were bright pink. She rubbed them occasionally, hoping to warm them up a bit.

We hadn't been walking five minutes, and Summer's complaining was already getting on my nerves. We won't even make it to the bus stop if she keeps this up, I thought.

"No, we won't," I replied.

"Yes, we will."

"No. We'll be fine." I tightened my grip on the straps of my backpack. "Eden knows where we're going."

Finally, silence. But only for a moment.

"My feet hurt, and I'm cold," Summer whined. "I'm hungry. Sending us out in the middle of the night with no food in our bellies is torture."

"Maybe you should go back," Eden said. He didn't

sound frustrated, which was shocking to me. Perhaps I was frustrated enough for the both of us.

Summer shook her head. "Without me, you two knuckleheads would get yourselves killed for sure. Besides, I've been dying to go on an adventure. There's no way I'm gonna sit back and let you two have all the fun."

"This isn't about *fun*," Eden said firmly, and stopped in his tracks. "This is about rescuing Rylan! It's about making things right, and if you don't get that then—"

"Hey, I get that. Okay?" Summer rolled her eyes and crossed her arms. "Stop trying to make me go back. I know what you're doing, Eden."

The two shared a look. "What? I-I'm not doing anything," he stammered.

The look lasted a moment longer, and Summer squinted at him. "You guys need to stay focused if we're going to get him back, and something tells me *you* will need me."

"Whatever," he muttered, and continued walking. "Come, but don't think of this as a crazy, fun adventure."

Summer smirked to herself.

Trees swayed gently as the wind picked up, and autumn leaves fell to the ground. Summer and Eden zipped up their jackets and shivered. They both stared at me in shock. "Aren't you cold?" Eden asked.

I shrugged. "A little, I guess. But you two are acting like you're about to freeze to death."

Summer's teeth chattered noisily, and it only grew

louder as the temperature dropped. We passed the alley Kaiden and I used to live in, and I glanced over to see if he'd returned. I sighed quietly when I saw no sign of him. How could he leave me like that?

We eventually passed another alley, and I saw two women sitting with their backs against a brick wall. I recognized one of the women. I'd seen her at Greeny's a couple times trying to steal food in her oversized coat. The woman couldn't have been more obvious, and she was banned from the store when Aaron finally caught her.

I put my hood up over my head and started walking a little faster.

Summer looked at the women and tilted her head. "Do you know them?" she asked.

Saw that coming, I thought with a groan. "I don't know every homeless person in the state," I snapped. "It's not a club."

"Okay," she said, making a face at me. "I was just asking. I don't know every Hispanic person either, but do you think that stops people from asking me if I know random people? No. And you know what? I don't bite their heads off when they ask!"

Summer was right. I shouldn't have snapped like that, but I couldn't help it. When anyone found out I lived on the street, they always asked if I knew some homeless person they'd met, and it was infuriating.

It never occurred to me that she would get asked similar questions.

After a while, we turned onto a highway where several cars zoomed past us. Nearby stores turned their signs from open to closed. Streetlights flickered on overhead. Our stomachs were empty, and grumbled loudly. I wondered how close we were to the bus stop.

"When are we gonna stop for the night?" Summer asked. "It's really late, and I'm freezing my ass off out here."

"Pretty soon, I guess," Eden said, and checked the time on his dying phone. "We've been walking a few hours already, and will probably cover more ground when we're not as cold and tired."

"Good." Summer exhaled on her hands and shoved them into her jacket pockets.

"So, here's something we haven't thought of," Eden said, eyes darting around. "Where are we gonna sleep?"

Summer looked at me. "Where did *you* sleep?"

"Usually Kaiden's car," I said. "But before that, I slept on the sidewalk. Sometimes I'd break into an abandoned building, but not very often."

"Who's Kaiden?" she asked.

I stared down at my shoes. "He's a friend of mine."

"The one from the alley?" Eden asked.

I nodded.

"I don't want to sleep on the ground," Summer groaned. "There are bugs."

"Gotta do what ya gotta do," I replied. "It's not so bad."

"I don't like bugs."

I rolled my eyes, and Eden stopped in front of an

old dollar store. "Maybe we can break into one of these buildings," he suggested. There was graffiti all over the front of it, and boards over the windows.

Summer's eyes widened. "Can't we get arrested for that?"

"Maybe," he said. "Do you have a better idea?"

She went silent.

The three of us walked a bit further, and came to a bench in front of a 24-hour Laundromat. Without a word, Summer sat down near the edge, and rubbed her sore feet. I sat on the other end, and Eden plopped between us.

Summer looked over her shoulder at the building behind us. "What's the point of a 24-hour Laundromat? Who does laundry this late?"

"I used to," I said, shifting nervously in my seat. "But Kaiden and I never saw anyone else."

"Why would *you?*" she asked, a judgmental look on her face. "Why not go during the day like normal people?"

"Just…because."

"Because why?"

I didn't reply. Instead, I closed my eyes, and leaned back against the bench.

"Just want to be different?" she asked.

"I'm different enough," I muttered.

"Then why?"

"Because I didn't like getting beat up all the time!" I snapped, eyes wide with annoyance. "Kaiden and I couldn't go anywhere without someone starting shit with us. Sometimes, someone would ask for money and if we didn't give it to them, they'd fight us, and try to take what little we had. Or we'd run into one of the assholes from school. So, we tried to avoid going places during the day; it was easier to go out at night."

"Oh" was all she said.

I pulled my knees up to my chest, and rested my chin on them. Calm down, I thought. Now that I knew I was so easily angered because of the wolf, I had to try harder to control myself. But that was easier said than done.

Eden then got up to read a flyer nailed to a telephone pole. It flapped in the wind, and he held it still as he looked over it.

A heavy teenage boy joined us, and took Eden's seat next to me. He held out a box of Saltines he'd been munching on. "Cracker?" He was very tall with no hair, and no jacket. The boy must've been freezing.

"I'd like some!" Summer reached for the box, her eyes wide and happy. "Thank you, kind sir."

"No problem." The boy glanced at each of us, a quizzical look on his face. "What are you guys doing out and about so late?"

"We're looking for someone," I said. "Well, looking for their house." Were we looking for a house? I honestly had no idea.

"Oh." The boy nodded and shoved some Saltines into his mouth. "How far ya headed?"

Summer and I exchanged glances. "Eden?" she asked.

Eden scratched his head, and returned to the bench, standing behind it. "The directions weren't very specific. I'm not exactly sure."

I wondered if Eden was lying to him, or if he really didn't know where we were going. Wouldn't Tealios have told him everything we needed to know? If I didn't know any better, I'd think the Elders didn't want us to succeed...

"Your name is Eden?" the boy asked him, and grinned. "That's my brother's name."

"Oh, cool. It's my name too!" Eden's cheeks flushed. "But that was obvious." He shook his head, clearly embarrassed, and I couldn't help but laugh. "Shut up, *Crispy*."

The boy shook Eden's hand. "I'm Shawn, by the way."

Summer reached for some more crackers, and chomped loudly on them. "I'm Summer. Pleased to meet ya."

Shawn turned to me, and arched an eyebrow. "And you're...Crispy?"

I glared at Eden, who shot me a wide grin. "Crispin. Eden was just being a dick."

"Well if you need help finding this place, I'm sure I could help." He glanced between the three of us. "I travel a lot."

"We'll be okay," Eden assured him. "But do you know where the bus stop is?"

"Up that way. Can't miss it." Shawn wiped the cracker crumbs off his shirt and pointed. "Well, I should get going. Good luck getting to wherever it is you're going!"

"Thanks," Eden and I said in unison.

We watched as Shawn walked off, and I silently wondered where the strange traveler was going next.

"I wish he'd left the crackers," Summer said. "And we still don't have a place to sleep tonight."

I got to my feet and crossed the street, heading down a narrow road toward an old building with wooden boards over the windows. Unlike the dollar store, there was no graffiti, but the paint was chipping badly. Trash was strewn about in front of it. Needless to say, it looked very inviting. "How about over here?"

Summer frowned as she and Eden joined me in front of the building. "But it'll be cold," she complained. "No heat."

"Look." Eden pointed to the roof. "There's a chimney. We can build a fire, okay?"

Her shoulders slumped. "Oh, all right."

We climbed a few wooden stairs, and stood in front of the door. There was a massive padlock on it. Eden stared at it thoughtfully, bringing his hand up to his chin. "Does anyone know how to pick locks?"

"We could break the door down," I suggested with a shrug. "Or maybe bust a window. Breaking down the door will make it colder in there."

"Um, guys?" Summer's voice sounded distant.

"Hold up," Eden said.

We made our way to the window we were about to break, but something caught my eye. "Wait!" I shouted. "Someone's in there." A dark figure approached the window as Eden and I inched away.

The figure in the window pressed its face against the glass and chuckled. "The other window was open, *geniuses*." Summer nodded toward the window to our right.

Eden and I sighed with relief, and laughed nervously. "I-I knew that," I stammered.

"Sure ya did, Chandler," Summer said with nod. "Sure ya did."

"It's Crispin!"

"Whatever."

As we walked inside the dilapidated building, mice scurried across the floor. A thick layer of dust coated the floor and a crooked sign hung on the yellowing wall. It read *Monica's Little Bakery*.

I coughed as I breathed in the musty air.

"Yikes! What is that awful stench?" Summer covered her nose.

"Probably moldy bread," Eden said, his eyes watering from the smell. "Hopefully a fire will cover it." He immediately went to work on the fire, and within minutes, it was blazing. The older boy stepped back and admired his work. "Damn, I'm awesome."

Summer snorted. "You do one cool thing and that makes you awesome?"

"I do lots of cool things," he protested, throwing his hands up to his hips.

"May I ask for one other example?"

He thought for a moment, tilting his head. "I've...oh, um..." He frowned, and then met her gaze. "Nope."

Summer laughed and unzipped her jacket. "Whatever. Doesn't make you awesome, though."

"Yes, it does."

The three of us gathered around the fire on the dusty floor, and Summer sneezed. A rat ran across the floor, leaving tiny footprints in the dust. "Disgusting!" Eden shrieked.

Summer eyed the rat tracks on the floor and wrinkled her nose. "Anyone see somewhere other than the floor we could sleep?"

I squinted at her. "You mean somewhere *you* could sleep?"

She averted her eyes. "Perhaps."

I looked around the abandoned bakery, and saw nothing except a counter that was way too small for any human to sleep on. "Looks like you're outta luck."

She sighed heavily. "Well, crap." She put her hood up over her head and lay down with her head resting on her arm. "This is gonna be a long night."

Eden and I did the same, and he shivered. "Try to get some sleep," he said softly.

My feet were sore, and my eyelids were heavy. I hadn't realized how tired I was before. Cockroaches darted from one end of the bakery to the other, but Summer and Eden were asleep, so neither was bothered. I shooed the bugs away when they got too close to one of my friends. It wasn't long before I fell asleep too.

CHAPTER FIFTEEN

Waking up to the sound of a car horn blaring in my ears wasn't how I'd planned to start the day. My head felt heavy and my heart was racing. Definitely not the best way to wake up.

Eden shot up, breathing heavily. He glanced at his phone and shouted, "It is four o'clock in the morning! What's going on out there?!"

We'd been sleeping less than two hours, and I felt like I could barely move. "I'll find out," I mumbled. I stumbled to my feet, rubbing my eyes, and nearly tripped over Summer, who snored quietly. My legs were wobbly. My back was sweaty.

"Hold up!" Eden rushed over to me, and grabbed my hand. "There could be hunters. No one should go alone." He dropped my hand, then turned to Summer, who ran her fingers through her hair. "Come on. We'll all go. There's safety in numbers."

The girl stretched and rubbed her droopy eyes. "Ugh, why are you such a fraidy-cat," she groaned. "You know, there's also death in numbers. Bloodbath, genocide, massacre." Eden and I glared at her, and she shrugged. "Ring any bells?"

"Well, thank you for making me feel worse, Summer," Eden said.

"You are most welcome."

"Whatever," he said, and waved a hand in exasperation. "Do what you want." The two of us trudged outside to see what was going on. By the time we got outside, the alarm had been turned off. Summer joined us outside after a minute, probably feeling guilty about what she'd said to Eden.

For a while, I didn't see anything. A single streetlamp illuminated a small section of the road, but the rest of the area was hidden from view by the darkness. I focused, felt my wolf's eyes take over my own and, after a few seconds, I spotted a black bag across the street.

"Wonder what that is." As I crossed the street, nervousness crept into my stomach. Something didn't feel right. My nerves were tingling, and I wondered if perhaps my wolf knew something I didn't. Was that even possible?

"Wait!" I heard Eden stagger down the stairs behind me.

But I kept going. My gut told me I needed to get to

the bag—or perhaps my gut was telling me to run like hell back into the bakery. Sometimes it was hard to tell.

A black van then pulled up behind me, its tires screeching against the pavement. No one made any attempt to get out. On the other side of the street, I heard Eden gasp, and I swallowed hard. The doors swung open and heavy footsteps hurried after me. Before reaching the bag, I turned around and was knocked to the ground by a large woman wearing an eye patch. Her big black boot connected with my face, and my vision doubled for a few seconds.

"Cris!" Eden shouted.

I shot to my feet and the woman pulled a dagger from her coat, gripping it tightly. "Kill 'em!" she shouted over her shoulder.

A man then hopped out of the van. He ran toward my friends, who were standing on the sidewalk in front of the bakery. Summer's eyes doubled in size, and Eden's breath caught in his throat.

My eyes darted around. I tried to think of something to do, anything other than transforming. But it was useless. Changing was the only thought coming to mind. I can't do it, I thought hopelessly. Not only was I worried I'd be unable to trigger it, but the thought of accidentally hurting one of my friends was unbearable. What if I ended up killing them?

Eden met my gaze and mouthed the word *Hunters,* a panicked expression on his face. The man approached him, and Eden's eyes turned red as his wolf began to take shape. He screamed from the pain of the change, but the scream was soon replaced by a growl. The man whipped out a gun and held it to Summer's head. He glared at Eden, who was now fully transformed.

The woman stepped up to me, eyeing me. She raised her dagger and held it to my throat.

Eden's wolf knocked the gun from the man's hands. It skittered across the road, and the hunter clumsily ran after it.

My friend lunged toward the eye-patch-wearing woman beside me. He knocked Eye Patch and me down, and the woman's head hit the cracked sidewalk. Unfortunately, that barely slowed her down. Groaning loudly, she got to her feet and raised her weapon, pointing it at Eden this time. He growled at her and pawed the ground.

I rolled away, ignoring the pain in my side from the fall. I was pretty sure I'd cracked a rib.

My friend threw himself at Eye Patch again, and slashed his claws across the hunter's mouth. The skin split open, blood coating the lower half of her face.

I wanted to help Eden fight off the hunters, but I couldn't; I felt paralyzed and useless. Was this mission going to be nothing but my friend trying to keep us alive while I stood around like a sack of potatoes? I thought I'd be a little more useful than that.

Eye Patch swung her dagger around like a madman. Screaming maniacally, she plunged her weapon into

Eden's side, and my friend retreated. He dropped to the bloodstained sidewalk, writhing in pain. She crawled over to him and slammed the blade into his back, her eyes wide with anger.

Why am I just sitting here? HELP HIM! But I still couldn't make myself move. My body wouldn't obey my commands.

Eden slowly shifted back to human, his wounds actually steaming. I concentrated on his heartbeat, and his short, ragged breaths. His face contorted in pain.

Please let him be okay.

"Wolf's bane," the woman chuckled as she walked over to me. I was still sitting on the ground, a few feet away from Eden. "All our daggers, swords, and bullets are made with bits of monkshood. A little bit won't kill you, but it will certainly cause a great deal of pain, nausea, and even hallucinations. It can knock you out, but it looks like your buddy is putting up quite a fight." Eye Patch gestured toward Eden, who was lying on his stomach in a puddle of his own blood. "He's still conscious…for now." The hunter pointed her knife at me, her eyes piercing into mine. "Do it now, Lincoln."

Summer screamed as Lincoln, who retrieved his gun from the ground, smacked Summer across the face with it. Her cheek turned red, and she staggered back. Lincoln's hand was trembling, but he aimed as steadily as he could.

And pulled the trigger.

Boom!

Summer fell to the ground. She wasn't moving.

"No!" I shouted as Eye Patch inched closer to me. I listened for a heartbeat, but all I could hear was blood roaring in my ears. I silently willed her to get back up. When I realized she wasn't going to, I began feeling dizzy. My head throbbed and my heart was racing in my chest.

My entire body was jittery and tingly. When my clothes started ripping, I knew my wolf was coming. My bones broke and snapped like twigs, shifting around for the wolf. Shifting still hurt, but it wasn't as painful as the first time. I wondered if I'd have the ability to control the wolf, but at that moment, I wasn't sure I wanted to. If I tore these hunters apart, I don't think I would feel bad about it.

Don't think like that, I told myself.

Now in wolf form, I pawed the ground and bared my teeth. I glared at the hunter who shot Summer, ignoring Eye Patch.

"I've got enough ammo for you and your other little friend too, pup," said Lincoln, who was standing over Summer's body. "But don't worry. It'll be quick."

Eye Patch furrowed her brow. "Wait," she said. "Which one did Wes want?"

But Lincoln ignored her. Filled with newfound confidence, he aimed the weapon at Eden. My friend struggled to get up, but his arms were wobbly. Blood still oozed from his wounds.

My heart stopped.

Before the hunter had time to shoot, I pounced on

Lincoln, gnawing on his hand. I chewed on Lincoln's arm, and clawed at his chest as he struggled to get away. He tried unsuccessfully to shove me back, but I was too strong. I took the man's neck between my teeth and chomped down hard, blood spilling into my mouth. A low growl ripped from my throat. I almost felt as if my wolf were laughing at the scene before him.

I couldn't tell if I were in control.

After what just happened, I hoped it wasn't me behind the wheel this time.

The noises around me began to fade until the only thing I could hear was the slow *thump, thump, thump* of Lincoln's barely beating heart. His eyes were wide and glazed over, but he was still alive.

I hovered over him, blood dripping from my open mouth as I barked.

Eye Patch's eyes darted between Eden and me. She seemed confused, showing no concern for Lincoln. "Which one does Wes want?" she asked again.

Lincoln didn't look frightened, even though he was lying in a pool of his own blood. He just looked pissed off. "Kill it!" he shouted, choking on the blood in his throat. "Kill it!"

It? I unleashed every ounce of rage, no longer caring whether the hunters lived or died. I ripped the man's throat completely open, blood squirting all over my furry face. His scream came to an abrupt stop, and his body stilled.

My body shook with rage. I breathed heavily, eyes

glued to the corpse on the ground. But my strength and anger vanished, leaving me feeling heavy and weak. I collapsed next to the corpse as my wolf disappeared, painfully returning my body to its original shape. I was on my stomach, face pressed into the concrete.

Out of the corner of my eye, I saw Eye Patch kick Eden in the face. My friend shot back when his nose crunched, his eyes fluttering closed. His body was covered with bruises. I figured he must've gotten them when I was distracted by Lincoln.

Eye Patch ran to me and raised her dagger. Her blade sliced through skin. I cried out in pain as it went deeper and deeper into my lower back. My blood poured out, mixing with Lincoln's on the ground. She kicked me in the ribs a few times, yelling in my ear. She asked my name, but I didn't respond.

Why would she ask me that?

My eyes were half-closed. I could barely move.

I could see that Eden's nose and other wounds were trying to heal. When he opened his eyes, they were bright red, though he remained human. A menacing growl erupted from the older boy's throat as he hobbled toward us.

The hunter jumped to her feet, holding her dagger out in front of her. "Stay back!" she shouted.

I gathered all my remaining strength—which wasn't very much—and slashed my claws across the back of her legs. She jerked away and screamed.

Her gaze shifted between the two of us once more.

I saw her mouth moving, but I couldn't focus on her words. I had no idea what she was saying. But Eden responded, and her shoulders slumped. She lowered her weapon and backed away, her eyes never leaving my face.

Then she grabbed the black bag I'd seen earlier, and retreated to the van. I watched her drive out of sight, the van swerving uncontrollably along the way.

I wanted to ask Eden what the woman said, but my energy was depleting. I could barely hold myself upright. Every inch of my body was screaming in pain, and my eyes burned from lack of sleep.

Eden's eyes were back to their normal bright blue. His black hair was messier than usual, and fell into his eyes. He grabbed our ripped up clothes from the street, and we threw them on.

My new Bristol Manor shirt now resembled the clothes I used to wear. There were huge holes in the seams, and the neck was stretched out. The pants were just as bad, and I knew we'd have to change them before going back to sleep. Fortunately, our shoes weren't in bad shape. They must've fallen off our paws during the transformation.

When we were both fully dressed, Eden sat beside me, bringing his knees up to his chest. His eyes landed on the body on the ground. Lincoln's body. "Are you okay?" he asked.

I groaned. "I feel like I'm gonna die."

Eden nodded as I gently wiped the blood from under his nose. "We'll heal," he said quietly. "It will take a bit, but we'll heal." He paused and wrinkled his nose. "You know, that was the first time I've ever been touched by wolf's bane. Before adding monkshood to their custom-made weapons, they were just pure silver, which doesn't do anything special to us if it's just a knife. It has to stay in our bloodstream to be fatal."

"If it'd been a silver bullet, would we die?" I asked, trying not to look at Lincoln. I could see him out of the corner of my eye, and it made my chest hurt. I couldn't believe he was dead. And I killed him. How was I going to live with myself? How could I have killed him so easily?

The older boy nodded again. "Unless you can get it out of your body in time. Most hunters don't work with daggers or swords, so we got lucky this time." He lowered his head, and his voice became softer. "Well, kinda."

With a heavy sigh, my eyes drifted to Summer. Is she really gone?

I stared sightlessly at the ground for a long while, thinking about what could have been done differently to prevent all this. What *I* could have done. I should have been able to help more.

Eden stayed silent for a long while as we sat in the middle of the road, surrounded by darkness. "You know," he said finally, "they would have killed Lincoln if you hadn't." He gestured toward the body on the ground.

I cocked my head to the side. "Why?"

"Because you bit him." He shrugged, and made a face, as if I should have known this. "The hunters kill *all* werewolves, even if you bite one of their own. A hunter would kill their own child before they let them become one of us." Eden shuddered.

It was hard for me to believe a parent could do that. Hunters really are heartless bastards. My thoughts then drifted to what Eye Patch had asked earlier. She kept asking about the one Wes wanted. I was about to ask Eden about it, but a sudden noise stopped me.

The two of us flinched at the sound of someone coughing. We jumped to our feet and stood back to back, preparing for another attack. Despite the pain from our wounds, we stood at the ready, waiting. When nothing happened, we exchanged puzzled looks. "What...?"

"Summer!" Eden shouted. We dashed toward her, and she pushed herself up with a groan. "You're alive!" He wrapped his arms around her, squeezing her tightly.

"How are you still alive?" I asked, feeling relieved. I was sure she'd been killed.

"The bullet went through my arm." She rolled up her sleeve, exposing a small hole that was slowly closing up. If she'd been shot a few inches to the left, the bullet would have hit her chest instead. "It really hurt at first." Eden hugged her again, and Summer closed her eyes. "It was unbearable. So I just lay there, waiting for death." When he pulled away, the girl shrugged casually. "But I'm still here."

"Are you sure you're okay?" Eden asked her.

"Am *I* okay? You don't look so good either." She rolled down her sleeve, and made a face as the fabric grazed the wound. "What are we gonna do now?"

Eden scratched his head, looking up at the stars. "Maybe we should go back to sleep for a while."

"Are you serious?" Summer yelled. "What if they come back?"

"Well, what if they spot us on the road?" I asked her. "I don't think any of us would be able to defend ourselves right now. We need to rest."

"Exactly," Eden whispered breathlessly. "And I..."

I shot him a concerned look. He was so pale. Well, paler than usual. His nose was still broken, and it was chin was stained with blood. I wasn't sure how his bruises and stab wounds were doing. "Are you all right?!" I asked. "What's happening? Is it poison? Are you gonna die?"

He waved off my concern. "I'm just not feeling well."

Summer studied him a moment. "You look like death, Eden."

"Well, thank you," the older boy said. "That's just what I needed to hear." The three of us trudged back to the building we'd slept in earlier, and Eden forced a smile when he caught me looking at him. "I'm fine. Don't worry about it."

"Are you sure?" I chewed my lip nervously. I couldn't let anything happen to him. "Seriously, you look like you're gonna keel over and die any minute."

"Aw, you two are giving me so many compliments," he said as he opened the bakery door. "I'm still kickin'. Well, maybe not at the moment, but I will be after a little more sleep." One thing I liked about Eden: the fight with the hunters didn't kill his spirit. He was still goofy.

We reclaimed our spots from earlier, and Eden fell asleep as soon as he laid his head down. I couldn't help but worry about him. He looked worse than I felt, and I felt pretty damn awful.

"Aren't you gonna sleep?" I asked Summer, who was sitting on the counter in Monica's Little Bakery. She looked pretty much as awake as one could be. Guess having a bullet go right through you will do that.

"Not right now, Curley," she said quietly. "I'm gonna watch for hunters. I figured someone should keep watch since you guys are incapacitated." She pulled her hood up over her head and crossed her legs. "Go on and get some rest. If something happens, I'll throw a shoe at you."

I frowned. "Please don't."

"Go to sleep," she said again, and gazed out the window.

This time, I didn't protest. I didn't even have the energy to care that she was *always* getting my name wrong. If a hunter *did* attack again, there was no doubt in my mind that I would die. I barely made it back to the bakery without collapsing. After getting comfortable, I drifted off to sleep, hoping the pain would soon go away.

I awoke later that night—morning, whatever—screaming my head off. All I could think about was the hunter I killed. Lincoln. In my nightmare, he threw glass bottles at me, and a few of them smashed right into my face. The wounds healed in my dream, but for some reason, now that I was awake, my face felt as if it were on fire.

I opened my eyes when I realized Summer was shaking my shoulders. She was saying something, but I couldn't understand her. Her words were distant mumbles in my ears.

When I didn't respond, the shaking became a little more violent. I stared blankly, straight ahead, wondering why my face was in so much pain.

"Wake the hell up! What did you do?" Summer's voice, now audible, echoed in my head. What was she talking about? I couldn't tear my eyes away from the nothingness my gaze was fixed upon even though I wanted to. I wanted to answer her, but couldn't make myself move. "Why did you do that?" she asked.

Every time I blinked, I saw Lincoln's face. I could still taste his blood in my mouth. His face grew larger and larger in my mind, the look in his eyes both angry and fearful. I could feel his hot, smelly breath on my face.

I lowered my head, and my eyes widened at the sight of blood. My fingers were *covered* in blood. I examined my trembling hands, my brow furrowed. The blood was dry and peeling off.

Whose blood was it? Did I kill someone in my sleep?

I caught a glimpse of Eden. He somehow hadn't heard

Summer and me screaming, and was still asleep. Or was he—? With my body unresponsive to Summer's pleas, I focused on Eden until I heard the soft *thump, thump, thump* of his heart.

He's alive.

So, where'd the blood come from?

Summer was no longer screaming at me. She just stared at me in horror.

The stinging I'd felt on my cheeks earlier began to fade. I brought my hands up to my face and felt around. My fingers slid across something rough on my cheeks. Scabs?

"Why did you do that to yourself?" Summer asked, her voice shaking. My eyes focused on her for the first time since I woke up. She was sitting beside me, her legs tucked under her.

"I scratched myself?" I asked. My throat was dry and my voice sounded raspy.

The girl nodded silently.

My dream of Lincoln felt so real; I remembered trying to dodge the glass bottles he threw at me, and the sudden pain I felt when I'd failed. I wanted to tell her about the dream, but was afraid it would only encourage the nightmare to return, torturing me every night for the rest of my life.

"I did it in my sleep," I whispered, shaking my head in disbelief. "I-I've never done anything like that before."

She looked at me sympathetically but didn't respond.

The pain was completely gone now. When I asked if

the scratches had faded, she nodded. "You're okay now."

But I wasn't. Taking a life, Lincoln's life, still haunted me, and I wondered if I would ever really be *okay* again.

CHAPTER SIXTEEN

It wasn't long after my nightmare that I was awakened by the sound of noisy kids passing the bakery on their way to school. I wasn't ready to get up, but we needed to get on the move anyway. The bus was running more than fifteen minutes late, so we decided to walk for a while. The morning air was cool and moist, refreshing against my face, which was still hot and sweaty.

Thick grey clouds blanketed the sky and the ground was a little wet. The scent of rain lingered in the air. I loved the smell of rain, though I hoped we wouldn't have to walk in it.

Eden looked much better now, and seemed to have more energy. I wasn't sure how I looked, but I certainly felt better. No signs of scratches on my face or lingering pain from the dagger.

Summer promised me she wouldn't tell Eden about what I'd done in my sleep. It was embarrassing, so I didn't want anyone else to know. When we were alone, she asked if I were okay and for the most part, I was. I still felt guilty about killing Lincoln, but I figured that would stay with me for the rest of my life, so I might as well get used to it. "It's not like you took an *innocent* life," Summer had said. "He's killed many werewolves, and would have killed all of us last night if you hadn't stopped him."

That was true, but it didn't make living with what I'd done any easier.

We walked along the road with our hoods up over our heads, and hoped no one would ask why we weren't in school. A passing car honked and the person inside threw a soda can at us. They shouted something unintelligible and sped off.

"What a dick," Eden muttered, shaking his head.

After a while, it started drizzling, and Summer and Eden zipped up their jackets. Thunder rumbled in the distance, and it wasn't long before the rain came down a little harder.

Great.

I was barely aware of footsteps and shouts behind us, increasing in volume. Someone yelled my name, but I made no attempt to acknowledge I'd heard. I was so lost in thought that I actually thought Eden and Summer were trying to talk to me.

"Lipton!" the voice yelled again.

Then it hit me. It couldn't have been my friends because Eden always called me Cris, and Summer just said the first C name that popped in her head. My last name was shouted again. When we made it to the other side of the street, I stopped dead in my tracks, finally recognizing the voice.

It was Marcus.

"You can't hide from me, Lipton!"

I turned to Eden, who was looking at me with a puzzled expression. "Do you know that guy?" He jerked his head toward the bully. "Because he certainly knows you, and he doesn't sound like he's coming to give you a hug."

"Who can blame him?" Summer muttered under her breath.

Exhaling a quivering breath, I turned to face the kid who'd made my life a living hell for so many years. Not today, I thought, my stomach filling with dread. Please go away.

"Well, well, well," Marcus said as he strolled up to me, a smug look on his face. "Where'd you disappear to? Haven't seen you at school."

I stared hard into his unwavering eyes, feeling my wolf's anger shoot through my body. "What do you want, Marcus?"

"Is that any way to greet your old pal?" He looked my friends up and down before returning his attention to me. "So why haven't you been in school?"

I crossed my arms. "What's it to ya?"

No matter what happens, I thought, transforming in front of him is not an option.

He laughed humorlessly. "Oh, I was hoping you would give me a reason to knock your teeth out." He grabbed the collar of my shirt and balled his fist. "And you just did."

I squeezed my eyes shut and prepared myself for a blow to the face, but it never came. My eyes shot open as his grip on my shirt loosened. Eden surprised Marcus by punching him in the face. Marcus's right eye was beginning to swell, turning a dark shade of blue and purple.

My old bully scowled at Eden, who had clearly pissed him off. My friend obviously didn't care. "Leave Cris alone," Eden said through gritted teeth. His fists were balled, and I could hear his heart pounding.

"Well, isn't that nice," Marcus said, staring hard at Eden and me. "You got your boyfriend to fight your battles for you. He's even got a cute little nickname for you." His voice made my skin crawl.

Eden's eyes grew wide and his faced turned bright red. "I-I'm not his—"

But he never got to finish his sentence.

Marcus raised his humongous arm and swung at my friend, who was then knocked off his feet. Summer stared in horror but not at Marcus or Eden. At me. I was hunched over on the ground, feeling my wolf fighting to take shape. For a moment, I resisted, trying my best to stay human. Then everything Marcus had ever done to Kaiden and me flashed before my eyes, and I smirked to myself.

It's payback time.

I closed my eyes and ignored the pain of the transformation as best I could. My body was stinging and aching all over by the time my wolf had finally taken shape. The power of my wolf surged through my veins, and I felt invincible. My senses heightened. I could hear conversations taking place a mile away, could smell Marcus's sweat and even his fear. At that moment, I felt more powerful than I ever had.

Maybe this werewolf thing wasn't so bad after all.

I growled at Marcus, who stared with his mouth agape and eyes widened. I bared my teeth, preparing for battle. Eden, who was still on the ground, stumbled to his feet and jumped out of the way as I threw myself toward my old bully. Marcus landed hard on the concrete, and I heard the unmistakable *snap* of one of his bones. Music to my ears, I thought. He cried out as I slashed my razor-sharp claws across his chest, and watched as his shirt turned red with blood.

There was no doubt this time. I was in control of the wolf, and I loved it.

An ambulance rushed by, the siren blaring in my ears. I tilted my head away, trying to shield myself from the screeching. When the ambulance was out of sight, I returned my attention to Marcus, who had gotten up and was looking for something to hit me with.

He cradled his broken arm, a look of pure terror on

his face. Marcus stumbled back when I ran toward him, and he tripped over a crack in the pavement, skinning his elbow. His face was red, his expression pleading, but I didn't care.

I wanted my revenge.

I bit down on his broken arm as hard as I could, sinking my teeth deep into his salty, sweaty skin. He screamed louder than I would have thought possible as I ripped away a small chunk of flesh.

The sounds of rain and thunder drowned out Marcus's cries for help.

"Cris!" Eden shouted, and ran to us. He grabbed my shoulders, trying to pull me away from Marcus. "Cris, stop!"

The urgency in Eden's voice made me pull back, and I admired my work on the bully's arm. Marcus clumsily got to his feet and whimpered. He squinted at me through the rain, wheezing. His injured arm shook violently.

My eyes landed on Eden, who looked sad and a little afraid. Wonder what his problem is, I thought.

The cold rain stung my face and drenched my fur. I shook the water off my back, and Marcus wiped drops of rain—or maybe tears—from his cheeks. He was on his butt at the edge of the sidewalk, his back pressed against a pole, too scared to move.

I plopped myself on the ground beside my backpack, and shifted back. Thankfully, the transformation from wolf to human was nowhere near as painful. This time, my clothes ripped too much to slip back on. I grabbed a new set from my backpack and wiped Marcus's blood from my mouth. Revenge never tasted so sweet. "This *never* happened," I said to him, my voice loud and confident.

He nodded quickly and took off, whimpering as he turned a corner.

A smile tugged at my lips as I watched him disappear.

Eden stared down at the bloodstained sidewalk, and knelt down to pick up my shredded clothes. He balled them up in his hands before throwing them into a nearby trashcan. "Would you have killed him if I didn't tell you to stop?" He was obviously upset, and a heavy feeling settled in my chest.

Honestly, for a second, I wasn't sure if I would have killed Marcus or not. But then I thought of Lincoln. Killing the hunter may have been my wolf's choice, but I didn't know for sure. I hated myself for killing him even though he was dangerous to our kind. Remembering what it felt like when he died, and knowing I was the cause, I shook my head.

"I don't think so," I said finally. "I probably would have done a little more damage, but I don't think I would have killed him."

Eden nodded, fidgeting with his purple bracelet. The three of us began walking again. "You need to be more careful, though," he said. "You can't change like that out in the open. If someone saw you—"

"I know."

"Who was that, anyway?" Summer asked with a shiver.

"Just an asshole I went to school with." I shoved my hands into my jacket pockets. "He deserved what I did to him. Trust me."

Running into Marcus made me wonder how many people would lose their lives on this quest. Would any of us ever make it back to Bristol Manor?

CHAPTER SEVENTEEN

Summer groaned as a loud clap of thunder boomed overhead.
I looked up as lightning flashed, spreading across the sky.
It was still raining, and the three of us were soaked to the
bone.

"Can we please find a bus stop?" Summer asked. "I'm
cold and wet and miserable."

"Yeah," Eden said, and gestured up ahead. "There's
one." We squished together on a bench that was being
occupied by an elderly woman. She held a bright pink
umbrella above her head. The woman nodded politely at
my friends and me, but inched away from us. I thought
that was a little strange, but didn't think much of it.

Then I realized why she'd moved. Marcus's blood still
stained my hands and chin.

As if reading my mind, Eden handed me a few napkins

from his backpack. They were wet from the rain. "Here," he said. "You look like a serial killer with all that blood."

Summer chuckled and the woman scowled.

I wiped away as much blood as I could, and the bus arrived a moment later. The old lady with the pink umbrella was the only other passenger. As Summer, Eden, and I took seats in the very back, the old woman sat in the front row. Two more teenagers hurried onto the bus before it pulled away, and they plopped down in a middle row.

Eden was seated in front of me, eyeing the teens. "What do you think they're up to?" he whispered.

"Probably not what we're up to," I replied.

I studied the pair of teens a moment. The boy looked to be a bit older than us, maybe seventeen or eighteen. His light blond hair was nicely styled, and his eyes were green. He looked as if he hadn't shaved in a while. There was a tattoo on his neck and several on his long, muscular arms. He wore a black short sleeved shirt and dark blue jeans. When he saw me staring at them, I averted my eyes and awkwardly glanced around the bus.

When I decided it was safe to look again, my eyes landed on the girl next to him.

She had strawberry blonde hair with big curls that spilled down her shoulders, and like the boy, her eyes were green. She was wearing dark eyeshadow, and her lips were plump and covered with shiny lip gloss. Her tight plain black shirt matched well with her blue jean mini skirt. Her black boots were long, stopping just below her knees.

There was a small skull on her skirt that appeared to have been drawn on with marker. When she flipped her hair, the smell of cherries filled the air.

The two of them were whispering very quietly, and I considered eavesdropping.

Summer nudged me. "Stop staring!"

"I wasn't staring at her," I protested.

She arched an eyebrow. "I didn't say you were staring at *her*." Summer giggled. "I just said stop staring. It's not polite."

"Oh." I blushed and covered my face with my hand. "Not polite? You get my name wrong every time you talk to me."

"So, *were* you staring at her?"

I blinked. "No."

"I think you were."

"I wasn't."

"Suuure." Summer eyed the girl a moment before turning back to me. "No offense, but I don't think you'd look good with her. I see you more with... someone else." She grinned mischievously.

Eden sank in his seat in front of us.

"Why not?" I asked her, a hint of annoyance in my voice. "You don't think I'm good enough for someone like her?"

Summer's eyes widened. "I didn't say that!" She crossed her arms, a frown on her face. "Anyway, I'm pretty sure that guy she's with is her boyfriend."

I looked them up and down. "He could be her brother."

"They don't look alike."

"They both have green eyes!" I protested.

"You also have greens. Well...eye. Does that mean you're related to them too? Doesn't Rylan have green eyes? Is he secretly your brother, and you just didn't bother to tell us?" I groaned and Summer straightened in her seat. "Face it, Coily. They're dating."

"Coily?! Really?"

"You know," Summer began, raising a hand to her chin, "there is one way we can settle this."

Oh, god, I thought. "Don't!"

Summer ignored me. "Excuse me," she said to the girl. "Is he your boyfriend?"

The girl looked at me, and then back at Summer. "Is *he* yours?" She spoke with a thick Russian accent.

Summer's face turned red as she leaned back in her seat, bringing a hand up to her face.

"Bet that wasn't what you were expecting," Eden said dryly.

"Shut up," Summer murmured.

I stared at my friend a long moment, annoyed by her reaction. "I know I'm not a big, strong idiot like Zak, but damn. Rude, much?"

Summer pulled her hood up over head. "Don't talk about Zak like that."

"Why?" I asked. "You don't like hearing the truth? That he's an asshole with a tiny brain—"

Eden interrupted, "And an even tinier—"

"STOP!" she yelled.

The three of us fell silent. Everyone on board looked back at us for a second. "Yeah, Zak is an asshole, but there's nothing I can do about that. I felt obligated to say yes when he asked me out, so I just have to put up with it."

I knit my eyebrows. "Why did you feel obligated to say yes?"

Summer took a deep breath and stared down at her hands. "Guess I should tell you the whole story. You need to know some stuff about my past, so everything makes sense."

I shifted uncomfortably in my seat. "Okay."

When she spoke, her voice was but a whisper. "My mother left when I was four. I don't remember very much about her, though I *do* remember watching her walk to the car with nothing more than a grocery bag full of clothes, and a few personal items. She got in and drove away without saying a word to me, or even a glance over her shoulder as I screamed my head off." Tears welled in her eyes, and her lip quivered. "I begged and pleaded for her to come back. But I haven't seen my mother since."

"My dad remarried when I was six," Summer continued, a sad look on her face. She tucked her hair behind her ear and sniffled. "Her name was Talia. I never liked her because she was so horrible to me. It was obvious Talia didn't like children. Every little thing I did annoyed her, and she made sure I knew it. She'd yell and scream at me over absolutely nothing." She held her breath a moment, and wiped her eyes. "After a while, my dad stopped defending me. He told me I needed to make this work because my mom wasn't coming back, and I couldn't drive another one away." She was crying now. Tears slid down her cheeks and dripped onto her hand.

"Oh, my god," I said as I leaned back against the window.

"So, I ran away," she said with a small shrug. "I ran away about a couple days after I was bitten. It wasn't because of the bite though; I was planning on running for a long time. But after I was bitten, a guy at Bristol Manor came to me. He apologized, and explained what he was and what was happening to me. He took me to Bristol Manor and stood up for me."

I tilted my head. "What do you mean, stood up for you?"

Summer bit her lip before responding. "At first, the Elders denied me."

My eyes widened. "What? Why?"

She shook her head. "All I know is that he went down and spoke with the Elders. He convinced them to let me join their pack, and basically saved my life by giving me a home and a new family." She met my gaze for the first time in a while.

My stomach felt queasy once I realized who she was talking about. "So that's why you're with him?"

"Yes," she said softly. "I owe him everything, and just

couldn't bring myself to say no."

I didn't know what else to say. Who knows what would have happened to her if Zak hadn't helped her get accepted by the Elders. But why would they have denied her in the first place?

"I'm really sorry, Summer," I said, my voice low. "About everything."

She wiped the remaining tears from her face. "It's okay. He really is a dick, you know? Not just to you. I hate him, but I tolerate him because he made sure I had a place to go. That's why I wanted to go with you and Eden so badly."

I stared at her. "To get away from Zak? But if we don't bring Rylan back alive, they'll kill us."

"Exactly," she said.

And suddenly, I understood what she meant. "Oh…"

Summer wiped her eyes again, and stared down at the floor. "Please don't tell anyone. I just—I feel so trapped. I'm not happy and leaving Zak won't solve that. I've been unhappy a long time, ever since I can remember. It'd be easier if I just didn't exist anymore." She got quiet and chewed her lip.

"You can't—I don't—You just—"

"Not a word to anyone." Her voice was firm but quiet, so no one could overhear. "No one else knows, so you have to promise not to say anything. Okay?"

I nodded my agreement, but I wasn't planning on keeping that promise. How could I? Surely Eden would know what to do. Summer didn't seem unhappy, but I guess you never really know what's going on in a person's head. I felt so bad for her. She deserved to be happy.

After that, no one said anything for a long while. Eventually Eden was the one to break the awkward silence. "I'm kinda hungry." He turned back toward us, and propped his arm up on the top of his seat.

"So am I," Summer said, and looked at me. "Check your phone to see what time it is."

"I don't have one," I admitted.

Her eyes widened. "You don't? Why didn't you get one? I can't live without my phone."

I rolled my eyes, not wanting to get into my money problems. "Since I don't have one, can you check yours?"

With a groan, Summer glanced around the bus. She then pulled her phone out from the middle of her shirt, her cheeks reddening. "It was in my bra," she whispered. "Anyway, we boarded the bus about four hours ago."

Eden turned back. "Four hours?" he shouted. "No wonder I'm so hungry! Did I hear you say your phone was in your bra?"

Summer shushed him, and the girl from earlier stared at us. "Announce it to the whole bus, why don't ya?"

"Sorry." Eden shot her a goofy grin. "We need to get to eat, though."

"We have no money," I said plainly. "How do you expect us to eat?"

"We *have* to eat," Eden said.

"Thank you, Captain Obvious. That doesn't answer the—" I stopped, suddenly realizing how he planned on getting food, and lowered my voice. "You want to steal?"

"I don't *want* to, but we may have to," he said as Summer crossed her legs. "You're telling me you've never stolen anything?"

I shook my head. "I had a job, thank you very much."

"Well, where is all your money then, Crispy?"

"Oh, god, I hate you." I squinted at Eden and he grinned, obviously quite pleased with himself. "It was a part time job for which I got paid minimum wage. I used the money from my last check forever ago."

"Then, unless someone presents a better plan, we'll be stealing some grub," he said. He didn't sound as nervous as I would have expected.

I eyed him. "Have you ever stolen anything before?"

He frowned and averted his eyes. "Yeah," he muttered quietly. "When I was seven, I stole a pack of gum. My foster parents found out, and beat the shit out of me for it. I never stole anything again, but the beatings never stopped."

"They hit you?" I couldn't hide the surprise in my voice.

"Oh, Eden," Summer said softly, and placed her hand on his arm. "I'm so sorry."

He waved off her concern, but couldn't meet our eyes.

When the bus stopped, the green-eyed strangers rose, and the girl smiled happily. "You guys could grab a bite to eat with us," she said. "Our treat."

Summer, Eden and I stared blankly at the girl. "Really?" Eden asked. The look on his face was skeptical.

She shrugged. "Sure. Why not? There's a great little place just across the street." The two of them headed down the aisle, and waited by the door. "You're coming, yes?"

Eden looked from Summer to me. "Should we?"

Having no better options, the three of us hurried after them, hoping we weren't making a big mistake.

CHAPTER EIGHTEEN

After we hopped off the bus, I stared up at the restaurant standing before us. Dimitri's Bar and Grill. The door opened and as a young couple strolled out, the smell of steak filled the air. My mouth watered instantly, and my stomach growled.

I wondered why the two strangers were being so nice. I hoped they weren't tricking us. Order a big meal and then ditch us, leaving us to pay the bill. But my friends and I decided to give them a chance. None of us were too comfortable with the idea of stealing anything.

Still, we were on the lookout for any suspicious behavior on their part. Just in case.

We walked up to the door and Summer halted. "Wait," she said, furrowing her brow. "They serve American food here, right?" Eden and I exchanged embarrassed glances, and I nudged her. "What?" She looked around innocently.

The girl eyed Summer. "Yes, it is American food."

Summer sighed with relief and Eden scowled. "What is wrong with you?" he whispered.

"Shut up!" Summer whispered back.

Eden and Summer made their way inside, and the blond boy stayed behind a minute. He glanced around the parking lot, occasionally sniffing the air. He shifted his gaze from one end of the parking lot to the other, and his body tensed.

Why was he sniffing the air like that? Could he be a…?

The girl held the door open. "Aleksandr, come on," she said, and waved him over.

Aleksandr turned toward the door, and I followed. "What were you looking for?" I asked.

"Nothing," he said quickly, his Russian accent just as thick as the girl's. He suddenly seemed on-edge, and I didn't like it. But I pushed my concerns out of my mind as I followed the others through the restaurant.

All I wanted to think about was food.

The two strangers were talking quietly at the front of the group, and I heard Aleksandr call the girl Lydia.

We took a seat at a large round table that reminded me of the ones at Bristol Manor. Aleksandr sat beside Lydia, who was sitting next to me. My face turn red as Lydia's hand gently brushed against mine when we reached for the menus in the middle of the table.

Eden, who was on my left, rolled his eyes.

"What?" I asked.

He met my gaze. "What?"

"Why did you—"

"Hello," said a voice from behind. "Welcome to Dimitri's Bar and Grill. I'm Kale and I will be your server today." She placed glasses of water in front of us. "Do you need a few moments to look over the menu?"

"Yes, I think we will need a minute," Lydia said.

"Okay, no problem." Kale stared at me with a look on her face I couldn't read—and didn't care for—then turned away. I was used to getting strange looks from people, but something about the way she stared at me left me feeling uneasy.

I watched as Kale spoke to a dark-haired guy near the entrance until she looked back in our direction. My gaze turned to Lydia, whose eyes were quickly shifting from one corner of the restaurant to the other.

"What's wrong?" I asked as I swallowed the lump in my throat.

Lydia met Aleksandr's eyes. "Do you smell that?"

Aleksandr sniffed the air. "Damn." His voice was a whisper, barely audible. My stomach felt queasy as the color drained from his face. He had a look of horror in his eyes. "I knew it. He's here."

Summer, Eden, and I exchanged worried glances. "What's going on?" Eden asked, chewing on his nails.

Lydia and Aleksandr said nothing as they shared a knowing look.

"If something is wrong you need to tell us," Summer demanded. "Now!"

"Shh!" Lydia held her hand up. "This hunter. He's been following us, and we thought we lost him a while back but—"

"Wait," I said, running a hand through my hair. "A hunter?"

"Yes," Lydia said plainly. "You guys are werewolves. How do you not know about the hunters?" The three of us exchanged nervous glances but didn't respond. "We heard you guys talking on the bus. If you don't want people to know, I recommend talking more quietly."

"Plus, you smell like dog," Aleksandr added. "No way to hide that. But hunters can't smell you, so it doesn't matter. The only people who will know are werewolves and other shape shifters."

"Other shape shifters?" I asked, wondering what else could be lurking around out there. "Wait. So, are you werewolves too?" I made a mental note to ask about the other shape shifters later.

Lydia nodded, her eyes glued to the front entrance. "We have to get out of here."

"Do you see the hunter anywhere?" Summer asked, a puzzled look on her face.

The two of them shook their heads.

Summer arched an eyebrow. "Are you absolutely positive he's here?"

Lydia straightened in her seat. "We know what Tom

smells like. Alek and I have been tracking his brother's scent for a while, and they smell very much alike."

"Why were you tracking his brother?" Eden asked, and folded his arms across his chest.

Lydia's eyes hardened and her tone darkened. "Because Carter killed our parents, and we wanted revenge."

"Your parents? You guys are related?" Summer asked, clearly surprised.

I tried to keep myself from smiling. *I was right!*

"Yes," Lydia said. "We finally took out Carter, but now his brother is after us."

"Are both of your parents were werewolves as well?" Eden asked.

The blond boy nodded. "We weren't bitten or turned."

"Enough of this," Lydia said, anger in her voice. She rose from her chair. "Now, come on. We need to leave. It's not safe here."

As the rest of us got to our feet, seven heavily armed people rushed to the door, blocking our exit. I recognized one of them, and shuddered. It was Wes. He stood in the middle, three hunters at each side. Wes stared hard in my eyes, not blinking. "I knew we'd meet again sooner or later, pup."

CHAPTER NINETEEN

Blood roared in my ears as the hunter grinned at me. I was really getting sick of seeing his ugly face. Once was enough.

"You know him?" the werewolf siblings asked in unison.

"Barely," I replied, not taking my eyes off Wes. "He tried to kill me."

The man squinted and cocked his head to the side. "Skyler. Ty." Two hunters on the left aimed their weapons at my friends and me. Their faces were scarred. Skyler had blood on her hands—literally—and looked anxious to add more. She grinned, exposing crooked, yellow teeth.

The hunter I recognized as Tom then stepped forward, aiming his gun at the siblings. "You fuckers killed my brother!" His extended arm wavered slightly, and sweat formed along his forehead. I could hear his heart beating rapidly. He was pissed.

Lydia backed up, but not from fear. "He killed our parents," she said calmly. Then her eyes turned red, and her voice wavered with anger. "That bastard got what he deserved, and so will you!" Light brown fur sprouted all over her body, and her transformation was over within seconds.

Lydia lunged at Tom with her teeth bared, and slammed him against the restaurant wall. The gun fell from his hand, but not before a single bullet escaped, barely missing Eden. My friend's eyes were wide with panic as he ducked just in time.

"Stephanie!" yelled Tom. Another hunter rushed to Tom's side, desperately trying to pull Lydia off him. She stabbed at the girl, but missed every time; Lydia was just too quick. She snapped and clawed at Tom, seemingly unaware of Stephanie trying to pry her away.

Aleksandr turned as well and pounced on Stephanie. He ripped into the woman, tearing her head right off her body. Buckets of blood spilled from the headless body. Loose flesh dangled from the head that Alek carried around the room, probably as a warning to the remaining hunters. Stephanie's face was permanently frozen in fear, and the pool of blood surrounding her body grew larger.

Diners inside the restaurant screamed, and fled the building. Several employees ran for their lives as well, leaving behind their coats and purses and wallets.

Our server Kale, who didn't seem at all fazed by what

was happening, approached Eden with a determined look on her face. When he wasn't looking, the woman whacked my friend across the face with something hard. Eden's skin began to sizzle and redden, and his hands flew up to the wound on his face. "Aaaaaaaaggghh!" he shouted as Ty rushed toward him.

Lydia and her brother teamed up to take on Skyler and another hunter, who had very long, black hair. He fired a few silver bullets into the siblings, but the two kept fighting.

Summer was helping a few remaining diners out of the building. One was a pregnant lady, who had tears sliding down her cheeks.

Kale swatted at Eden again as Ty dragged him away. Eden struggled in his grasp. I started toward him, concentrating on shifting to the wolf, but Long Hair fired a bullet into my thigh. Then Wes grabbed a fistful of my hair, dragging me toward the door. I stumbled along beside him, the silver bullet burning my leg.

I wanted to scream. The pain was growing stronger, and I couldn't stop worrying about my friends. Once again, I was a useless sack of potatoes. What is wrong with me? I have to do something! Eden was nowhere in sight, and Summer was lying on the floor, clutching her leg. Gunshots filled my ears, and windows shattered throughout the restaurant.

When Wes and I reached the door, he knocked me to the floor and rummaged through a big black duffel bag. I tried to push myself up, but the pain in my leg shot through my entire body. I cried out in agony. After pulling out a syringe, Wes grabbed my head and injected whatever was inside into my neck.

"I'm saving you for last," the man said with a sneer. "I want him to watch you die."

"Who?" I asked, my eyes feeling heavier and heavier.

The hunter replied, but I couldn't focus on his words. I wasn't even sure he was talking to me.

My eyes fluttered closed. My heartbeat slowed. Shouts and other sounds became nothing but a muffled hum in the background. The fire alarm went off, though I could barely hear it. I smelled smoke, but my body felt too heavy to move.

Then I heard a scream.

"Cris!" Eden shouted, and my eyes flew open.

My heart pounded in my chest, and I felt a little more in control. My fingers twitched slightly, and I knew it wouldn't be long now. Not dying today, dickhead! Whatever Wes injected me with was rapidly leaving my system as adrenaline pumped through my body.

The air was hot and dry. The fire was spreading quickly.

"Shit," the hunter said, and zipped up his duffle bag. He glared at me before fleeing the building. The remaining hunters ran after them, all of them bloody and bruised. There were a couple bodies on the floor, consumed by the flames.

Eden called my name again, and I finally struggled to my feet. I rushed around the restaurant in search of my friend, but there was no sign of him anywhere. Where could he be? My legs were wobbly, but my strength was returning.

Summer, who was hiding under a table, screamed loudly. Fire formed a circle around her, trapping her. "Help me!"

Without thinking, I leapt over the flames, meeting her under the table. I blinked the fuzziness from my vision, but the world was still blurry, and I felt out of it. What had been in that syringe?

"Are you all right?" Summer asked, but I didn't reply.

I knocked the table over onto the fire and for a second, there was an opening. We ran across the table before the fire spread, and stumbled out the door. Summer sat on the hood of a random car, clutching her chest and coughing.

I started toward the restaurant again.

"Wait!" she shouted, her eyes doubled in size. "What are you doing?"

"Eden," I said breathlessly. I inhaled too much smoke, and my lungs burned. "He's still in there."

"Are you *crazy?!* At least wait for the others!" She gestured behind her. "They're chasing the hunters but will be—"

Ignoring her, I dashed inside the flaming building and frantically searched for Eden. I couldn't let anything happen to him. Tables were engulfed in flames, and I launched them across the room as anger boiled inside me. "Eden!" I shouted with a cough. The smoke burned my eyes, and I could barely keep them open. I coughed and coughed, but didn't stop searching. I won't leave him behind, I thought.

Over the roar of the fire, I heard a small voice. It was very quiet, but somehow, I heard it coming from the kitchen. Tripping over chair legs and broken plates, I found my way to the kitchen. I couldn't see my hand in front of my face; the smoke was too thick. After crashing into a table covered with pots and pans, I heard him again.

"Cris," he said between coughs. His voice was weaker now and a little hoarse.

I got down on my knees and crawled around. The smoke wasn't as thick down here, but I could still barely see. Feeling around with my hands, I finally found him. He was tied to a pole, his hands wrapped behind his back.

Blood slid down the side of his face. "Maybe newbies," he muttered. "I don't think they knew how to kill me."

"Or they wanted you to suffer." My heart sank.

He shrugged and then shifted around uncomfortably. "Please hurry. I don't think we have much time."

"Right."

But the knot was too tight; I couldn't untie it. I felt around the floor for something, *anything* I could use to free my friend. Eventually I came across a knife, and sliced a chunk out of my finger when I went to pick it up. "Gah!" I shouted and jerked my hand back. Warm blood slid down my hand.

I cut through the rope and within seconds, Eden was free. But there was no time to celebrate.

The two of us stared in horror at the kitchen door. The way I'd come was now completely blocked by the fire, and we couldn't see another way out. There must be a back door, I thought. There had to be. We crawled around, sticking close to the walls, and searched for another exit. Eden and I yelped when a piece of burning wood from the roof landed on our skin, but we couldn't stop even for a second.

My skin was hot and my limbs ached. Eden was still bleeding.

The older boy finally managed to find the back door. I barely heard him over the roaring of the fire, though it didn't help that he couldn't exactly shout. Neither of us could speak louder than a whisper; our lungs were basically on fire. "Over here."

As I reached for the doorknob, a flaming chunk of the ceiling detached itself and slammed down on my legs. Somehow I managed to pull my legs out from under it. I patted out the fire, trying my best to keep from crying.

The door swung open. Eden grabbed me and helped me to my feet. We stumbled outside, and he took a deep breath of the fresh afternoon air. He was shaking and gasping for air.

We staggered toward the front of the building, but I had to stop. I just couldn't make myself go on. I'd never felt pain like this before.

"We have to keep going!" Eden said, his hands on my shoulders. "We can't stop. Not yet."

Breathlessly, I shook my head and waved him away. "I can't..." I leaned my back against the restaurant, unable to care anymore. I was fighting to stay conscious. At least I didn't go down without a fight, I thought.

"Guys!" he shouted, desperation in his voice. "Come here. Quick!"

Everyone rushed toward us, but I didn't acknowledge them. The slightest movement sent tears to my eyes.

I placed a trembling hand on my burned leg, and screamed as loud as I could. The skin was raw and hot. My eyes stung, and my throat tightened. Someone wiped the tears from my face, but I couldn't see who.

Everyone whispered around me—or perhaps they were speaking normally, and I could barely hear them. But I couldn't focus on their words.

"...going to die?"

"He'll be..."

"We should get him out of..."

"...doesn't look so good."

"Just give him some space."

My breath was coming in short gasps now. I knew if I didn't calm down, I'd pass out. The world was spinning, and I felt as if I were about to throw up.

Was it too much to ask for a normal day?

"Calm down," someone said. Alek, maybe?

Soon their muffled voices were drowned out by a loud

ringing in my ears. My head throbbed. I felt my body stiffen just as the ground rushed up to meet me, and everything went black.

"He's been out way too long," a muffled voice said. "I hope he's okay." I couldn't tell where I was, but I could no longer smell smoke. Where were we?

"Are you sure he's not dead?" said another voice. It was completely unrecognizable, though I had a feeling it was probably Summer.

I tried to work up the strength to move, but I wasn't quite there yet. So, I focused on the voices of my worried friends. Everyone sounded distant, a million miles away.

"Has he started healing yet?" Was that Lydia?

For a moment, I felt pressure on my legs where the burns should have been, but there was no pain. "Yeah, he's healing. He'll be fine."

My eyes rolled under my closed eyelids. I worked up the strength to turn my head, but that was all I could do. Even that was exhausting.

"He's alive!" a girl shouted.

"Cris?" I knew who that was instantly. Eden. "Can you hear me?"

After a silent moment, my eyes fluttered open, and I waited as the blurry figures around me slowly took shape. Lydia pushed my damp hair out of my face, and I groaned. She then picked up a damp cloth napkin from Dimitri's, and gently dabbed my cheeks and forehead. The water was cold against my warm skin, and a shiver ran down my spine.

I forced myself to sit up, and looked around. "Where are we?" My voice was so hoarse it made me cringe. I half-expected to find myself in a hospital or even a police station.

We were surrounded by shelves of moldy old books, cobwebs draped over them like a blanket. A thick layer of dust coated a table that our backpacks had been placed upon, and a broken chandelier lay only a few feet from me on the old hardwood floor.

"An old library," Aleksandr said. He was wearing completely different clothes than he was before, and I wondered where he'd gotten them. "We needed to get away from Dimitri's. Fire trucks and police were on their way, so we brought you here."

Everyone was sitting cross-legged on the floor beside me. Summer wrote something in the dust on the floor in front of her, paying no attention to the conversation.

"We were going to hide out in the woods," Lydia added, "but when we found this place, we decided it would be safer for you."

"You're okay, right?" Eden asked. He looked much better now. His wounds healed, and he was no longer trembling. There were a few holes in his shirt, though. "No pain, dizziness or anything?"

I shook my head. Thankfully, I felt almost normal.

"We didn't know if you were gonna make it." Eden had a sad look on his face as he fidgeted with his bracelet. "You've been unconscious for hours." Seeing how much he cared, I couldn't help but smile. My stomach filled with butterflies—or maybe flying elephants.

I scratched my head. "Really?" It felt like I'd only been out a few minutes.

"And your burns weren't healing," he said, his gaze shifting to the floor. "We thought they weren't going to."

I blinked in confusion. "What? Can that really happen?"

He nodded. "If it gets too bad, you won't heal."

Aleksandr got to his feet and shoved his hands into his pants pockets. "Whatever that hunter injected you with could have delayed the healing process."

I thought back to that moment, and furrowed my brow. "He said he wanted someone to watch me die."

Summer looked up, suddenly interested in the conversation. "Who?"

I shrugged. "I asked, but couldn't hear his answer."

Eden frowned. "That's strange," he said. "I wonder who he was talking about."

"Why would he want someone to watch you die?" Lydia asked, eyeing me. "Sounds like you're pretty important to someone."

I chuckled humorlessly. "Yeah, right." Wes's words repeated in my head. *I want him to watch you die.* Who was he talking about? Why was it so important that he watch *me* die? My brain began to hurt, and I shoved the thoughts aside for the moment.

The sun began to set, casting an eerie shadow through the windows. "Well," Eden said, "we really need to get going. Rylan needs us."

"We still haven't eaten, though." Summer crossed her arms. "Are we planning on doing that tonight or no?"

"There's a McDonald's down the street," Lydia said, perking up. "We can find something there."

Eden extended his left hand in an offer to help me up. We grabbed our bags and made our way to the library door.

Summer zipped up her jacket. "I can eat anything, especially McDonald's."

"Good," Lydia replied. "Let's go." She opened the door and the five of us headed out into the approaching darkness of nighttime.

CHAPTER TWENTY

"Are you sure you can afford all this?" Eden asked as he shoved the last bite of his burger into his mouth. There was ketchup all over his fingers, and he licked it off as Summer tossed him a napkin.

"Yeah, we've got plenty of money," Alek said with a shrug. "Don't worry about it."

I wasn't sure how I felt about our new friends. I was pretty sure they were trustworthy, but I knew very little about them. Still, it was nice having them around.

"Is Bristol Manor private school or something?" Lydia asked as she pointed to our shirts.

"We call it a Wolf House," Summer corrected her. "It's a school for werewolves."

"And a home," Eden chimed in. "For those of us who have no other options."

"Which is, like, everyone there," Summer replied.

"A school full of werewolves." Lydia tilted her head to look at Alek before finishing up her fries. "That sounds fun. Can anyone live there?"

"If the Elders accept you," I said, though I felt odd answering questions when I was still so new.

"Why do you care, Lydia?" Aleksandr asked as he leaned back in his seat with a scowl.

She shrugged. "I don't know. It would be nice to have someplace to go where we could be with others like us."

Aleksandr rolled his eyes.

"You're not tired of always being on our own?"

"We're *not* on our own," he muttered angrily.

"The butler doesn't count," Lydia said plainly.

"Butler?" Eden and I said in unison.

But the siblings ignored us.

"If we could get accepted into Bristol Manor, we would have people to talk to," Lydia said. "Kids our age." Alek stared down at the table. "It has just been Alek and me for a long time," she said to no one in particular. "That's why I was so excited for you guys to join us at Dimitri's." She looked at me and tucked her hair behind her ear. "It's nice being around kids like us. Most teenage werewolves don't last long on the streets, so it's rare to run into any."

Alek muttered something under his breath, and then met his sister's gaze. "Am I not enough for you anymore? Does family mean nothing to you?"

"Family means everything to me!" she snapped. "You

know that! I just don't want to go through life alone. What if something happens to you? Who will I have then? Or what if something happens to me? You will be completely alone. Is that how you want to live our lives?"

Alek slammed his fist on the table, and Eden flinched. "These people are strangers!" the blond boy shouted. "We know nothing about Bristol Manor, Lydia."

"We'll be fine," she said firmly, and took a sip of her soda. "We can take care of ourselves. But it can't just be the two of us anymore."

"We won't always come out on top," Alek grumbled. "You know that."

Lydia stared daggers at him before turning her attention to the rest of us. "Would you guys like some company?" She scooted away from her brother.

Aleksandr loudly slurped the last bit of his water. "I think we should head home. We've been gone too long."

Lydia shook her head. "I'm going with them. I love you, brother, but I need friends too."

Eden cleared his throat. "We're not supposed to ask for help," he whispered.

"We didn't ask," I said. "She volunteered. Do you think that counts?"

Eden shrugged. "I'm not sure."

"We should be fine," Summer said, waving away his concern. "We didn't ask for help, so we're not breaking their rules."

"I guess."

"Good," Summer said, and shoved one last fry into her mouth. "Are we ready to go?"

Eden shot her a puzzled look. "You do know it's like, thirty degrees outside, right?"

Summer nodded. "So?"

"I've just never seen you so anxious to get out in the cold," he said as he gathered the table's trash. He tossed it into the trashcan, and gazed out the window. The sky was practically black, dotted with tiny twinkling stars.

"We're taking the bus, right?" Summer asked.

"Yup."

"Then all is well." She grinned.

Eden and I exchanged a look as she headed out the door, and the two of us ran after her. There was a bus stop right across the street, and it was scheduled to come any minute. I was freezing and dead tired. It was obvious my friends were as well. Summer's teeth were chattering, and her eyes were droopy, though she looked a little less out of it when Alek joined her.

Lydia latched onto my arm as Eden exhaled on his hands to keep warm. I shoved my hands into my jacket pockets and shivered as the bus pulled up.

Again, we were the only ones on the bus. We flung our backpacks into the first couple seats as we drove away.

"Where exactly are we headed?" Summer asked Eden. "You're the only one who really knows where we're going."

"First, I have to check in with someone at a Quick-Mart," Eden said. "There are two checkpoints until we

227

get to the SFT. I guess so the Elders can keep track of us."

But Summer wasn't listening to Eden, and she stretched out on a couple seats in the back of the bus. "I'm going to sleep, guys," she said. "Wake me when we get there."

Lydia did the same in the seat next to mine as Aleksandr stared blankly out the window. I looked at Eden, who was staring at his phone. "Almost dead," he said with a sigh. I sank down into my seat and pulled my hood up over my head. "You look tired."

"I'm not," I lied.

"Tell that to your eyes." There was a short silence. "Just go to sleep."

"I'm not tired."

Eden chuckled. "You know, that would be a lot more convincing if your eyes were open."

"Mm," I said, wondering what he was talking about. Then I bolted upright. "Oh." I rubbed my heavy eyes, and ran my fingers through my hair. "Maybe I am a little tired." That was one hell of an understatement. I was so tired that I was actually seeing double. I didn't feel like I'd be able to move if my life depended on it. "I guess I'll...go to sleep...for just..."

"Aaaaaaagggghh!" Eden yelled as I fell to the floor of the swerving bus.

"What's going on?" I shouted as we made a sharp

228

turn. We must have been going a hundred miles an hour.

Eden was also on the floor, holding on to his seat to keep from rolling around. "Hunters! They took over the—"

The bus came to a sudden stop, causing us all to shoot forward, and sending Alek right through the windshield. "Alek!" Lydia screamed at the top of her lungs.

Then the bus tipped over and rolled down a steep hill, windows cracking from the rough tumble. I slammed against a window and shards of glass embedded into my palms. My head banged into the edge of a seat when the bus did another flip. It finally came to a halt at the bottom of the hill, and I fell forward, landing on top of Lydia. She groaned as I rolled off.

"Sorry," I muttered, rubbing my head.

Summer was in the back, screaming. She clutched on to Eden's arm as several hunters tried to drag them away. We were outnumbered, and I knew we wouldn't win this fight. This is it, I thought. I can't just sit around. I have to protect my friends.

My heart pounded in my chest as I focused on the change. But everything went black. I blinked several times, hoping it would clear my vision. *What's going on?!* I felt a hand on my shoulder, shaking me. Someone called my name.

Eden was trying to get my attention, but I couldn't see him. I stared blankly at the nothingness around me until...

"WAKE UP!" Eden slapped me in the face.

Heart racing, I shot up, gasping for breath. "What the—"

Eden jumped back, startled.

"Calm down, Calvin!" Summer shouted as she pulled her knees up to her chest.

Lydia stared at her. "Who?"

Eden and I were on the floor of the bus, but none of the windows were broken, Alek was alive, and there were no hunters on board. "I'm fine," I murmured, and rubbed my head. "I guess I had a weird dream. It felt so real." I looked from Eden's blood-smeared face to Alek's. "To be honest, I'm not completely sure it wasn't real. What happened to you guys?"

Eden helped me to my feet, but neither of them answered my question. I then realized they were about as far away from each other as they could possibly be while still on the bus.

"They got into a fight," Lydia said, glaring at her brother. "Alek recognized some hunters on the street and said some things he shouldn't have."

"Such as?"

Aleksandr shrugged. "All I said was I wanted to kill them. And I do."

"*All* of them," Eden said angrily.

Alek nodded, not a bit ashamed. "Yes, all of them. And anyone who stands in my way. The hunters fucking killed my parents!"

Eden frowned. "I'm aware of that. But killing everyone isn't going to bring them back."

Aleksandr walked over to my friend, and stuck his face
in Eden's. "I don't expect someone like you to understand.
If you lost both of your parents, maybe you'd—"

"I've never even *met* my parents!" he shouted angrily.
Everyone stared at him, and his cheeks flushed. He shoved
Alek out of the way and retreated to the back of the bus.

Alek rolled his eyes and stomped to the front row,
taking a seat next to Summer. They spoke in low voices,
and I looked back at Eden, who threw his hood up over
his head. I approached my friend, who was staring out
the window. At first, I wasn't sure he realized I was there.
"Hey," I said quietly.

Eden looked up at me. "You can sit down, you know."

I sat next to him, and chewed my nails. "Do you want
to talk?"

He shrugged.

"You don't have to," I said.

He ran a hand through his hair pushed it out of his
eyes. "I know." Eden lowered his head and flicked the
bracelet on his wrist. "I feel bad for getting so worked up
about this, though."

"You shouldn't. The world needs more people like
you."

Eden chuckled humorlessly, and met my gaze. "Then
how come everyone around me seems to want someone
dead?"

For a second, I got lost in his bright blue eyes. I shifted in my seat. "Wanting someone dead and killing them are completely different things."

"I just...I hate violence. But everyone else seems so indifferent about it." Eden sighed, and brought his knees up to his chest. He wrapped his arms around his legs, and rested his chin on his knees. "Has anyone told you about the other Wolf Houses?"

My eyes widened. "There are others?"

Eden nodded. "Brighton Falls isn't too far from Bristol Manor. Its Tealios's house, like Bristol Manor is Perinious's. Newcastle Hills belongs to Lusious."

"I thought they all lived at Bristol Manor?"

"They do," Eden said. "Tealios chooses who stays at Brighton Falls because that's his House. And Lusious chooses who stays at his Wolf House. But Perinious doesn't find many who are worthy of *his* approval, so the other Elders help fill up Bristol Manor, otherwise you'd be the only one there." He stopped talking momentarily when Summer burst into a fit of giggles. I wondered what she and Alek were talking about. "Anyway," he continued, "the Elders stay at Bristol Manor because it was the first House built. They visit the others occasionally, though."

The sun crept higher, turning the sky beautiful shades of pink, orange and yellow. There were only a few visible stars remaining. The sunrise made me think of Kaiden. Wonder what he's doing, I thought.

"I used to live there," Eden said, pulling me from my

thoughts. "At Brighton Falls."

"You weren't always at Bristol Manor?" I asked. The bus hit a bump in the road, and our backpacks went flying. But Lydia quickly gathered them up.

Eden shook his head, eyes glued to the window beside him. I saw his reflection in it. He looked so gloomy. "I was turned when I was ten, didn't get to Bristol Manor until I was thirteen."

I remembered Ian telling me how young Eden was when he was bitten. Part of me didn't believe him until now.

"Jack, the guy who bit me," Eden said, "he told me about Brighton Falls. He said I could live there permanently, and being a foster kid my entire life, I jumped at the chance to have a real home." He swallowed hard, and leaned back in his seat. "It was always one place after another, getting used to a new family, new rules, new neighborhoods, and schools. For me, it was really frustrating. Some of my foster families were nice, but towards the end, I got stuck with some really shitty ones."

I suddenly remembered Eden telling us he'd been beaten by his foster family. The thought made me both sick and angry. How could anyone treat a child that way?

"So, I let Jack take me to Brighton Falls." He smiled faintly at the memory, but the smile didn't reach his eyes. "I was quickly accepted by everyone there, and made a bunch of friends." Then his body tensed a bit. "You know how you got into that fight with Zak?"

233

I nodded. I'd never be able to forget that.

"Well, I got in a fight with someone too," Eden said. "It was with this older kid named Bret. He was a jerk, just like Zak, always picking on those who were smaller. I saw him beating up Jack, who had been my best friend for three years. I wasn't gonna just stand there and let him get the shit beaten out of him." The older boy frowned. "I was angry, you know? Furious. So naturally, I turned. But Bret didn't. So—" Eden stopped himself. He took a quivering breath before starting back up again, and his hands trembled. "I killed him."

My mouth dropped open.

Eden's eyes filled with tears. "I...I didn't mean to." He tried to blink the tears away, but they slid down his cheeks anyway. He wiped his eyes and covered his face with his hands. "I just wanted him to leave Jack alone. I was kicked out of that House, and that's when the Elders told me about the others. They said I could go to Bristol Manor, but this was my last chance."

How could the Elders force teenagers to participate in those barbaric cage-fights in which there's only one survivor, but punish a kid for defending his friend? If I didn't already hate the Elders, I sure did now.

Eden sniffled and I looked at his tear-stained face, trying to think of something to say. I couldn't believe what I'd just heard, but it made everything so much clearer. "That's why you're so strongly against killing."

"And basically, all forms of violence unless *absolutely*

WEREWOLVES OF BRISTOL MANOR

necessary. Even then, I still hate it." He wiped his eyes
again. "The kid I fought to secure my place at Bristol
Manor, she was new too. Her name was Morgan." He
shook his head in disbelief, staring down at his hands.
"I killed two sixteen-year-olds in one week. I don't even
know how I live with myself."

My heart broke for him. "I'm so sorry, Eden."

"It's okay," he said as the tears came to a stop. "And
thanks."

I tilted my head. "For what?"

"For not judging me."

"I'd never judge you," I said.

The look on his face made me think there was
something else he wanted to tell me. Was he unsure how
to say it?

"Is there something else?" I asked finally.

He opened his mouth to speak, but stopped himself.
"I'll just tell you later."

I had something to say too, but Summer plopped
down in the seat in front of us, and I decided now wasn't
the best time. She eyed the two of us suspiciously. "Everything all right back here?"

"Yup," Eden said with a sniffle. "I'm good now."

"Good, because we're about to pass a Quick-Mart."
She pointed out the window as the bus drove by the Quick-
Mart sign. "We need to get off now, right?"

"Yeah, we do." When the bus came to a stop, Eden
made his way to the front, and grabbed his backpack.

I got to my feet, but Summer made no attempt to move. "You coming?"

"Yeah," Summer groaned. "I just don't want to be out in the cold again."

Summer and I met our friends at the front of the bus, and shouldered our bags. When the door opened, we were met with a blast of cold wind, and the five of us trudged toward the store. I couldn't stop thinking about Eden's story, and wondered what else he had to tell me. Could it be the same thing I was going to tell him?

CHAPTER TWENTY-ONE

|We hurried inside Quick-Mart and gathered inside near the entrance. Eden and Alek were still a little angry, so they kept away from each other. The wind whistled as the automatic doors screeched closed behind us.

I didn't notice I'd been tuning out the conversation until Eden snapped his fingers in front of my face. "Hello? Anybody home?"

I blinked and stared blankly at him for a second. "What?"

"I'm supposed to meet up with some guy named Bob Wellington," he said, eyes darting around the store. "I have no idea where he is; all I know is that he works here. I think. Anyway, this is checkpoint one of two." He led the way through the building, and motioned for us to follow. "Let's see if anyone here knows Bob."

Summer threw her hands up to her hips. "What are you gonna do, ask every employee we see?"

Eden shrugged. "Couldn't hurt."

"Actually, it could," Summer said. "The person we ask could kill us."

"That's a *cheery* thought," I said as we passed a large candy display. Eden eyed it before hurrying after us. "But I don't think it will happen."

"Why not?" Summer arched an eyebrow.

"One regular, possibly annoyed human against five werewolves, and the human comes out on top?" I shook my head and wrinkled my nose. "That isn't gonna happen."

"Ya never know. . ."

The five of us then made our way back to customer service because Eden figured that would be the quickest way to locate Bob. But something caught my eye. There was a man hiding behind a rack of clothes, tracking our movement. We walked past him, and when I turned back, the guy was gone.

I came to an abrupt stop, feeling his eyes on me. But where could he have gone? And why was he watching us?

Lydia noticed I wasn't with the group, and came back for me. "Why did you stop?" she asked, and tucked her hair behind her ear. "Do you feel it too?"

I shot her a puzzled look. "You mean—?"

"That someone is watching us."

I nodded back toward the others, who were now at the customer service desk. "Why do they not feel anything?"

The hairs on my arm stood on end. Were we being followed by a hunter? Could it be Wes? I focused hard on the scents around me, but couldn't remember what he smelled like.

Were we jumping to conclusions? Maybe we weren't being watched. Maybe we were just being paranoid. But my gut told me otherwise.

"We have stronger senses than everyone else," Lydia said.

"Why is that?" I hated how little I knew about being a werewolf, and suddenly wished I'd read those books Kaiden was obsessed with.

"Alek and I are full-blooded werewolves." She looked me up and down. "Are you?"

I shook my head. "I was bitten a few days go."

The girl narrowed her eyes in disbelief. "Seriously?" Lydia brought her hand up to her chin. "That's strange. I've never heard of a newly turned werewolf with senses as strong as yours."

I groaned quietly as I was beginning to feel like a mutant. A freak. "Does your brother not feel anything?"

"I'm sure he does," she said confidently. "So, can you smell him? Whoever is following us, I mean."

Deciding to give it a shot, I closed my eyes and I sniffed the air. The man's scent filled my nose. It was strong, and made me want to sneeze. I could tell he was to our left, no more than sixty feet away. When I realized that he was a werewolf, I gasped. Why would a werewolf be creeping up on us? The man was wearing cologne I recognized, but I couldn't remember where I'd smelled it.

"You do smell him, don't you?" Lydia's eyes were wide with excitement.

"Yeah," I murmured, much less enthusiastically.

"Why does that bother you so much?" she asked. "Do you know how many werewolves would kill to have our abilities?"

"I just want to be normal for once." I averted my eyes and lowered my head. "Being different is—"

"Being different is the best thing anyone can be, and don't let anyone tell you otherwise." Lydia's voice was loud and confident. "There are billions of people in the world, and far too many of them want to blend in. If the ones who were different and special had the courage to be themselves, the world might be a more interesting and accepting place." She smiled sympathetically. "I understand how difficult it can be, but the more people out there who embrace their differences, the safer and better the world will be become."

My cheeks turned bright red. I knew she was right. But so many people made fun of me for being different. I wasn't sure I was ready to embrace even more differences just yet.

It wasn't long before the others came back for us.

Summer narrowed her eyes and folded her arms. "Why did you stop, Cairo?" she asked. "We thought you'd been taken too!"

I stared at her, a blank expression on my face. "You

can't possibly think that's my name," I muttered. "And I was away from you guys for *maybe* sixty seconds." I then turned my attention to Eden, who now had a half-empty bottle of water in his hands. "Did you find Bob Wellington?"

"Yeah," the older boy said. "He told the Elders that we've made it this far. They found out about our guests"— he gestured toward Lydia and Alek—"and they weren't too happy. But since our new friends *volunteered* to come along, the Elders are letting it slide."

"How thoughtful of them," I said.

"Some guy named Asher is the next person we have to meet up with," Summer said. "He'll be waiting for us at PetsLuv. And it looks like it's going to rain soon, so we better get moving. I'm tired of walking in all this rain."

Summer linked her arm through Alek's and took off toward the entrance with Eden following behind. When I went to follow them, Lydia caught my arm. "Crispin," she said.

Before I could respond, she placed her hand on my cheek, leaned in, and pressed her lips against mine. Her lips tasted of strawberries, and I breathed in her cherry-scented hair as she pulled away. For a moment I forgot what we were supposed to be doing, and I blushed.

"Don't ever forget how special you are," she said. "Trust me. It's good to be different."

The two of us then joined the others by a bench next to the exit. They were zipping up their jackets as clouds in the sky darkened.

Eden looked at me, his brow furrowed. He must have seen the kiss, I thought. Damn it.

He sighed heavily and trudged out the door. "Come on, guys," he called over his shoulder. "We need to go."

Why did he have to see that kiss?

We exited the store and hurried across the street. Eden led the way and was walking much faster than usual. Lydia and I trailed behind.

"Is anyone else starving to death, or is it just me?" Summer asked. "We should have bought something to eat at Quick-Mart." But she perked up when a convenience store came into view. "We can get something there." She pointed straight ahead.

But Eden kept going. "Do you have money?"

Aleksandr took out his wallet. "I do," he said, and motioned for Summer to follow him inside. "I'll get you something."

"Thank you, Alek!" Summer kissed his cheek as they ran inside.

Lydia held the door open. "Do you either of you want something?" We shook our heads, and she closed the door behind her.

Once we were alone, I pulled Eden aside. "Can I talk to you for a second?"

"What's up?" he asked, staring down at the ground.

My stomach was in knots. "I know you're upset," I began.

"I'm not upset."

I blinked. "Angry?"

He shook his head. "Nope."

"You seemed pretty upset a few minutes ago," I said, eyeing him.

He took a wobbly step back. "I don't know what you're talking about...."

"Is it because—"

"I'm not upset!" Eden threw his hands up in the air, clearly frustrated with me. "You can do what you want, Cris. Kiss whoever you want. It's your life, and none of my business."

"Eden, I just—"

But the door swung open and our friends came stumbling out, putting our conversation on hold. There were a million things I wanted to say to him.

When we started walking again, I remained at the back of the group so I could think. But Summer joined me when she finished her bag of chips. "So," she began, "are you two together now or something? You and Lydia?" She licked her fingers noisily, and I cringed.

I shrugged. "I like her, but...."

"You like her butt?!" she shouted, and everyone glanced back.

That wasn't embarrassing at all.

"You know what I mean," I said impatiently.

We then passed a vacant six-story building that used to be a very fancy hotel. In front of it was a marble fountain, and it was filled with dark brown, almost black water topped with layers of leaves, old fast food bags, and discarded candy bar wrappers. I was pretty sure there was a dead squirrel inside as well. The stench of the water was so bad it made my eyes water.

"But what?" Summer asked, her tone a bit more serious now. "Do you want to be? Or would you rather be with... someone else?" There was a mischievous grin on her face.

"Someone else?" I swallowed nervously. Was it that obvious?

"You like him, don't you?"

Eden shouted, interrupting my uncomfortable conversation with Summer. "Cris! Come here for a second."

Summer returned to Alek as I jogged over to Eden, who was standing several feet in front of them. The group had come to a stop, though I wasn't sure why. "What is it?"

"Lydia said she sensed something," he said quietly.

"Sensed what?"

His eyes shifted side to side before he spoke. "She said there's another pack around here."

"Of werewolves?" I asked.

Eden arched an eyebrow. "No, of gummy worms. Ya want some?"

"I'm more partial to gummy bears, actually."

He made a face. "Really? I love me some gummy worms."

I gasped when I finally smelled the other pack. My stomach twisted uncomfortably. Something didn't feel right.

Eden's eyes widened. "What's going on? What do you

244

smell?" The older boy sniffed the air and groaned disappointedly. "I smell nothing."

I focused hard and tuned in to everything around me. All sounds amplified, sending a shiver down my spine.

Four werewolves with heavy footsteps and a pungent odor were headed our way. They smelled as if they'd each rolled around in excrement before walking a hundred miles. "There are four of them," I told Eden. "I think they're pretty close."

"You can't tell for sure?"

"No," I said disappointedly. "They're hard to focus on. The way they smell is too—"

"Horrible?" Alek said as he and the others circled around us.

"We're having the same problem," Lydia said.

Summer glared at me and stomped her foot. "How come you have this special power that Eden and I don't have? We've been members of this club longer than you, Chauncey."

"I found that interesting as well," Lydia said.

"Um, guys?" Eden interrupted as several figures came into view. "Should we be worried? Most street packs are wild and violent. This could get ugly." I could tell he was trying to hide his fear.

The five of us stood frozen in place as the other pack of werewolves crept toward us. *Wild and violent* Eden had said. I held my breath until I could see their eyes glowing bright red.

CHAPTER TWENTY-TWO

Sweat slid down my face as the werewolves approached. I know Eden said street packs were dangerous, but that couldn't apply to every pack, could it? No. There had to be a few good ones out there, I thought. But the looks on my friends' faces told me they believed otherwise.

Eden shuddered as the pack stopped right in front of us.

The guy to the left was huge. He was probably six and a half feet tall with bulging muscles everywhere. He looked to be mid-twenties, but something told me he was just a teenager.

The kid next to him was just as bulky. She was several inches shorter though, and her skin was darker. She looked so young, but so angry. Her clothes, like the others', were dirty and bloody, and smelled terrible.

The guy next to her, probably the youngest of the group, was short and skinny with no visible muscles. He had a messy mop of blond hair that kept his face hidden, but his long nose poked out of it.

The girl on his right was the smallest of the bunch. She had long black hair and her glowing red eyes were filled with hate. Her face was splashed with freckles, and long scars trailed up her forearms. She had electric blue streaks in her hair, and I thought she might be kinda pretty if she didn't look like she wanted to rip my head off my shoulders.

"Jeremy," the tiny girl said as she folded her arms across her chest. She smirked, revealing her fangs.

"Now, Zee?" the blond mop—Jeremy—asked.

Zee then turned to the muscular guy. "Jabari?"

He nodded eagerly, rubbing his hands together like a cartoon villain.

"Do it," the tiny girl said, her voice loud and commanding.

Summer pursed her lips as Lydia and Aleksandr stepped back, preparing to transform. "What do you want?" she asked Zee. "We've done nothing to any of you."

Jabari stuck his ugly face in hers, and she whimpered. He towered over her. "We just want to see your insides... on the outside," he whispered, and licked his lips. He laughed manically and kicked Summer to the ground. The concrete knocked the wind out of her.

When I went to help her up, Jabari knocked me aside

with so much force that I went flying back twenty feet. I scraped my hands against the sidewalk when I landed, the skin peeling off painfully.

Lydia darted toward Zee, who already looked bored. Zee ducked and dodged the other girl's punches with ease. She gracefully maneuvered around Lydia, landing some punches of her own every now and then, smiling the whole time.

But Lydia quickly picked up on Zee's fighting style, and was finally able to do some damage.

I stumbled to my feet, and winced when I put pressure on my palms. Jabari shot over to me and kicked me in the jaw. It made a loud crack and I spat out blood.

Alek and Eden were now struggling to stay alive as the other two members of Zee's pack beat them black and blue. Jeremy sliced his claws down Eden's back, and it wasn't long before his shirt was ripped to shreds.

Cars driving by ignored the fighting, which was probably for the best. If a human intervened, they could get seriously hurt. Or worse.

Jabari was knocking Summer around when I finally stopped spitting out blood. He kicked her in the ribs, and she doubled over, grimacing in pain.

Eden was on all fours. His face was bruised and swollen, and his eyes were closed. Jeremy had a few scratches on his arms, but he was a skilled fighter, and evaded most of Eden's attacks. When my friend fell to the ground, a knot formed in my stomach.

My bones slowly began to break and shift, and I knew my wolf was coming. Each time a bone moved into a different position, it made me want to scream. My eyes turned red, and my senses sharpened. Right before my wolf was able to completely take shape, Jabari grabbed a fistful of my hair and slammed my head into the edge of the fountain.

My body reverted back to its normal shape, and I saw stars circling around my head. My shirt was on the ground, leaving my upper body exposed. I was shivering. Goosebumps dotted my forearms.

The world was spinning and it left me feeling sick. Jabari laughed as he reached for me again. I tried to roll away so my wolf would have plenty of time to take shape, but Jabari was fast. He grabbed the back of my neck, digging his sharp claws deep into my skin as he lifted me to my feet. He threw me inside the fountain and held me under the murky water.

I squeezed my eyes shut as the freezing water rushed over my face. Jabari wrapped his fingers around my shoulders and forced me to the bottom of the fountain, refusing to let me come up for air. He chuckled at my futile attempts to escape. No matter how much I struggled, I just couldn't break free.

Eventually, his hands slipped as I flailed wildly, and I took his wrist in my mouth, biting down as hard as I could. The disgusting water filled my mouth and I gagged, but didn't let up. Jabari howled in pain and jerked his hand away long enough for me to sit up. I threw myself out of the fountain and onto the hard ground.

I couldn't stop shivering. My skin appeared blue, but I figured it was just my imagination. I wanted to crawl away, but my body wouldn't move. It was like I was glued to the ground.

Jabari leapt out of the fountain and wrapped his hands around my throat. Blood trickled from the bite on his wrist. I couldn't breathe, and I couldn't fight back. I'd never felt more helpless.

That's when Alek joined our fight.

He launched himself at Jabari, and they went flying through the air. They landed with a thud right next to the mutilated corpse of the bulky girl from Zee's pack.

I threw up the filthy fountain water as blood roared in my ears. For a while, it was the only sound I could hear. My throat burned as the water poured from my mouth.

Summer and Eden were lying on the ground, covered in battle wounds. Jeremy stood over them, his white teeth stained with blood. I couldn't hear what he was saying to them, but the look on Eden's face told me he was scared to death.

Lydia back-flipped over Zee. Her foot collided with the side of Zee's head, and the tiny girl stumbled back, falling into a pile of garbage bags. Jeremy's face paled as he ran to her.

Alek and Jabari were still going after each other, but they were closer to the abandoned hotel now. Jabari flung

Alek into the wall, and I heard a few of his bones snap. Alek grabbed the other boy's neck, but Jabari knocked my friend's hands away.

Aleksandr was obviously exhausted, and I didn't know how much more the poor guy could take. He and Jabari were bleeding all over, but Alek's movements were rapidly slowing down.

I have to help him, I thought. He saved my life.

I stumbled toward my friend, still deaf to the sounds around me.

Alek's lip was busted open, and his nose was obviously broken. His eyes landed on Zee's unmoving body in the pile of garbage bags, leaving him unprepared for an attack. Before I could reach them, Jabari slashed his claws across Alek's stomach and slammed them deep into his chest.

I gathered every ounce of strength in my body and focused solely on Jabari. Screaming in anger, I ran up to him and shoved my claws through his throat. They poked out the other side, and Jabari went down with a thud.

My body was suddenly drained of energy and rage, and I fell to my knees.

I hadn't realized Alek was on the ground too. He was lying on his back, blood gushing from his wounds. But Jabari's claws had broken off inside Alek's chest, preventing him from healing. When he spoke, his voice was soft, and barely audible. "Get...Lydia."

I called for her, and she froze in place. She was bent over Eden and Summer, helping them to their feet. Jeremy

251

and Zee stumbled away without even a glance over their shoulders.

Lydia's eyes widened as she yelled her brother's name, and ran to his side as quickly as she could. Eden and Summer slowly limped over, but kept their distance. Everyone knew what was happening.

Lydia knelt down and took hold of her brother's trembling hand. Tears spilled from her eyes as she pushed his hair out of his face. Her cheeks turned red as her body shook. "Don't leave me, Alek," she said between sobs. "You can't leave me all alone." Her voice was a strained whisper. "You're all I have. Please don't leave me." She squeezed his hand tightly, bringing it up to her face. Her tears landed on his fingers.

"Lyds…" Aleksandr whispered, blood trickling from his open mouth. "I…"

"No," Lydia said, her voice quivering now. "You can't leave me! If you want to return home, we can. We don't have to stay out here anymore." She sniffled as tears streamed down her face. She refused to let go of her older brother's hand. "You're all I need, Alek."

I lowered my head when his eyes glazed over, and his chest stopped moving.

Lydia buried her face in Aleksandr's chest, and sobbed inconsolably. Her shoulders shook as she cried.

"He was the only family I had," she said, her voice muffled. "I feel like I can't breathe."

"I'm so sorry, Lydia." I said. "I swear I tried to help

him." But I was too late.

I looked down at Alek, his eyes staring sightlessly up at the sky. He didn't deserve this, I thought. Alek didn't deserve to die.

Lydia's hands trembled as she carefully closed his eyes. She pulled her knees up to her chest and wiped her nose. "When our parents were killed, Alek and I were determined to get revenge," she said. "Having the hunters to focus my anger on helped me keep it together. It kept him together too." She paused and looked up at the sky, trying to keep from crying again.

She leaned over, resting her head against my shoulder. "I don't think I can help you find your friend, Crispin."

The warmth of her touch sent shivers down my spine. I tried not to concentrate on how cold I was. What Lydia was going through was much worse. "It's okay," I said. "Where will you go?"

"Maybe back home." Her voice was unsteady and hoarse. "That might be the best place for me to be right now. Or maybe I'll visit one of the packs my brother and I met when we were hunting the hunters."

"Why not go to Bristol Manor?" My heart was heavy. I didn't want her to be all alone in the world, and she was so excited to learn of the Wolf House.

"I might go there after I've had time to think." Lydia ran her fingers through Alek's hair. Her eyes were glued to his unmoving chest, refusing to look at his face. "Maybe Bristol Manor is the right place for me to be. Maybe it

253

isn't." She shrugged, and pulled away from me, meeting my gaze. "I need to think about who I have left in this world, and how I'm going to stay alive. I don't know anyone at Bristol Manor except you three, but I know several packs around here." She leaned forward, resting her chin on her knees. "I just don't know anything right now. I need some time to think."

I wrapped my arms around her in a hug, and she closed her eyes. "I hope you decide to give Bristol Manor a shot," I said. "But I know you need to do what's right for you. You're the only one who can make that call." I squeezed her gently in my arms. "I hope you'll be okay."

She looked at me and wiped her eyes. "Can you help me move his body?" she asked. "I want the cops to find him so he can be given a proper burial."

We waited until there were no cars passing by, and then Eden and I gently dragged Aleksandr's body to the grass between the road and the sidewalk. "He should be easily spotted here," Eden said.

Summer bit her lip to keep from shedding tears of her own.

Lydia picked a few resilient flowers from the garden of a nearby building and placed them in Alek's hands as a couple more tears spilled down her cheeks. "I'm sorry, Alek," she said to him, struggling to breathe. She leaned forward, kissed his forehead, and whispered something in Russian before getting to her feet.

She sighed heavily, pulling me into one last hug. She

squeezed her arms tightly around me. "I'll miss you," she said. "I hope you understand why I need to leave."

"I do," I said when she pulled away. "I hope to see you again, though." Saying goodbye made me feel sick.

Lydia smiled half-heartedly, and then turned to Eden and Summer. "Goodbye, my friends. I wish you the best of luck."

"Lydia—" I began.

"We *will* see each other again," she promised me. "I know we will." She kissed my cheek. "Goodbye, Crispin."

Eden and Summer joined me as I watched her walk away, fading into the distance. I turned to face my friends, feeling lower than I'd felt in a very long time. "Alek saved my life," I murmured. "But I couldn't save his."

"Hey," Eden said softly, placing a hand on my shoulder. "None of this is your fault, okay? Those guys obviously kill for fun. They were crazy, and we tried our best to defend ourselves."

Summer handed me a clean shirt from my backpack. As I put it on, she said, "They were just too strong, Crispin. His death isn't your fault."

How could this have happened? How could things go so wrong so fast? I couldn't shake the feeling that I was partially to blame. If I'd been just a little faster, Alek might still be alive. I had a feeling his memory—like Lincoln's—would haunt me for the rest of my life.

CHAPTER TWENTY-THREE

I couldn't get Aleksandr out of my mind. Every time I closed my eyes, I saw him on the ground, taking his final breath. We continued our journey in silence. My hands began to tremble, so I shoved them into my pockets, hoping neither of my friends had noticed.

As we made our way across the street, a dark blue car pulled up next to us. We kept walking, but stopped when someone got out and ran after us. Eden and I exchanged worried glances.

They're back.

I still felt sick from swallowing filthy fountain water, and my entire body was sore. There was a nasty cut on the side of Eden's face that hadn't healed yet, and Summer couldn't walk without limping. We were in no condition to fight.

"Well, well, well," Zee said, her tone oddly cheerful. She and Jeremy hadn't completely healed either, but neither of them seemed to mind. "I was hoping we'd run into you guys again. We need to finish what we started." Zee's hair was messy and tangled, and her face was dirty. Claw marks on the side of her neck were still red but, no longer bleeding.

Jeremy had a black eye, but the bruises on his arms were fading. He looked around, a puzzled expression on his face. "Where's the other girl?" he asked. "We didn't scare her away, did we?"

"Why are you doing this?" I asked, ignoring his question. My entire body trembled with rage. How could they be so heartless?

Zee cocked her head to the side. "Why *are* we doing this, Jeremy?" She pressed a finger to her chin as if in deep thought. "Oh, that's right. Because we fucking *can.*" The girl shrugged. "And because it's fun. There's nothing I like more than feeling someone's warm blood on my hands, watching the life leave their body, and hearing their heart finally stop. It gives me a rush. I've become quite addicted to it."

Addicted to killing? I could feel myself losing control as my body shook.

I started toward them, but Eden pulled me back. "What the hell are you doing?!" he shouted. His eyes were wide and his palms were sweaty.

I shook free of his grasp, glaring at the psychopaths in

front of us. "I'm avenging Alek."

"Put her down!" Summer exclaimed, and Zee chuckled humorlessly.

"Cris, no," Eden said, inserting himself between Zee and me. "I know you feel like you have to do this, but you don't. You can't—"

"I'm not asking you to help me," I said, trying to keep my emotions under control. I was angry and terrified, and just wanted this to end. "If everyone backed away from a challenge, nothing would ever get done. If I fail, I fail. I at least have to try."

"Tell that little bitch to back off," Zee said, eyeing Eden. Her voice sounded sickeningly sweet. "If he talks you out of it, fighting you won't be as much fun."

I held my wolf back for as long as I could. But I fell to my knees, and my muscles burned as they stretched. My bones shifted and my eyes turned red. My clothes ripped from my body as my wolf took shape.

When the transformation was over, I stood calmly in front of Zee and Jeremy. I let out a deep, low growl before pouncing on Zee. We landed hard, and I smacked my head on a metal pipe on the sidewalk. Zee screamed as her wolf came out as well.

Jeremy shot toward me, but Zee growled at him, and he stumbled away.

Zee sliced through my fur, and I yelped. She let out an earsplitting howl when I ripped her ear off. I dropped it on the ground, and Summer gagged.

Zee was foaming at the mouth. She raised her paw and slashed her claws across my face.

I felt blood trickle down my cheek. I ignored the pain and knocked her over, sinking my teeth deep into her back. I dragged her around in a circle while she howled in pain and clawed at the ground. I twisted her fur with my teeth as she pawed at my chest.

When I risked a glance at my friends, I saw Jeremy slam Eden's face through the window of the blue car. Glass shattered around my friend's head. He pushed Jeremy away and sank to his knees, his back pressed against the side of the car. Tiny shards of glass were embedded in Eden's lips and cheeks, barely missing his eyes.

Rage filled my body. It surged through my veins, filling me with power. A shiver ran down my spine, leaving my entire body feeling tingly and more alive than ever before.

I sank my teeth into Zee's skin and ripped away a chunk of her furry neck. Blood spilled from the wound and coated the lower half of my face. The girl staggered away, reverting back to human. She didn't move when the transformation was complete. Zee remained still, lying face down in a humongous pool of her own blood.

I killed another one. Was it intentional? I honestly didn't know and was sort of afraid to find out. My stomach hurt at the thought of killing Zee. She was just a kid.

I couldn't make myself look at her. What am I becoming? How could I have done this? Was it truly unavoidable? She and Jeremy chose to attack us twice, knowing there had been deaths on both sides. Still, seeing her lying on the ground left a heavy feeling in my chest.

I shifted back and threw on some clothes, no longer feeling powerful.

Summer ran up to me as a long cut across her chest closed up. She pointed at Eden and Jeremy, who were still fighting near the car. "I tried to help him," she said, her bottom lip quivering.

Jeremy had his hands wrapped around Eden's throat. My friend's face was turning purple as he desperately tried to pry the other boy's hands away. I snuck up behind Jeremy, but something didn't feel right.

Summer was staring at me in horror, though I couldn't understand why. My heart nearly stopped when I saw that Zee's body was no longer on the ground. I had to be ready for an attack. When I looked down, I suddenly felt sick. The metal pipe I'd come across earlier was protruding from my stomach.

"Cris!" Eden managed to shout. His eyes were bloodshot, and his hair was plastered to his forehead with sweat.

Blood poured out of my stomach and dripped out my mouth. My ears were ringing as the coppery taste of blood filled my mouth. My legs wobbled. My head throbbed.

It was the worst pain I'd ever experienced, and I wasn't sure I was going to live through it.

Zee kicked Jeremy out of the way and stared down at Eden, her eyes turning red. Her throat wound had stopped bleeding, but it wasn't closing up, which meant it wasn't healing.

I spat out a mouthful of blood and shuddered. My body was hot and I felt lightheaded. But Zee was closing in on Eden, going in for the kill.

I am not about to lose another friend to this blood-thirsty monster, I thought.

I struggled to my feet, doing my best to ignore the pain in my stomach. I willed my wolf's strength to fill my body as I grabbed Zee's head and gave it a quick twist. Her head bent at an unnatural angle before she collapsed.

Jeremy stood there paralyzed, staring at the dead girl. The bone broke through the skin of her neck, and Jeremy puked at the sight.

My knees suddenly gave out, and all I felt was pain when I hit the pavement. I would have smacked my head on the sidewalk, but Eden rushed up to catch me. He lowered me to the ground, and Summer yanked on the pipe, trying to pull it out of my stomach.

I couldn't stop myself from screaming at the top of my lungs. I was sure my throat was bleeding after that. "STOP!" I yelled. It felt like my stomach was on fire.

"What are you doing?!" Eden shouted, and swatted at her hands. "You're gonna make him bleed out!"

"He'll be fine." Summer smacked his hand away. "Hold him still."

Eden cringed, but did as he was told.

I squeezed my eyes shut. Summer yanked one last

time, and the pipe slid out. I stared down at the hole in my stomach. "Is—is that my—?"

"Intestines?" Summer looked at me with sympathetic eyes. Then she got to her feet and raised the pipe with a crazed look in her eye. She swung it and screamed maniacally.

Eden and I exchanged a terrified look as she stood behind Jeremy, who was still puking.

Summer whacked Jeremy on the side of the head as hard as she possibly could, and he fell forward onto the car. She then shoved the pipe through his left eye socket. When it was obvious the boy was dead, she pulled the pipe out, and did the same thing to Zee. She then dropped the pipe, and it made a loud *clang* as it hit the ground. "I just wanted to make sure they were dead."

Eden stared at her in horror and gulped. "Tell me to look away next time," he said.

Summer sat down beside him and began picking the glass fragments from his face. He winced and pulled away, but she kept at it. "Oh, Eden, don't be such a baby."

When his lip was free of glass, be turned his attention to me, his eyes full of concern. "Have you started healing?"

The pain in my stomach was just as bad as when the pipe first burst through. My insides burned so badly I wanted to scream, but I forced myself not to—which took every ounce of willpower left in my body. If I was going to heal, I wished there was something I could do to speed up the process. I could still taste blood in my mouth. "I don't know," I said weakly.

Summer placed her hand on my stomach near the open wound, and pressed down. This time, I couldn't stop myself. I screamed as she pressed down harder and harder, but she didn't stop. My trembling hands reached for hers, trying to knock them away. "Hold on," she said in a firm voice.

"What are you doing?" Tears filled my eyes as she continued pushing harder and harder on my stomach. "Stop! Please stop!" My voice was hoarse, and it hurt to talk as I choked back sobs.

"You're gonna kill him!" Eden shouted.

Summer rolled her eyes. "You two are so dramatic." She finally stopped, but the pain didn't ease up. "You're healing, Clayborn. The wound is slowly but surely closing up." She lifted my shirt so Eden could take a look. "See?" The pain was starting to fade, only slightly though. "I'm sorry I hurt you, but I'd do it again if I needed to," she said with a shrug.

Eden frowned. The cuts on his face from the glass were completely gone now. "If he'd been unable to heal—"

"Then he would have died anyway," Summer snapped. "My pushing on his stomach would have sped it up, but we needed to know."

"I do prefer quick deaths," I said to no one in particular.

Eden smiled weakly and shook his head. "You sure are a crazy one. You did great though."

263

"I must say," Summer began, "you're a little scary when you're angry. The calm way you snapped Zee's neck? Creepy."

"You're one to talk," I muttered. "You screamed like a maniac when you killed Jeremy."

I then turned my attention to Eden. "I'm sorry I couldn't help you sooner."

"It's okay," he said. "I'm all right."

"Maybe next time you won't be." I tried to sit up, but my arms were too weak to lift me. "I always try to help, but it never works out. I thought I'd be able to help you rescue Rylan, but I'm just dead weight."

"No, you're not," Eden said, scooting closer to me. "Do you know how far I would've made it on my own? I would have died at the very first attack."

"Maybe not," I said, chewing my lip. "For some reason, the hunters are after me. Maybe if I weren't here, they wouldn't have attacked you."

"I know you have a hunter after you," he began, "but they kill *all* werewolves. I would have died on my own. Even if the hunters hadn't showed up, there's no way I would have survived the fight with Zee and her pack by myself. And I know I'll need your help when we reach the SFT." Eden's blue eyes stared into mine. "I need you, Cris. I can't do this without you."

I looked away sheepishly.

"I'm really glad you fought so hard to come along," he said.

Summer cleared her throat. "Hi! Remember me? I'm here too."

He smiled and pulled her into a hug. "I'm glad you came too, Summer."

The sun was setting and the temperature started dropping. I knew we needed to get going, but I secretly wished I could have a few hours—or days—to heal.

"Can you stand?" Eden asked.

I put my hand on his shoulder and pushed myself up, cringing from the pain.

"The next checkpoint is right there." Summer pointed to a large blue building off in the distance. "You can rest here in Zee's car while Eden and I—"

"No," I interrupted. "I'm fine, guys."

I wasn't, but there was no way I was going to stay behind.

My body was still very weak, so I wrapped my arm around Eden's shoulder as I hobbled along. Summer trailed behind us, carrying my backpack and eyeing the Krispy Kreme that was next to Quick-Mart.

"Mmm, doughnuts sound good," Eden said.

"You can say that again," Summer replied.

Eden licked his lips. "Mmm, doughnuts sound good."

I chuckled. "Smart-ass."

People stopped at a traffic light gawked at us as we crossed the street. Guess it's not every day you see three blood-soaked teenagers out and about, I thought. Summer threw her hood up over her head to avoid their lingering gazes.

After a while, I began walking slower. My stomach hadn't fully healed yet, and every step I took sent a sharp pain throughout my body.

"You're walking slower than my grandpa," Summer complained. "And he's dead."

"Thanks for the concern," I muttered.

"Why don't you sit down for a minute?" Eden asked, and pointed to a bench in front of a dollar store parking lot. It was wet from the rain, but I didn't care. I plopped myself down and groaned, clutching my stomach.

Summer sat next to me, and wrinkled her nose. "Great. Now my butt's wet."

"I'm gonna run inside and grab some bottles of water," Eden said, gesturing over his shoulder to the dollar store.

The girl narrowed her eyes. "I don't think any of us should be alone right now."

"I'll be okay," he assured her. "He's the one who shouldn't be left alone."

She crossed her arms and lowered in her seat. "Leaving me out here with the smell of doughnuts," she muttered. "That's just rude."

But Eden disappeared inside the store, and Summer and I were left alone. The parking lot was dimly illuminated by a single streetlamp. I stared down at the shadows on the ground until something familiar caught my attention.

The scent of our stalker had returned! I rose from my seat in a panic. What if he hurts Eden? I couldn't let that happen. Yeah, I was probably being a bit paranoid, but considering everything we'd been through recently, I had a right to be. "Come on!" I shouted to Summer as I dashed toward the store. I didn't know how I was able to run, but I knew I couldn't stop until we found Eden.

"What's going on?" Summer yelled as she clumsily ran after me. "Slow down!"

As we approached the entrance, I filled Summer in on everything that happened at Quick-Mart. Whoever had been watching us back there had come here, and that couldn't be a coincidence.

"You're sure this guy is a werewolf too?" Summer asked, a puzzled look on her face.

"Absolutely."

The two of us came to an abrupt halt at the front of the store. I sniffed the air once for Eden's scent, and once for the stalker's. I took off in search of my friend without making sure Summer was keeping up. As I dashed around the corner, I slammed into someone, and we both fell to the floor.

"Watch where you're going," a familiar voice said. "Cris?"

"Eden!" I pulled him into a hug. "Are you okay? Are you hurt?"

When we pulled apart, he gathered the bottles of water he'd dropped. "I'm fine. What's going on?"

Summer finally joined us, panting heavily. She placed her hands on her knees as I explained everything to Eden as well.

"I'm fine, by the way," Summer muttered. "Don't worry about me."

"Sorry I left you," I said. "I panicked."

She waved away my concern. "It's all right. Everyone is okay, and that's all that matters."

I helped Eden to his feet, and as we walked toward the front of the store, the stalker's scent grew stronger. *We're getting close.* The familiar scent nearly knocked me off my feet. I wasn't exactly sure how to proceed, but we rounded another corner, and I looked up into the eyes of our stalker.

CHAPTER TWENTY-FOUR

Eden and Summer rushed to my side as the man looked down at me, an odd look on his face. I tried to move, to say something, anything. But my body wouldn't obey my commands. So I just stood there, staring up at the stranger. I remained calm, but my heart was pounding in my chest.

The pain in my stomach was flaring up again, and I had to fight to keep my face as emotionless as possible. We needed to figure out why this man—this werewolf—was following us. When I confronted him, he seemed surprised to learn I actually knew that he'd been watching us.

The man's dark green eyes silently studied us. My gut told me something wasn't right. He looked so familiar, but where could I have seen him? His rough-looking face had some stubble, and his arms were long and muscular. Such a normal-looking guy, yet something definitely seemed off. "What makes you think I've been following you?" he asked calmly.

My cheeks reddened. What's happening? Could this be the wrong guy? I began to panic internally until I closed my eyes, and let my nose do its thing. That scent was unmistakable. "I know you've been following us," I said, my voice filled with confidence I didn't feel. "Now tell me why."

He shifted his weight to his other foot. "I need to speak with you, Crispin." He eyed my friends. "You've made it quite difficult to track you down."

"I made it difficult?!" I frowned and crossed my arms. "You didn't have to *follow* us! You could have come up to me and...wait. How did you know my name?"

The man went silent, his face unreadable. I looked him up and down before he finally answered me. "I knew your mother," he said softly. "I heard about her passing. So sorry for your loss." He lowered his head. "She and I were once very close."

I averted my eyes, not wanting to talk about my mother. "What did you want to talk to me about?"

He tilted his head, gazing at Eden and Summer, who were standing quietly at my sides. "Can we speak in private?"

"No," Eden said and stepped in front of me. "You were *following* him, and that's just creepy. We have no reason to trust you."

"I don't believe I was talking to you," the man snapped,

his jaw clenched. "We need to talk, Crispin, but not with these two around."

Eden opened his mouth to speak, but I stopped him. "It's okay, Eden. Can you guys wait for me here?"

My friend bit his lip and sighed. "Fine. Just be careful, Cris. We don't know what he's capable of."

"Stranger danger," Summer added with a thumbs up and a huge grin. "Wouldn't want you to go missing too."

"I appreciate your concern," I said plainly, unsure how genuine her words were.

She nodded and tucked her hair behind her ear. "Knew you would."

The stranger and I walked far enough away so that we couldn't be overheard. My friends were still visible, and they kept a close watch on us. "What do you want?" I asked the man.

"Your friends are quite protective of you," he said with a smile. "It's sweet."

I knit my eyebrows. "Is that what you wanted to talk to me about? My friends?"

He shook his head. "I needed to tell you something pretty important. I was hoping to tell you much sooner than this." He took a deep breath as if preparing for some huge revelation. "I'm the one…."

I blinked in confusion. "What one?"

"The one who bit you," he said. "It was me in the woods that night." He reached forward, but I shot back.

I couldn't believe he did this to me. "Don't touch me!"

I shouted, louder than I should have. "Why the fuck did you bite me? You did it on purpose, right?"

"Shh!" He held a finger over his lips, signaling me to be quiet. "I was gonna talk to you sooner, but they took you to Bristol Manor before I got a chance." He ran a hand through his dark brown hair. "I bit you because I wanted you to join my pack. We need you, Crispin. You should never have been taken to Bristol Manor."

"You want me to join your little wolf pack?" I asked, glaring at him. "You think you can tell me that you bit me, and all of a sudden I'll want to join you? I don't even know you!" My voice was filled with anger. "I've made friends at the Wolf House, and I'm not leaving them." Rage bubbled in my stomach, and if I wasn't careful, I feared my wolf would come out.

So I sucked in a deep breath, trying to calm down. "I have a new life," I said. "I'm not gonna leave that and my new friends behind. There is nothing you, a man I know absolutely nothing about, could say or do that would change my mind."

He covered his mouth with his hand. "Oh, I'm sure you've been told a thing or two about me."

"My mother never mentioned some random guy who stalks teenagers," I muttered.

He laughed to himself. "No, I guess your mother wouldn't have talked about me. And I didn't stalk you."

"Yes, you did."

He shot me an annoyed look. "Crispin."

I shrugged. "I'm just saying."

The man held his look of annoyance a moment longer. "My name is Pierce."

I felt my breath catch in my throat as I took a step back. "Pierce? As in…?"

He nodded, and I looked him over. I didn't know what I'd expected Pierce from Bristol Manor to look like, but this certainly wasn't it.

"Well, that doesn't change anything," I said, and looked over at my friends. They were talking quietly, and Eden chewed his nails. "I might know your name and *very* little about you, but I'm not leaving my friends to join your pack. Why do you even want me, anyway?"

"Because you're powerful," he said, and zipped up his dark blue jacket. "More powerful than you know."

"No, I'm not." I stared down at my shoes, my shoulders slumped. "Trust me on that."

"Crispin—"

"Well, you've got your answer," I said, walking back toward my friends. "I'm not joining you, so you can leave us alone now."

Pierce sighed, and shoved his hands into his pockets. "Your friend is gonna be very disappointed."

I stopped and met his gaze. Oh, no.

"What friend?" I asked, dreading the answer.

"Kaiden." Pierce tilted his head. "The kid with the fingers? Used to be your best friend?"

"I know who he is!" I shouted, and shoved him. "What

did you do to him? Tell me you didn't turn him."

"When I realized that you'd been taken to Bristol Manor," Pierce began, "I knew it wouldn't be easy getting you to leave. There are lots of kids your age, and I knew you'd make a few friends. So, I turned your *best* friend." He gestured toward Eden and Summer. "Well, I *think* he's still your best friend."

Dread filled my stomach, and it became harder to breathe. How could he have done this to him? "Kaiden joined you?"

Pierce nodded. "I told him what we are, what *you* are, and asked if he would like the bite as well. He was pretty excited to join my pack, and I know he's been looking forward to seeing you again."

My head was throbbing, making it difficult to concentrate. "All this just to get me?"

"Like I said, you're more powerful than you know."

"How do *you* know?" I eyed him suspiciously. What is he not telling me? "If I don't know what I'm capable of, how could you?"

"I just do," he said with a shrug. "I can't explain it. Not here, anyway." He waited for me to reply. When he realized I wasn't going to, he added, "If Kaiden doesn't die, I'm sure he will be an excellent addition to my pack."

My eyes doubled in size. "If he doesn't die?!"

Pierce waved his hand casually. "If he were going to die, I'm sure he would have by now." His words were not very comforting. "We'll know for sure after his first change though, which should be very soon. You don't want to miss your best friend's first werewolf transformation, do you? I'm sure you'll agree that it's a traumatic experience, especially if you're facing it all alone."

I remembered how terrified I was when it happened to me. Knowing Eden was there definitely helped me through it. How could I let Kaiden go through it all by himself?

"What if it kills him?" I asked. My voice sounded so small. So quiet.

"If he is strong enough, he will survive."

"Well, what if he isn't? You might have sent my friend to his grave just to get me to join your stupid pack!" My legs trembled, and my mouth went dry. "If he dies, I swear I'll kill you."

Pierce laughed. "A bit dramatic, don't you think?"

"I mean it, Pierce!" I balled my fists. "If he dies, I'm coming for you."

"He's still alive, boy," he snapped. His heart beat faster as his frustration with me grew. "Do you honestly think you, a newly turned werewolf, could kill me? Your threats are empty, buddy." He shook his head, and brought his hands up to his face. "I promise he'll be fine. Everyone is outside if you want to meet them and see your friend again."

I stood frozen in place. I wanted to see Kaiden, but I didn't want him to think he was getting to me. "Can my friends come too?" I asked. Seeing Kaiden was more important than avoiding Pierce's pack.

"Crispin—"

"Either we all go, or not at all."

"Well look at you, making demands," he said. I stared down at the floor, awaiting his response. "All right. They can come."

I gathered my friends, and the four of us made our way out to the parking lot. Pierce walked ahead of us as we approached his pack. "That's Pierce," I whispered.

"Are you serious?" Eden asked. "That's him?"

I nodded.

"I expected him to look a little...meaner." He lowered his voice. "What did he talk to you about?"

I quickly filled them in the conversation I'd had with Pierce.

Summer wrinkled her nose. "Why is everyone acting like you're so special?" she asked. "Seriously, you're nothin' to write home about."

"Thanks," I muttered.

"I disagree," Eden said, and lowered his head so that his hair fell into his eyes.

Pierce finally stopped next to four people huddled around a bunch of shopping carts, and smiled warmly. "This," he began, "is Shiloh Moore, Fitzgerald Halls, and Zorya Roberts." He turned toward my old best friend. "And you already know—"

"Crispin!" Kaiden shouted as he pulled me into a hug, his backpack dropping to the ground. "I was so worried about you! I thought you'd been killed or maybe you got sick of me."

I squeezed him tightly. "I thought the same about you." Though I hated knowing that Pierce bit him as well, I was relieved to see my friend was okay. My heart nearly broke when I thought he might have abandoned me. "I went by your car to talk to you, but you weren't there." We pulled apart, and I saw sadness in his eyes. "You really scared me."

"Now you know how I felt," Kaiden murmured, and I was suddenly overcome with guilt. "I woke up one morning and you were gone. Why didn't you say anything?"

"I didn't mean to leave like that," I said as I squeezed the strap of my backpack. "I went out for a walk to clear my head and was attacked by werewolf hunters. Then I was rescued, and taken to a Wolf House. But I tried to come back and explain everything later."

Kaiden shrugged. "I guess I'd already been recruited by Pierce."

I glared up at Pierce, who looked away and ran his fingers through his hair.

"We live in a cool house, though," Kaiden said with a smile. "You should see it!"

"I'll bet it's not better than Bristol Manor," Summer muttered under her breath. Eden nudged her in the ribs, and she looked at him innocently. "What?"

Kaiden looked at Summer and waved flirtatiously. "Hello, there. We haven't been properly introduced. I'm Kaiden Davis-Smith. And you are?"

She made a face, clearly uninterested in my friend.

277

"Summer."

Pierce turned to Eden, eyeing him. "And your name is?"

"Eden."

"You were in the woods the day Crispin was attacked by the hunters." Pierce squinted and brought a hand up to his chin. "You're one of the kids who brought him to Bristol Manor."

Eden nodded. "And Bristol Manor is where he's gonna stay."

"We'll see about that." Pierce arched an eyebrow before turning his attention to me. "I'm surprised the Elders accepted you."

"Why?" I asked. "If I'm as powerful as you claim I am, why wouldn't they want me?"

"Because you're powerful," he said with a shrug.

I groaned. "That doesn't make sense."

"The Elders still make everyone participate in the caged wolf fights, right?" he asked. "How did your initiation fight go?"

I paused, trying to figure out where he was going with this. "I fought Eden." Memories from our fight flooded my brain. The pain, the horror, the frightened look in Eden's eyes. Then I remembered something else. That was when I first took control of my wolf. "How did you know?"

"The Elders' fights wouldn't be as interesting for them with someone like you in there," he said. "And I guarantee they won't put you in again, now that they know you can

278

control it."

But how could he have known about that? Could that skill have been passed to me through the bite? Was that possible?

"We really need to get going," I said. "We've wasted too much time already." My friends and I turned to leave, but Pierce rushed over to me and grabbed hold of my arm.

"Wait!" he shouted, and I jerked free. "When was the last time you kids had something to eat?"

"Why do you want to know?" I asked as my stomach growled.

"How about the three of you come back to our place for a while?" he asked. "We'll get you some food and you could rest a few hours. Whatever you're doing, you can't continue in this condition." He looked us up and down.

"No," I said firmly. I wanted to get to Rylan as quickly as possible. Out of the corner of my eye I saw Eden put a hand on his stomach, and I knew he was just as hungry as I was. Were we making a big mistake? Should we trust this strange man who claimed to know my mother?

Summer inserted herself between Pierce and me. "We're not seriously turning him down, are we?" she asked. "I'm starving and tired and cold and probably a few more things."

"We don't even know him," Eden said to her, and Pierce backed up a bit, giving us a little privacy. "We're supposed to trust him?"

Summer stomped her foot. "He hasn't given us a

reason not to. Besides, he wants Collin. What's he gonna do? Poison us? Charlie can't join him if he's dead."

I frowned. "Girl, you just called me two different names in the same breath."

"If you come with us," Pierce called to me, "I'll loan you kids my car. I'm sure you're all tired of walking."

I gripped the straps of my backpack, tugging lightly on them. "You would really loan us your car?" I asked. "Why would you do that?"

"Like I said, I was close with your mother, and I don't like seeing her son like this. Starving, weak, and covered in blood." There was a look of genuine concern on his face, and it was hard not to trust him. "Do any of you have a license?"

Eden raised his hand. "I do!"

"Good." Pierce clapped his hands together. "Then it's settled. You'll come with us, get some food, sleep a few hours, and in the morning when you leave, you can take the car. Sound good?"

I looked at my friends. "But—"

"Excellent!" Pierce exclaimed as he and his pack hurried across the street to a couple cars parked along the side of the road. My friends and I followed. After everything we'd been through, we figured we deserved a break. I just hoped trusting Pierce wouldn't come back and bite me in the ass.

CHAPTER TWENTY-FIVE

Fitzgerald, Zorya, Shiloh, and Kaiden hopped in one car, while Eden, Summer and I climbed into another. Pierce drove us back to his place, and the others pulled up behind us. The two-story house was grey, and the paint was chipping badly. It looked almost identical to the other houses on the street.

"Nice place," Summer said as we waited in front of the front door. "Ours is bigger."

I nudged her.

We drove farther than I would have liked, but I figured we'd make up for it tomorrow. I still couldn't believe he was going to loan us his car. Could this man really be trusted? Did he just want to help?

When we entered, Pierce motioned for us to have a seat on the couch. It was against the wall in front of the window, facing the television. My friends and I sat down and I couldn't stop myself from smiling. The couch was so comfortable; it was like sitting on a cloud.

Shiloh, Fitzgerald, and Zorya accompanied Pierce in the kitchen, flicking on a few lights throughout the house.

Eden was beside me and my hand accidentally brushed against his. I chewed my lip nervously, and he blushed. Kaiden took a seat in a nearby chair, and things quickly got awkward.

"How long have you guys been friends with Crispin?" Kaiden asked. I felt like we were at job interview.

"Not long," Eden admitted. "Just a few days, actually."

"Feels like forever," Summer muttered, and threw her arm up on the arm rest.

I turned to her a moment, unsure how to take that.

"I've known him a long time," Kaiden continued. He leaned forward and clasped his hands together.

I averted my eyes when he looked at me. He was my best friend. Why was this so awkward? "Are you still going to school?" I asked him.

He nodded. "Unlike you." There was a brief pause, and his face turned red. "I didn't mean that. I mean, I did. But I didn't mean—"

"It's okay," I said. "I know."

"Do you think you'll take Pierce up on his offer?" he asked. "I think you should."

Eden leaned back in his seat and fidgeted with his bracelet.

"Um, I don't know."

"You don't know?" Kaiden tilted his head.

I frowned. "Can we talk about this later?" I didn't want to have this conversation in front of Eden and Summer. Fortunately, Kaiden seemed to understand.

"Why don't we go to my room? We can talk there."

I followed Kaiden up to his room, leaving my new friends in the living room. It was great to see Kaiden again, but things felt so different between us now. I could tell he was jealous.

"Are you seriously not gonna join us?" he asked as he shut the door to his bedroom. There wasn't much in it. His backpack and blanket were on the bed, but the shelf by the window remained empty. Kaiden stood in front of me when I sat on his bed, and folded his arms across his chest. I felt like I was getting a lecture from an adult I'd disappointed.

"I really don't know, Kaiden. I would love to come here with you, but it's complicated now. If I hadn't been taken to Bristol Manor and hadn't met Eden—"

"Didn't you miss me at all?"

"Of course, I did."

"Then screw them! Join us!" He paused, and when I didn't respond, he groaned. "Oh, come on, Crispin. I'm your best friend, aren't I?"

I remained silent, trying to decide how to respond.

Kaiden furrowed his brow and his body tensed a bit. "Have I been replaced this quickly?"

"You haven't been replaced," I assured him. I pulled my leg up to the bed and wrapped my arm around my knee. "But I can't just agree to come here with no thought. There are things I have to figure out and I can't leave—"

"You can't leave them, but you can leave me?"

"Oh, calm the hell down, Kaiden," I snapped. "You and your friendship mean the world to me. You're like my brother. But you have no idea what Eden, Summer, and I have gone through."

"Whatever you've gone through with them can't possibly be worse than what you and I went through." He paced angrily around his room. "You do remember all those fights, right? The bullying? The isolation? The homelessness? You can throw away our friendship for two random people you just met?"

"Kaiden, stop!" I shot to my feet. He backed away as my face turned red with anger. I inched closer as I spoke, gesturing wildly with my hands. "They're not random people, okay? And don't say anything about what the three of us have gone through, because you don't know shit. One of our friends has been kidnapped, and I don't even want to think about what the SFT are doing to him right now. Another friend was killed. Aleksandr was killed after saving my life. His sister left our group after his death, and I have no idea where she is, or if she's okay. We've had to kill people to stay alive and are basically on a suicide mission, but we have no choice. Eden was given this quest, and I refused to let him go alone. We have to get

Rylan back but no one at home believes we'll make it and honestly, sometimes I don't either."

By the time I'd finished my rant, my body was stiff and sweaty. I backed away and exhaled a quivering breath.

Kaiden stared down at his feet. "I'm sorry, dude," he said quietly. "I didn't know."

"Exactly," I said, trying to calm down. I ran a hand through my hair as I reclaimed my spot on his bed. "I'm sorry I yelled, and I'm sorry I left. But I can't leave Eden."

My friend tilted his head curiously. "Oh?" He went silent and nodded.

There was an awkward moment where no one spoke. I broke the silence when I asked, "Did Pierce really bite you?" Unlike the other werewolves, Kaiden didn't smell like a dog.

He raised his jacket sleeve, exposing a bite mark on his forearm. I knit my eyebrows as I examined the wound.

"What?" Kaiden asked, and gulped nervously.

"Why hasn't it healed yet?" I looked up at him. "How long ago did he bite you?"

He shrugged, pulling the sleeve of his jacket back down over the bite. "I'm not sure. It wasn't long ago, though." He went quiet and there was an odd look on his face. "Can I ask you something?"

"Of course you can."

Kaiden opened his mouth, but no words came out. He sat next to me on the bed and took a deep breath. "Does— does it hurt? Turning, I mean."

285

I nodded slowly, unsure how he would react to the news. I knew I couldn't lie to him about something like this. "It felt like I was being ripped apart and set on fire simultaneously. But that was just the first couple times. It gets easier. Are you afraid of the pain?"

"Not exactly," he said quietly.

"Then what's wrong?" I asked. "You know you can tell me anything."

Kaiden's mouth was a thin line. I knew he was hiding something. "I guess I'm just nervous about this whole werewolf thing," he said after a while. "And yeah, you know I'm not a big fan of pain. That really scares me."

Something didn't feel right. I could smell fear on him, but I knew becoming a werewolf—and the thought of possibly killing someone—was scary. I wrapped my arms around him in a hug. "You'll be fine," I said softly. "I'm still here, and you're way tougher than I am. You'll handle it way better than I did."

We pulled apart and he nodded. "Any tips?"

"Just don't freak out," I said. "Stay calm and relax as best you can."

"Will do," he said. "Will I...be naked?"

"Werewolves don't usually wear clothes."

He chuckled. "I meant when I shift back."

"Yeah, but it's not as weird as it sounds."

Kaiden flashed a very fake smile. "Greeeeat."

He opened the door, and the two of us made our way back downstairs, where everyone was sitting around the

WEREWOLVES OF BRISTOL MANOR

coffee table, deep in conversation. Eden scooted to the middle of the couch so I could next to him.

Shiloh Moore, who was sitting in a big recliner next to the couch, looked to be about eighteen. He was tall, and his blue-green eyes peered out from behind his long black hair. I noticed a tattoo of an hourglass on the side of his neck, and wondered if he had any others. His facial structure sort of reminded me of Alek. Images of Aleksandr's dead body flashed before my eyes, and I shuddered.

Fitzgerald Halls was probably about nineteen. His hair was short and brown, and he had big brown eyes. He was about five eight—the shortest guy of Pierce's pack—and had very muscular arms.

Zorya Roberts looked no more than seventeen years old. She was skinny, but fierce. The girl had dark brown hair and even darker eyes. Her tan skin was smooth, and there were several tattoos on her arms. Both Zorya and Shiloh had their nails painted neon green, except for the middle finger on each hand, which was painted black.

A timer went off in the kitchen, and Zorya and Pierce went to retrieve mugs of hot chocolate. Zorya came back and placed three mugs in front of us on the coffee table. Pierce gave out the others to members of his pack. "We thought hot chocolate would warm everyone up," Pierce said.

"Thanks," Eden said, and took a sip.

Zorya and Pierce returned to the kitchen, and Shiloh sat up in the recliner. The wind picked up outside, and it whistled loudly as rain began beating down on the roof. "So," Shiloh said, awkwardly glancing around. "What exactly are you guys looking for? We weren't filled in on everything."

"The SFT," Eden said. He gripped his mug tightly, and I was afraid he might actually break it in half.

"Ugh, I hate them." Shiloh wrinkled his nose. "Why are you looking for them? Just go outside and wait. I'm sure those bastards will find you soon enough." Shiloh didn't strike me as rude, but he did seem rather pessimistic. I could definitely relate to that.

"They took our friend," Eden replied.

"Oh." Shiloh looked down. "Are you guys planning some revenge?"

"No. We're rescuing him."

"Are you sure he's alive?"

"He's alive," I chimed in. I knew he was. "They said we could get him back in exchange for something."

"In exchange for what?" he asked, and took a sip from his mug.

Eden, Summer, and I exchanged looks. "I'm not sure," Eden piped up. "But we're just going to try and break him out of there. I don't know exactly what they do to us, and I don't want to find out."

"Good luck." Shiloh shrugged. "They haven't captured many of us, but those who have been taken were never the same again."

Eden gulped nervously. "What do you mean?"

Shiloh placed his mug on the coffee table in front of him. "They don't kill unless they think you being there will put them in danger. But they're not above torturing to get information or cooperation." He leaned forward, an intense look in his eyes. "A buddy of mine, his sister was taken a few years back. They wanted her to shift on a livestream, but she wouldn't." His eyes fell to the floor. "Or maybe she couldn't. I'm not sure." He covered his mouth with his hand and shook his head slowly. I wondered if he knew the girl he was talking about. "Nothing the SFT did to her worked. They tried all sorts of mind games and many different methods of torture, but they couldn't get her to shift when they wanted her to."

Summer sank down in her seat. When she spoke, her voice was quiet. "What happened to her?"

Shiloh met her gaze. "After torturing her, they tossed her out in the middle of the woods. She was wandering around for days, no clue where she was or who she was. When her pack finally found her, she was mumbling nonsense. Shadow, clock, spring, rat. Stuff like that is all she says now."

The room went silent, and I knew we were all thinking about Rylan. What was he going through right now? How different will he be when we get to him? I hadn't known him long, but the thought of him going mad like that broke my heart. He seemed like such a happy kid.

Summer brought a hand up to her face as tears fell from her eyes.

"Shiloh?" Pierce called from the kitchen. "Could you come in here a sec?"

"Sure." He hopped up from the recliner and turned to face us. "Good luck, guys." There was a hint of sadness in his voice. I wondered just how many lives the SFT and hunters have destroyed.

But then I thought about the fights at Bristol Manor. How many teens have the Elders sent to their deaths? Were they just as evil? And if they were, what did that say about us?

My gaze landed on Eden, who was looking hopeless and frightened. Bristol Manor wasn't a good place for him. If Pierce could leave the Wolf House without suffering any consequences, did that mean we could too? If I accepted Pierce's offer and joined his pack, would he let my friends as well? Could this be our ticket out of Bristol Manor and away from the Elders?

Shiloh and Pierce then returned with plates full of ribs, and my mouth watered as I remembered how hungry I was. My friends and I devoured our food in less than a minute, and Eden licked the barbecue sauce off his fingers.

"That was so good," I said when I was finished.

"Mmm," Summer agreed, her mouth full with one last bite. "So good."

"Would anyone like seconds?" Pierce asked as he grabbed the plates from the coffee table.

"Not me," Summer groaned, patting her stomach. "I'm full. Might have to burp."

"Just don't puke," Eden chimed in, and Fitzgerald stifled a chuckle.

"Eww!" She whacked his shoulder. "Don't talk about puking after I just ate!"

"I'm too tired to eat any more," I said.

"Me too," Eden agreed. "I just want to sleep."

Pierce nodded and returned to the kitchen. The bed we were going to sleep on was a fold-out couch bed, and Kaiden helped us get it out. He handed us some sheets and pillows as he rubbed his tired eyes.

"Good luck tomorrow," he said. "I hope you get your friend back."

"Thanks," I said, and hugged him one last time. It was so good to see him again, and to know that he hadn't abandoned me. I wanted to tell him about my idea. That I'd move in here if my friends could too. But I was afraid Pierce would say no and didn't want to get Kaiden's hopes up.

"Good night, Crispin," he said, and headed up to his room.

Summer fell asleep within minutes. She was on the far-left side of the bed, her arm hanging over the side. I plopped down in the middle, leaving room for Eden on the right, and beat the crap out of my pillow until I was satisfied with its fluffiness.

"I'm sorry we don't have another bed," Pierce said, gesturing around the living room. "We don't usually have guests."

"Is that recliner comfortable?" Eden asked.

Pierce shook his head. "I've been meaning to get a new one. I've had that one longer than any of you kids have been alive."

"This bed is huge, Eden," I said as I patted the space next to me. "Come on. I won't bite. Unless ya want me to."

He smiled shyly and sat down. The older boy stretched out on the bed and patted his pillow a few times like I had, only not as roughly. "Good night, Cris."

I looked at Eden before rolling onto my stomach. After turning out the lights, Pierce disappeared into his bedroom. I shifted positions one last time as Eden fell asleep beside me. "Good night."

I dreamt I was running in the woods barefoot, wearing shorts and a plain black shirt. Twigs snapped beneath me, sending sharp bursts of pain through my feet. Though I couldn't see Wes, I knew he was the one after me. Crickets chirped around me as I stumbled through the dark forest. Mosquitos hovered around my face, and I swatted them away.

I tripped over a small possum and tumbled down a leafy hill, screaming all the way down. Suddenly, I was surrounded by the faces of those who'd lost their lives on this quest. Lincoln, Alek, Jabari, Zee, Jeremy. Their faces were mutilated and angry. I swallowed the lump in my throat, and they started toward me.

"Wait," said Wes, who was now standing in front

of me. "I don't want him to miss this moment." The hunter pointed over my shoulder, where a man stood in the shadows. His face came into view when he stepped forward.

It was Pierce.

Wes raised a crossbow and shot an arrow at me, sending it straight through my stomach. I gasped and raised my hands to the wound. I felt no pain, but my hands came away bloody. The ghosts started toward me again. They put their filthy hands on my shoulders, and I screamed.

I awoke with a start.

My heart was racing, and my face and neck were damp with sweat. Was it a sign? Did Wes want Pierce to watch me die, or was I jumping to conclusions? Was there a bond between us that I didn't feel? He bit me and made me what I've become, but I felt nothing special. However, that didn't mean Pierce felt nothing.

There were too many things I didn't understand, and I knew I wasn't going to make sense of them at four o'clock in the morning. I shifted around in the bed but froze when Eden moved as well.

I closed my eyes and tried to fall asleep, but my dream left an odd feeling in the pit of my stomach. What could my subconscious be trying to tell me?

CHAPTER TWENTY-SIX

It was eight in the morning when I awoke to the sound of Fitzgerald going into the kitchen for something to eat. He then sat in the recliner with a big bowl of cereal. He smiled sheepishly. "Did I wake you?" he asked, and shoved a spoonful of Cheerios in his mouth. "I forgot you were here."

I rubbed my eyes. "It's okay."

Summer ran a hand through her hair as Eden's eyes fluttered open. The girl groaned and shielded her eyes from the morning light. "Too early," she muttered.

Pierce moseyed into the living room, his hair sticking out at the sides. "You kids are up early," he said. "When I was your age, I slept until noon whenever possible."

"Where are your keys?" I asked, gesturing toward the front door. "And which car are we taking?"

"Um, about that, I—"

I rose to my feet, a scowl on my face. "You said we could—"

"Calm down, buddy." The man stepped between the door and me. "I'm still gonna let you take the car. I just don't think you should leave right this second."

I eyed him suspiciously, unsure if I should believe him. "Why not?"

"Don't you hear the storm?" He pointed out the window. The wind blew a heavy trashcan into his neighbor's yard as thunder rumbled overhead. The rain was coming down so hard it was difficult to see through. "And it's only gonna get worse."

"But we have to go now," I argued. "We don't know what they're doing to Rylan. He may not have much time."

"Rylan?" Pierce suddenly seemed more interested. "He was the one taken? Do you have anyone else coming to help you?"

I shook my head. "No, it's just the three of us."

"Oh…." He clenched his jaw, straightening his back a little.

I wondered why he seemed so concerned. Was it possible that he knew Rylan? If so, how? A strange feeling settled into my stomach.

"Crispo," Summer said, forcing me out of my thoughts. "I don't want to wait either, but I think we may have to. This storm is really bad, and it's impossible to see through all that rain. We'll end up getting ourselves killed."

Eden shot to his feet. "No, I'm with Cris. We need

to get to Rylan as quickly as possible. He's already been with the SFT way too long." He swallowed hard. "It's my fault they have him, so if you don't want to go, Summer, I completely understand."

She shook her head. "I'm going with you guys," she said, and placed a hand on his shoulder.

Pierce narrowed his eyes at Eden as Fitzgerald took another bite of cereal. "Have you driven in weather like this before?"

Beads of sweat dripped from the sides of Eden's face. "Yeah, of course," he said, a little too casually. The kid was a horrible liar. "I've driven in storms way worse than this. Piece. Of. Cake." He chuckled nervously. "Yup."

I cringed. There was no way Pierce bought that. "So, can we have the keys?"

"Why did the Elders send you three to the SFT?" Pierce asked, and gestured toward Eden, Summer, and me. "They're *making* you go, right?"

"It's my punishment." Eden stared down at his feet, and I could hear his heart hammering in his chest. "When we came across the SFT in the woods, we ran back to the car and drove away." He fidgeted mindlessly with his bracelet. "I was the oldest one out there, but I didn't make sure everyone got back safely." He lowered his voice. "And Rylan was taken. The Elders said I had to bring him back, or I'd be killed."

Pierce's dark green eyes landed on me, judging me. "Why are you here, then? It's Eden's punishment. It has nothing to do with you."

Summer and I exchanged a look. "We couldn't let him go alone," I said as my cheeks flushed.

"You voluntarily put yourself in this situation?" he asked, anger rising in his voice. "Do you know what it's like for teenage werewolves out there? How easy it is for you to be killed? How many different groups you'll have after you?"

"Why are you so concerned?" I snapped. "I don't know you. What I do is none of your business!"

"Cris," Eden whispered. "Stop."

"It is my business!" Pierce paced in front of me and placed his hands on his hips. "The Elders are ruthless, Crispin. If they sent him to the SFT with no real backup, then they never intended for him to make it back alive."

I crossed my arms, meeting his frustrated gaze. "I know."

He looked away, muttering something under his breath. Fitzgerald awkwardly rose from the recliner and retreated to the kitchen with his cereal.

I grabbed my backpack from behind the couch and my friends did the same. "Are you letting us take the car or not?" I asked. "We really need to go."

Without another word, Pierce grabbed the car keys from a hook on the wall and tossed them to Eden.

Summer zipped up her jacket and grabbed an umbrella from an open closet.

"Be careful," Pierce said to me, a sad look on his face.

"Rescue Rylan, but don't get killed in the process. I'll do what I can to help too."

I studied him as my friends ran out to the silver car in the driveway. He obviously thought we were in over our heads. "I'll do my best," I said. "Is Kaiden up yet?"

Pierce shook his head. "Still asleep."

Damn. "Can you tell him that I want to talk to him when this is all over?"

"Of course."

I then dashed to the car at the end of the driveway and jumped in the passenger seat. Summer was stretched out in the back, snoring softly. Pierce closed the front door as we drove down the street.

I couldn't stop thinking about him. Pierce was a lot nicer than I'd expected him to be, and I kind of felt bad about the way I'd treated him. I wondered if I'd missed my opportunity to ask him about Eden. It was the perfect plan. If Pierce agreed to let Eden into his pack, then I would join as well. Neither of us would have to participate in those awful cage fights for the amusement of the Elders again.

Kaiden was another reason to consider going to Pierce's. He was my best friend, and life wasn't the same without him.

Pierce wasn't all that bad, though he was a bit strange. I found it hard to believe that he knew my mother. She never mentioned him, so he must have known her a *long* time ago.

The rain came down harder, making it impossible to see. "Ugh! I hate rain!" Eden groaned and gripped the steering wheel.

"Told you we should wait," Summer muttered and rubbed her eyes. Her hair was messy and frizzy, and she kept running her fingers through it. "We could be eating right now."

"We couldn't wait." The older boy pulled onto the shoulder and shook his head in frustration. "I can't see. We'll have to wait here until it eases up a bit."

"Great," Summer said sarcastically. "I wonder what we'd be eating at Pierce's right now."

"You're driving me nuts." He glared back at her.

She flicked her hair over her shoulder. "I know. It's part of my charm."

A car pulled up behind us, and Eden looked in the rearview mirror. "I wonder what they're doing." Their headlights were on, but that was all I could see through the heavy rain.

"Probably waiting for the rain to stop," Summer said. "No one is crazy enough to drive in this weather. Oh, wait a minute. You are!"

"You didn't have to come!" Eden shouted. "No one asked you to!"

"Calm the hell down!" she yelled back. "If Cyclone and I hadn't volunteered to go with you, you'd be dead right now. You said so yourself. We wouldn't even be in this mess if you put Rylan's safety above your own back in the woods, but you didn't! The Elders were right. You are a coward."

Eden sank down in his seat and lowered his eyes.

I wanted to comfort him. There were a million things I wanted to say to him.

But Summer folded her arms across her chest and met my gaze, silently asking for backup in the argument.

All I said was, "Cyclone? Really?"

She shrugged. "It's a name."

"Maybe, but it's not mine."

Two doors slammed shut. The three of us looked over our shoulders as blurry figures crept toward us. I gasped when I caught sight of a gun. "Eden," I said, my voice quivering.

"Shit." He started the car.

"Go, go, go!" Summer shouted, throwing on her seatbelt.

It was still impossible to see through the rain, but we took off anyway. However, it didn't take the hunters long to catch up. When we came to a traffic light, Eden knew we couldn't stop. Instead, he floored it.

And so did the hunters.

"Eden, watch out!" I yelled as we sped across a bridge.

The hunters' car rammed us, and we spun out of control. They slammed into us again, this time forcing us off the road, and into the small wall of the bridge. I held my breath, my eyes glued to the water below. The hunters hit our car a third time, and we flipped over the edge.

The car sank quickly. Within a minute, the front of the car was completely submerged. The windows were cracking, and icy water squirt through.

Eden couldn't catch his breath as he began to panic. "We have to get out of here."

"The doors won't open," Summer screamed, "and we can't break the windows." The car sank deeper into the river.

My head throbbed as I fought to stay calm. Eden's window cracked a bit more, and my chest tightened with fear. My window splintered, letting in another small stream of freezing water.

Then the back window busted open. A pair of hands reached inside and pulled Summer out as water gushed through the massive hole. "Boys! Get out now!" the man yelled. It was Pierce.

He swam over to my window as water continued to fill the car. I covered my face as he busted the window, shards of glass floating around us. After he did the same on Eden's side, Pierce returned to the surface for air.

I began to crawl out the window and cut my hand on a sliver of glass. Eden struggled to get out of his seat, but something was holding him back. "Cris!" he shouted frantically. I hurriedly swam over to him, and my heart nearly stopped when I saw his jacket was somehow twisted in the seatbelt. The water was almost over our heads now, and we needed to get out fast.

I did my best to free him, but it was no use. My

movements, like Eden's, were becoming more and more sluggish. The water was numbing my body, making it harder to move. "Can you take your jacket off?" I shouted over the rain.

My arms were heavy and sore. It was hard to stay afloat.

Eden desperately jerked about, hoping his jacket would rip off. The whites of his eyes were red. His body trembled. When he finally gave up, I grabbed his arm and pulled, hoping I wasn't about to pull his arm out of its socket.

We were completely submerged now, and neither of us had taken in enough air. No matter what we did, we couldn't get him untangled. My lungs screamed, but I wasn't going to leave him. I did everything I could think of to free him, though nothing worked.

Eden looked up at me with terrified eyes. He knew we wouldn't make it and mouthed a single word that sent chills down my spine. *Go.*

But I squeezed his hand. *Never,* I mouthed back.

There was no air left in my lungs, and I assumed the same was true for Eden. We knew the end was near. But then I looked at him. His eyes were closed, and I knew he'd completely given up. He accepted death, as I had only seconds before.

No, I thought as my wolf's strength filled my body. I can't let him die like this. My eyes turned red, and power shot through my veins. Grabbing Eden's jacket, I ripped as hard as I could, and my entire body shook. It finally ripped in half, and I couldn't believe my eyes.

I shook his shoulder, and his eyes shot open as the jacket floated away.

When he was free from the car, Eden took hold of my hand and tried to pull me to the surface. But I was dead weight. It was as if my entire body just shut down. I used up all my strength to help Eden, and the water had completely numbed my body.

I was fading out of consciousness. The world around me grew darker and darker until there was nothing left but blackness. And I knew I was dead.

CHAPTER TWENTY-SEVEN

I saw light despite the fact my eyes were closed. It wasn't a white light, as I'd expected, just brightness from the sun coming out from behind a dark cloud, shining down on me. The storm was passing, but it was still cold out. I was numb, unable to feel, move, or even hear anything. I wasn't dead, which came as a surprise. I just couldn't move.

Or breathe, for that matter.

I bolted up and coughed more than I ever had in my life. Huge mouthfuls of river water came pouring out of my mouth, and I clutched my throat.

It burned, but I couldn't stop myself from throwing up. My fingers were red and shaky. My blurry vision slowly came into focus.

When I was finally able to breathe again, Eden wrapped his arms around me. "You saved me," he said

WEREWOLVES OF BRISTOL MANOR

quietly. "Again." He pulled away, and I couldn't tell if he was crying, or if river water was sliding down his face.

"Are you all right?" Pierce asked.

A shiver ran down my spine. "C-cold," I murmured. "Other than that, just d-dandy." My clothes were soaked, which told me I hadn't been unconscious for long. Water dripped from my hair and I coughed once again.

Pierce offered a hand to help me up. "Come on," he said. "I'm going to take you kids to get some dry clothes."

"Oh, thank goodness," Summer said, rubbing her arms. "You're an angel." She ran to a car that was parked on the bridge and waited. It was dark blue and had several dents along the side.

"Were you following us?" I asked Pierce as Eden struggled to stand up.

The man sighed, avoiding my gaze. "Yes," he admitted. "I was worried about you."

Part of me wanted to be angry, but I couldn't. If he hadn't followed us, we'd probably be dead right now. So, I decided to let it go for now.

Summer hopped in the passenger seat as soon as Pierce unlocked the doors. He looked uncomfortable sitting next to her, and even asked if she'd rather sit in the back with Eden and me. "I'm good," she said with a grin.

Pierce turned up the heat, and drove to a small clothing store. The three of us stayed in the car, shivering. He quickly returned with a few bags of clothes and took us to an old motel where we could get changed.

After paying at the front desk, Pierce opened the door to room 113.

We each took a turn in the bathroom, and left our damp clothes on the floor in the corner. When I emerged from the bathroom, I found Pierce sitting on the bed, staring down at his ruined phone.

"Thanks," I said, "for saving us and for the clothes."

He nodded. "No problem, buddy."

I sat in a chair by the door, folding my legs underneath me. My body was still trembling from the cold, but I was starting to warm up. "I'm really sorry about your car."

The man shrugged. "It's not your fault. It's the damn hunters."

"I wish there was something I could do to make up for it."

He arched an eyebrow. "You could always join my pack."

I shook my head, hoping he wouldn't press the matter further. I needed to talk to Eden first, because I wasn't leaving Bristol Manor without him.

"Worth a shot." Pierce opened the door and stepped out. "Be right back."

Summer then picked up a towel and returned to the bathroom to dry her hair.

When we were alone, Eden paced the floor anxiously. There was a big purple skull on his new shirt, and it matched well with his purple bracelet. He folded his arms across his chest, a look of concern on his face.

I looked up at him as he walked by. "What's wrong?"

He paused, running a hand through his slightly damp hair. "I hope we're not in over our heads." I watched him fiddle with the zipper of his new jacket. "I just don't know if we have what it takes to save Rylan anymore."

I shot to my feet. "Eden—"

"We would have died in that river if Pierce hadn't been following us," he said. His shoulders slumped, and he brought a hand up to his face. "What if we can't do it?" His ears turned bright red.

I gently placed my hand on his shoulder. "You have to believe that we can do this," I said firmly. "Believe in yourself, believe in us. Nothing in life comes without a little struggle. We've overcome everything they've thrown at us so far, and we can do it again." I swallowed hard. "Rylan needs us. We have to save him."

"What if we get there and we're outnumbered? Or what if we die before we even get there?" He backed away from me, staring down at the floor. "What if they take us too?"

I reclaimed my seat by the door. "Fine," I said. "Then we won't go."

Eden looked at me. "What?"

"We'll just give up."

He glared at me. "I'm not saying we should give up!"

"Then what *are* you saying?"

"I don't know!" Eden threw his hands up in exasperation. "I'm not good at this, Cris! I'm not a leader; I don't know what to do. All I know is, I keep thinking of everything that can go wrong and everything that has gone wrong so far." His voice quivered as he struggled to breathe. "We barely survived this trip and I'm—I'm not ready to die." He sat on the bed, bringing his knees up to his chest. "The Elders will kill us if we return without Rylan, and the hunters will kill us if they catch us off guard. The SFT will do unspeakable things to us when we get there, so no matter what we do, we're pretty much fucked." Tears fell from his eyes, and my heart broke. "I really am a coward."

"What do you want to do?" I asked after a while. "I'm with you, no matter what."

He met my eyes, and wiped the tears from his chubby cheeks. "Really?"

I nodded.

He took a deep breath, regaining his composure. There was a thoughtful look on his face as he considered our options. "Let's go to the SFT and do everything we can to bring Rylan back." He straightened in his seat. "We have to try."

I joined my friend on the edge of the bed, and hugged him tightly. "You know, being afraid doesn't make you a coward. Despite the danger, you still want to help Rylan and that makes you a hero, no matter how this pans out."

Eden blushed. "You're crazy." He lowered his feet to the floor, shoving his hands into his jacket pockets. "You think we should ask for help, though?"

"Ask who? A god?"

"No." He nodded his head toward the door. "Pierce. I want to get Rylan out of there but let's be honest, there's no way the three of us can do it on our own. He and his pack could help us."

I didn't care for that idea. Pierce was nice to us and helpful, but there was something about him that left me feeling uneasy.

"I'm gonna ask him," Eden said.

"Do you have to?" I groaned, and voiced my concerns, but Eden didn't seem bothered.

"Usually I'm on your side," he said. "But if we stop trusting the one person who has been helpful to us, we're not going to make it."

I chewed my lip. Eden was right. "Before you ask him, I have something I want to talk to you about." I figured now would be the best time to ask him if he'd be willing to leave Bristol Manor with me.

He tilted his head. "What is it?"

But Summer emerged from the bathroom and clapped her hands together. "So, what's the plan, boys? Are we taking the bus or what?" She was dressed in a grey camouflage long sleeved shirt, and her hair was pulled up into a loose ponytail. She grabbed her backpack, which was still damp, held it tightly against her chest.

The door swung open, and Pierce stood in the doorway.

"I'll tell you later," I said to Eden, and he frowned.

"So," Pierce began, "Eden told me you guys need to

meet up with someone at PetsLuv? I can take you there but after that, you will have to take the bus. I have to look after my pack, and I shouldn't be away too long."

Summer smiled flirtatiously. "That's so sweet of you!"

I nudged her in the ribs. "He's like thirty years older than you. Chill."

She nudged me back, though much harder. "Shut up, Curtis."

Pierce narrowed his eyes at me. "I'm actually twenty years older than you all. I'm only thirty five. But thank you for assuming I'm in my forties, Crispin. That doesn't make me feel old at all."

I averted my eyes. "Sorry."

Eden and I grabbed our backpacks as Summer dashed out to the car.

"Since you kids destroyed my other car," Pierce said, "I'll take you to PetsLuv under one condition."

I sighed heavily. "I have to join your pack?"

Pierce shook his head. "No, but you have to consider joining. And I mean *seriously* consider it. Sit down and weigh the pros and cons. I really think you'd thrive with us."

"Okay," I said. "I'll consider it."

Just gotta talk to Eden first. He had to get away from Bristol have to and the Elders. They were destroying him.

"Great. Let's go, then." Pierce headed toward the car and motioned for us to follow.

As I took a step out the door, Eden pulled me back. "You're gonna leave Bristol Manor?" he asked. "You're going throing to all this trouble to save one of the new friends you made, only to abandon him when he gets back? And leave me after all we've been through?" The look on Eden's face made my stomach hurt. "I thought we..." He lowered his head, and shoved passed me. "What a *wonderful* friend you turned out to be, Crispin."

"It's not like that!" I shouted. "I wouldn't leave y—"

"Whatever."

Eden climbed into the backseat with Summer, and stared sightlessly out the window. Sitting next to Pierce in the passenger seat, I watched rain fall from the sky as we drove, trying not to think about Eden. But the drive was quiet, and he was all I could think about.

When we reached PetsLuv, Eden got out before Pierce even turned the car off. He stormed off and disappeared inside the store.

"What's with him?" Summer asked, leaning forward in her seat.

"He's mad at me," I replied.

"I can see that," she said. "But why?"

Pierce looked at me out of the corner of his eye, and I shrugged. "It doesn't matter."

Without another word, Summer grabbed her stuff and took off after Eden.

As I went to unbuckle my seatbelt, Pierce held out an envelope. "What's this?" I asked.

"Money," he said quietly. "It isn't a lot, but it's enough to buy you and your friends something to eat tonight."

"I'm not taking your money."

"Crispin, I promised your mother I would—"

My stomach twisted into a million knots. "When did you talk to my mom? She's never mentioned you, and if you two were as close as you claim to be, I feel like she would have."

"A few months before she died, she asked me to look out for you, make sure you were okay. And that includes keeping you from going hungry."

I held up a hand. "Wait. What?"

Pierce blinked in confusion. "What?"

"She asked you to look out for me? Why would you need to do that? Why would she randomly ask that of you?"

"Um, I just meant—"

"Did she think she was gonna die?" I asked and got out of the car. "Did she?"

Pierce ran around to my side and stood in front of me. "Crispin, please. Just—"

"Answer me, Pierce!"

He swallowed hard, unable to meet my gaze. "Yes," he said finally. "She thought she might die, and wanted to make sure you had someone who'd look out for you."

My heart pounded in my chest, and my throat burned. "Why did she think that?" I could feel myself losing control, so I squeezed my eyes shut.

"I can't tell you that, buddy. Not here."

"Why can't you?" When he didn't answer I yelled louder, "Answer me!"

312

He grabbed my shoulders. "You have to calm down. You can't—"

"No!" I tried to jerk free from his grasp, but his grip tightened. "Tell me what I want to know." My voice quivered. I tried to force my wolf away, but he was too strong. All I could focus on was my anger.

"Crispin—"

"TELL ME!" I had no choice but to give in. My bones snapped and cracked as they shifted. My insides burned. I screamed and fell to the ground as fur sprouted along my arms. When I came back up, I was no longer human; I was a wolf.

CHAPTER TWENTY-EIGHT

"Don't do something you'll regret, buddy," Pierce said calmly, and took a step closer. I growled and he halted, not daring to move another inch. "I'm not gonna fight you. Turn back, Crispin."

But all I could think about was how angry I was. He was keeping something from me involving my mother, and I couldn't stand it. I lunged toward Pierce with outstretched claws, and knocked him to the ground. I tried to pounce on him, but he was too fast and always seemed to be one step ahead of me. I snapped at him, and drool fell from my open mouth as I growled. I was going to kick his feet out from under him, but he saw it coming. Pierce walked up behind me and held me down.

I went to bite him, but he grabbed hold of my mouth and held it closed. At first, I wondered why he remained human. But I quickly realized that Pierce didn't need to be a wolf to defend himself. I struggled beneath him, trying desperately to wriggle free. His death grip tightened around my snout. "Turn back," he said again. "That temper of yours is gonna get you in trouble one of these days."

I growled in response, and finally jerked free. We stood face to face, panting heavily. Pierce narrowed his eyes, waiting for me to make my move. Just as I was about to pounce, someone fired a gun, and then I heard a scream. But there wasn't a soul in sight. Pierce and I looked at each other and instantly knew the fight was over...for now.

Someone was in danger.

I remained a wolf and took off in the direction of the screaming. Pierce ran after me. When the screaming stopped, I found myself standing in a junkyard, surrounded by crappy, worn-out cars. I sniffed the air as dread filled my stomach. Where is everyone? I knew my friends where here somewhere.

"Cris?" a voice whispered. "Is that you?" Eden was crouched behind a dirty old car, his hair plastered to his forehead with sweat. His eyes were wide with terror. "I don't know where they are," he began, still whispering, "or how many there are. After I talked to Asher at PetsLuv, Summer and I saw a hunter, so we ran. We got separated when we came here, and I have no idea where she is or if she's okay." He shook his head as if he couldn't believe what he'd just said. "I fucked up again." Eden buried his face in his hands. "What is wrong with me?"

I nudged him with my snout, and he placed a gentle hand on top of my head, scratching my furry ears.

He sniffled and looked away.

Pierce finally made it to the junkyard and stood in the middle with his hands on his hips. He dropped my backpack by his side, and I watched him sniff the air before turning in our direction.

Unable to speak, I nudged Eden with my snout again. He got the message and waved Pierce over. He explained the situation to him and lowered his head in shame.

"I'll find Summer," Pierce said. "You boys stay here." I let out a low growl and he eyed me. "I mean it, Crispin. Stay. Put."

But Eden and I didn't listen.

We followed Pierce at a distance, hoping he wouldn't notice we disobeyed him. Unfortunately, we weren't as stealthy as we thought. The man looked over his shoulder and shook his head. "I should have known you wouldn't listen," he muttered before continuing his search.

Pierce stopped, and my friend and I exchanged quizzical glances when he motioned for us to step back.

A man I recognized stepped into view, and greeted Pierce with an oddly terrifying grin. I'm really getting tired of seeing that guy, I thought. "What are *you* doing here?" Wes asked.

But Pierce ignored the hunter's question. "Where is the girl?"

"What girl?" he asked casually, and retrieved a gun

from a strap on his leg.

"Don't play dumb with me."

"I honestly don't know what you're talking about," Wes said, and gestured toward me. "It's the boy we're after. He's higher on our list than anyone, other than you."

Pierce looked back at me before returned his attention to the hunter. "Why not kill me right now then?"

"The others would like that," Wes admitted with a nod. "After all, it isn't often that we see you without your pack. You're quite good at evading us."

"Do it, then."

Wes raised his gun and aimed it at Pierce's heart.

I stepped in front of Pierce and bared my teeth, growling at the lone hunter, whose gun was now aimed at me.

"Crispin, get back," Pierce demanded, but I didn't listen.

The hunter laughed to himself. "I was hoping this would happen," he said with a chuckle. "Like you, that boy is too wild. He needs to be put down now, while he's still young and inexperienced."

"Leave Crispin out of this," Pierce said, his jaw clenched. He stormed toward the hunter, who kept his gun fixed on me. He stood in front of Wes, glaring down at him.

The hunter wasn't fazed at all. "There will come a day when the two of you are outnumbered," Wes began, looking Pierce right in the eye. "I'll kill him first, but it won't be a quick death. It will be very slow and painful.

He'll beg for the sweet release of death, and all you'll be able to do is watch."

I gulped nervously. Eden ran to my side.

"If you ever come near him," Pierce warned, standing almost nose-to-nose with the hunter, "I'll flay you alive." He wrapped his hand around Wes's throat and squeezed. Wes dropped the gun and raised his hands in surrender as his face reddened.

"Are there others?" Pierce asked, kicking the gun away from them. "I want to know how long the kids will have to escape after I slit your throat." He threw the hunter to the ground, and Wes coughed as he struggled to his feet.

"All right, little brother," Wes said breathlessly. "You win for now. Next time, I won't be alone, and your luck will have run out." He turned to walk away. "And don't worry about the girl. I shot at her, but she dodged the bullet. She's a quick one." Wes fled before I could shift back.

I grabbed Eden's backpack and pulled out some of the extra clothes Pierce bought us. I threw them on as quickly as I could before running after the hunter, who was long gone now. "You're letting him go?"

"What would you have me do?" Pierce asked.

"Kill him!" I turned toward him, gesturing wildly with my arms. "Isn't that what you threatened to do thirty seconds ago? Didn't you hear what he's gonna do to me?"

"He's my brother," Pierce replied dejectedly. "Family may mean nothing to him, but it means something to me." He paused briefly, studying me. "Don't worry, buddy. I won't let him hurt you. If I have to, I will kill him."

I stared down at my shoes. There was so much Pierce wasn't telling me. "Why didn't you tell me your brother was a hunter?"

"Why do you need to know?"

I crossed my arms. "I can't join your pack if I can't trust you, Pierce."

The look on his face suddenly changed. "You're right," he said. "I'm sorry. After we get Rylan back, I'll tell you everything."

"We?" I asked.

"I told you I wanted to help as much as I can," he said. "And I meant that. I'm going to get my pack, and we'll do all we can to help rescue Rylan from the SFT." Pierce pulled out the money he tried to give me earlier, and placed it in my hands. "Take it," he insisted. "I'll be back. Just don't go inside until we get there."

"How will you find us?" I asked. "Do you know where they are?"

"I'll find you," he said. "Trust me." And with that, Pierce disappeared, leaving Eden and me alone in the junk yard.

CHAPTER TWENTY-NINE

The silence was deafening as Eden and I stood motionless in the junk yard. I knew he was upset about me leaving. Maybe this was the perfect time to discuss my plan with him.

"I have an idea," I began, as Eden walked away.

"We have to find Summer," he said quietly. "She has to be here somewhere."

"I want you to come with me.

He stopped. "What?"

I jogged after him and took a deep breath. "If Pierce is that desperate for me to join his pack, he'll probably let you join if he knows I won't go without you. This could be the perfect opportunity for you to get away from the Elders. If Pierce can leave, so can we!"

Eden tilted his head like a curious puppy. "Do you really mean that?" he asked. "You wouldn't leave without me?"

I nodded, a smile tugging at my lips. "So? Will you come with me?"

"Cris—" He covered his face with his hands. "Have you talked to Pierce about this?"

"I bet he hasn't," Summer said, climbing out of a car.

Eden frowned as she joined us. "Have you been in there this entire time?"

"Yup." She dusted off her pants. "It was too cramped, though, and I had to get out. It hurt my butt."

Eden returned his attention to me, waiting for an answer to his earlier question. "I haven't asked him yet," I admitted bashfully. "I wanted to make sure you wanted to go before I asked."

"It's sweet that you care about me so much," he said. "I don't think we'd really be safe from the Elders there. I'll have to think about it."

Summer pulled a sweatshirt out from her backpack, and threw it on over her jacket as the temperature dropped. "Speaking of safety, that hunter said you're at the top of their list. I think it's too dangerous for you to come with us."

"We've made it this far and I'm not backing out now," I said. "We know the hunters want to kill us. This isn't new information."

She shouldered her bag and scowled. "But he said—"

"I know what he said, Summer!" I grabbed my own backpack and headed for the bus stop. "I'm not asking for your permission. I'm coming with you, and there's nothing either of you can say to make me change my mind."

My friends rushed to my sides. "We just don't want anything to happen to you," Eden said softly. He gripped the straps of his bag as we came to the bus stop.

"I know," I murmured. "But we all knew this would be dangerous. And we're so close to getting Rylan back. I can feel it."

The two of them exchanged glances. "No one would blame you, Chuck," Summer said. "If you wanted to quit, I mean. We agreed to come along before we knew the hunters were after you."

"They're after all of us."

"Especially you," Eden argued. "He wants to kill you slowly and painfully. Everyone else usually gets gunshots to the face. They'd die pretty quickly if they didn't fight back. But you wouldn't."

"I'll be fine," I said, more to myself than to my friends.

"If you're sure," Eden said as the bus pulled up. "The SFT's building is close to a place called Lola's. It's a restaurant, so I think we should eat while we wait for Pierce to show up."

"Sounds like a plan," Summer said as we boarded the bus.

The three of us slept for most of the ride. By the time we got there, the sun was setting, and my stomach growled. When we entered Lola's, there was a sign that read *Please wait to be seated.*

We waited patiently until a woman greeted us and led

us to a booth with a white tablecloth neatly draped over it. In the center of the table was a vase with a single white rose inside. I slid into one side of the booth as Eden slid into the other. Summer sat next to me and scanned the restaurant with her eyes.

"Mo will be here shortly to take your order," the woman said, placing a few menus down in front of us.

Summer picked up the menu and looked it over right as our waiter strolled up.

He was a tall guy in his early thirties. "I'm Mo, and I will be your server this evening," he said, seeming very uninterested in his job. "Do you know what you want?"

"We haven't decided yet," Summer said politely.

"Well, let me know when you're ready and I'll rush right over!" Mo rolled his eyes and walked away.

"That was rude," Summer said, still staring at Mo. "We had the menu maybe fifteen seconds. Jeez."

Eden made a face. "He's gonna spit in our food, isn't he?"

It wasn't long before Mo came back and took our order. The three of us practically inhaled our food, and left a generous tip when we left, despite our waiter's poor attitude.

We strolled outside the restaurant to wait for Pierce, and Eden came to a halt. "Do you think Pierce will find us?" he asked nervously.

"I think he can probably track us pretty well," I said. "Why?"

"We've got company."

A very tall, heavily armed man was headed our way. I figured he didn't need half the weapons he had on him because of his humongous muscles. The hunter began running toward us, his eyes fixated on me.

"Run!" Summer shouted.

We bolted down the alley behind Lola's and climbed a tall chain-link fence that was topped with barbed wire. It ripped holes into my clothes and tore up my arms and legs. Blood oozed out from countless places on my body. I hopped down from the fence and ignored the stinging pain.

Eden and I landed hard on our feet. We started down a dark street, but were stopped dead in our tracks when Summer yelled, "Help me!"

I looked over my shoulder and saw that she was caught in the barbed wire, and Tall Guy was closing in on her.

Panicked, I turned to Eden, who looked just as frightened. "Go," I said, fighting to stay calm. "I'll get Summer."

Eden grabbed my hand. "I'm not leaving you!" The two of us ran back to our friend.

When we reached Summer, the hunter was only a few feet away. My trembling fingers fumbled around where her shirt was hooked to the barbed wire. My hands were sweaty and my heart was pounding.

"Please hurry," Summer said, tears forming in her eyes. Her arms were bleeding and her body shook with fear.

A terrifying scream of rage erupted from the hunter's

lips. He reached us before I could free Summer, and I froze. He grabbed her ankle and yanked her down. The barbed wire sliced through her skin, and she hit the ground with a thud, banging her head on the concrete.

Blood pooled around her head.

"Summer!" I slammed my fists against the fence, eyes glued to the motionless body of my friend. The hunter landed on our side of the fence, and I pushed Eden away just as the man retrieved a gun from his vest.

"We can't just leave her," Eden said as I dragged him away. We dodged a couple bullets, but one hit my calf, and I wrinkled my nose in pain.

"She's already gone," I said, my throat burning.

Eden felt awful; I could see it on his face. I hated to leave Summer, but we had no choice. If we stayed, we'd all be killed, and Rylan would never be freed.

Eden and I ran as fast as we could until we came to an old abandoned house. There was a tree house in the fence-less backyard. The ladder was rotting and couldn't support much weight, but we had to get away.

Eden shot up the ladder and scurried into the tree-house. When I was halfway up the ladder, it snapped in half. I grabbed hold of my friend's hand, but my palms were too sweaty, and I kept slipping. Tall Guy flung to-ward me and grabbed my leg, squeezing it tightly. He yanked me down and my hand slipped from Eden's grasp. My friend jumped to the ground, and hunched over as his wolf painfully took shape.

"Eden, no!" I shouted.

But it was too late.

Eden lunged toward him, but Tall Guy knocked him aside effortlessly. He circled around the hunter, snarling viciously. His dark red wolf eyes stared unwaveringly at the hunter, who tossed aside his gun when he realized it was out of bullets.

Tall Guy retrieved another weapon from his vest—a dagger—and I quickly jumped on his back, wrapping my arms around his neck. Eden snapped at him as Tall Guy slammed the dagger into my leg. I cried out in agony as he pulled the weapon from my thigh and threw me off his back.

Tall Guy darted over to me with his dagger raised, and Eden rushed up to him, sinking his sharp teeth deep into his neck. Blood squirted out like a fountain as the man collapsed.

I took the dagger from his hands as my heart hammered in my chest. Tall Guy was barely clinging to life. When I raised the dagger, I had every intention of killing him. But when I looked into his eyes, I couldn't do it.

As I turned to walk away, Eden whined, and I heard the unmistakable sound of bones crunching. When I looked back, Tall Guy was on his feet, and Eden limped away from him.

The hunter sneered as he ran at me, and pinned me down to the ground. His blood rained down on me as it continued gushing from his neck.

I twisted the dagger around in my fingers. This time I didn't hesitate.

I plunged it into the hunter's heart. His eyes glazed over, and I shoved his body off me. I killed another one...

My hands were covered in Tall Guys' blood, and they shook uncontrollably. My thigh wound burned, but I could feel it trying to heal.

For a moment, I forgot Eden couldn't control the wolf. When his leg healed, he crept closer and growled, exposing his sharp teeth. I swallowed hard. "Eden," I said softly. "It's me." I stepped back, my eyes glued to his. "I know you can hear me." My voice quivered. "Try to turn back, okay? Can you do that?"

Eden snarled as he dug his claws into the ground, and I shuddered. He's going to kill me.

CHAPTER THIRTY

Eden snapped at me, tearing into my flesh with ease. I kicked him back as my wolf took shape. I hated to do this, but saw no other option. I had no idea how to get him to shift back.

I stood on all fours, growling at my friend in hopes of intimidating him, but it just instigated the fight. He flung toward me, and I met him in the air, sinking my teeth into his silky black fur.

He yelped but didn't back down. Eden's angry red eyes burned into mine as he charged toward me. Rising to his hind legs, he knocked me down as I tried to shove him back with my paw. Sharp claws dug into my side, and I howled in pain as I rolled away. Eden sank his teeth into my wounded leg, causing even more blood to spill out.

Don't hurt him, I told myself. Don't hurt him. Don't hurt him.

He yanked back, and skin and fur ripped from my leg. Ignoring the excruciating pain, I forced him back and jumped onto an old picnic table I hadn't realized was there before.

I hoped my friend, who was trapped inside his wolf, would soon return. My own wolf was becoming harder and harder to control.

Eden raised his head, waiting for me to make my move, and flicked his tail. I leapt forward and knocked him down. I had him pinned. He squirmed about, trying unsuccessfully to get away. He wiggled around a bit more, and I put my paw on his chest. A loud roar erupted from my throat and he cowered beneath me.

My friend was finally starting to change back.

I removed my paw from on top of his chest and lay on the ground, hoping it would make my own transition back to human a bit easier on my aching body.

It didn't.

Our clothes had been ripped to shreds during the change, but my backpack wasn't far. We threw on the last sets of clean clothes, and rested on the blood-soaked grass so our bodies could heal. The air was chilly, but I was dripping with sweat.

When Eden caught his breath, he wrapped his arms around his knees, unable to meet my gaze. "I'm sorry, Cris," he said quietly. "I didn't want to attack you. I just—"

"It's okay," I said. "I know."

"Did I hurt you?"

Eden looked so worried and concerned that I considered lying to him. But I figured he'd probably prefer to hear the truth. "Yeah, but it's okay because I think I hurt you too."

The two of us trudged along, and came to a stop when we reached Summer's body. We stood silently beside her, and Eden knelt down. "I'm so sorry, Summer," he whispered as he took hold of her hand. He looked up at me, tears sliding down his cheeks. "This wasn't supposed to happen," he said. "I swore to myself I wouldn't let either of you get hurt."

"This is not your fault, Eden." I sat beside him and lowered my head. "Nothing that happened during this trip has been your fault. It's the fucking hunters and SFT." My eyes burned with unshed tears. I couldn't force myself to look at Summer.

She's really gone.

Eden squeezed her hand and wiped his tears away. He sniffled as he closed her eyes, and his lip quivered. "She was one of my best friends. She drove me crazy sometimes, but I know I drove her crazy too." He smiled faintly at the memory, but it quickly faded. "I wasn't strong enough to save her."

Eden and I were silent for a long while, not wanting to leave her alone. The wind picked up, and a shiver ran down my spine. "We should send someone back for her," he said finally. "After we get Rylan somewhere safe."

My chest tightened. "We will," I promised him.

He nodded and got to his feet, but I didn't move. Though she and I hadn't been the best of friends, I really cared for Summer, and it was hard to see her this way.

The hunters needed to be stopped. The SFT as well. They shouldn't get away with doing this.

The two of us walked back to Lola's where we planned on waiting for Pierce. We were dirty and covered in blood, so it came as no surprise when an employee came out and told us to get lost.

I started to cross the street, but Eden stopped me. "What are you doing?" he asked.

"Going to the SFT," I replied. "That's their building, right?" I pointed straight ahead. It was a tall brick building that was painted white. There were no cars in the parking lot, but I knew it was full of people. I could practically smell their hate.

Eden crossed his arms. "We're supposed to wait for Pierce."

"I'm just going to look around," I said with a shrug. "I won't go in."

He frowned. "You're still going on SFT property without a plan! What if they take you too? Are you *crazy*?"

"Possibly."

"We need to wait for Pierce's pack, so you can just sit your crazy ass back down, mister." Eden threw his hands up on his hips.

"I'll be fine." I tried to shove past him, but he wouldn't let me.

"No!" he shouted. "We're not risking it. I can't lose you too."

A smile tugged at my lips. "Listen, we need to get Rylan back, and Pierce was confident in his ability to find us. I think we should get as close as we can so we can see what we're dealing with."

"Don't you ever think about the consequences of your actions?" he asked, chewing his nails nervously. "What if it's a trap? What if there are fifty people in there with weapons worse than what we've come across so far?"

"You think too much!" I shouted. "You overthink everything and at some point, you just have to make your move."

"You're too impulsive!" he argued, and stomped his foot. "You need to weigh the pros and cons of your actions. Sometimes you need to be a little cautious."

"You're *too* cautious! You never take any risks, even when you should!"

Eden paused, eyes staring hard into mine. "What's that supposed to mean?"

I looked away, my heart pounding. "Nothing."

He chewed his lip, and brought a hand up to his face. "You're right," he said finally. "Let's go in."

"Really?"

"Yeah." He sighed, and looked up at the big white building. "Let's go get Rylan back."

As I suspected, the first floor was completely empty, though now I was starting to worry we'd made the wrong decision. But I didn't want to tell Eden he was right, so we kept going.

There were no cameras that we could see. There were no locks or weapons or computers. Not even a garbage can. When we found the stairs, we climbed up to the second floor, which was also empty.

"Maybe we should have waited for Pierce," I finally admitted.

Eden stared at me, a look of annoyance on his face. "Ya think?"

Come on, Pierce, I thought. Where are you?

The two of us searched the third and fourth floors and again, found nothing. I was beginning to think we'd been led to the wrong place, but my gut told me otherwise. We just needed to keep looking.

We made our way up to the fifth floor, and entered a room with a big wall of windows. Inside the room was a kid about our age, and I realized I knew them.

Xayden Mavis went to my old school. I only had one class with them, so I didn't know them very well. Still, it was a shock to see them in the SFT building.

"What are you doing here?" I asked, and narrowed my eyes.

Their short blonde hair was neatly styled. Their big brown eyes were full of fear, and there were huge bruises along their skinny arms. "People like you shouldn't exist,"

Xayden said, shaking their head. "It's not right." They inched closer, eyes trained on Eden. "We just want the world to see what's out there. They need to know so they can join the fight."

I tilted my head, knowing these were not Xayden's words. They sounded like they were reading from a script, being told what to say. "You don't have to do this," I said.

Xayden retrieved a small silver knife from inside their jacket, and their arm wobbled unsteadily. They raised the knife, a horrified expression on their face, but I knocked it from their hand, and grabbed it midair. I held the knife to their throat and felt them tremble.

"I'm sorry," Xayden said, squeezing their eyes shut. "I wasn't going to do anything. I mean, I was gonna try but… Please don't kill me."

"Do you really believe that shit you just told us?" I asked.

"No," they said, trembling still. "Everyone else here does. My whole family is here, so I had no choice."

Eden and I exchanged glances. "Do you think they'd trade Rylan for Xayden?" I asked him.

Eden shrugged, then turned his attention to Xayden. "Do you think they would?"

Xayden shook their head. "A werewolf is worth way more to them."

Damn.

Eden stood in front of them. "If we let you go, are you gonna tell anyone we're here?"

"They already know," Xayden whispered.

I let out a heavy sigh before releasing them. "Go," I said. I didn't know what else to do. There was no way I was going to kill an innocent kid who didn't want to be a part of this. And Xayden wasn't a bad person. They were one of the few kids at Valley Park High who never laughed when Marcus tormented me.

Without another word, Xayden bolted out the door and ran up the stairs.

Right as Eden and I were about to go out into the hall, an angry woman blocked the doorway, trapping us in the room. "We were just expecting one," she said, her voice deep and raspy. "Guess this is our lucky day! Surely one of you will give us what we need."

I eyed her. "And that would be?"

"Proof that your kind exists."

"Why does it matter?"

"We won't get in trouble for killing your kind if we have proof of what you are," she said plainly. "We want to make this world a safer place, but we don't want to go to prison for it."

The woman reached for a weapon on her back, but Eden and I leapt toward her before she could grab it. She whopped me upside the head with her bulky fist, and I fell to the floor. I looked at Eden, who was now right in front of the unguarded door. Please don't leave me, I thought. Would he really abandon me?

The woman now stood over me as heavy footsteps

descended the stairs. She grabbed my hair and slammed my face through one of the windows. I squeezed my eyes shut as the glass broke around my head.

She chuckled joyfully. "No reason we can't have some fun first, though!" She tried to push me farther out the window and I grabbed hold of whatever I could to keep myself inside. I tightened my grip on a metal pole that was separating the large windows, and the woman knocked me out the window. My legs dangled, and my shaky arms couldn't hold my weight much longer.

"Eden!" I yelled. My sweaty hands were losing their grip, and the woman above me grinned. "Go back down and wait for Pierce!"

She turned toward Eden, whose eyes doubled in size. "Think a drop from this high would kill him?" the woman asked. "Let's test it, shall we?"

My heart pounded, and blood roared in my ears. Was I really going to die when we were this close to saving Rylan? Eden was right. I was too impulsive, and this never would have happened if we'd waited.

"Eden, go!"

The woman banged her fist against my fingers, trying to force me to fall to my death. Right when I felt my fingers slipping, Eden darted toward us, and my heart stopped. He threw his body against the woman, and they both went crashing through the window beside me, plunging toward the concrete that lay five stories below.

CHAPTER THIRTY-ONE

"EDEN!" I pulled myself back inside as tears streamed down my face. My knees were too shaky, and couldn't support me. I looked out the window he'd thrown himself out of and screamed in frustration. The bodies on the ground were motionless, and my heart suddenly felt heavier than ever before. Cold wind blew the hair out of my face through the gaping holes in the windows. Tears stung my eyes, and my throat tightened.

Is this really happening? It felt like a nightmare I would awaken from, but deep down, I knew I never would.

The room filled with people, all with angry expressions on their faces. A tall woman grabbed my upper arm, pulling me to my feet, and shoved me toward the stairs. I didn't struggle. I didn't have it in me anymore. One of the men surrounding me chuckled as we climbed the stairs and said, "Good dog."

They led me to the tenth floor and into a room that was filled with at least a dozen people. Along the walls were several black filing cabinets and safes. Several collapsible chairs were scattered about the room, as well as a few opened coolers filled with beer. I saw a table of what appeared to be trophies from werewolves they've killed, and shuddered.

The woman behind me shoved me to the middle of the room, and a man and woman approached me.

"Xayden," the man said, staring hard at me. "Go to the roof."

"Why?" they asked as they cowered in the corner.

"Your brother is up there. He'll show you what to do."

Xayden looked at me with sympathetic eyes before climbing the final flight of stairs.

"Alverna, the other boy killed Flynwood," the woman behind me said. "The kid's dead too. They both fell through a window."

I felt sick. This couldn't be real. Eden couldn't be dead.

The man and woman in front of me exchanged glances, and then Alverna looked at me, cocking her head to the side. "Why did they send two of you?"

When I didn't reply, the man balled his fist and yelled, "Answer the question!"

"Calm down, Theo. We'll get answers." She smiled coldly. "He doesn't want any trouble. Do you?"

"I-I came along to help my friend," I stammered. I

could barely speak as tears still rolled down my cheeks.

"The dead one?" Theo asked.

Holding my breath, I closed my eyes and nodded. I was barely keeping it together, and was sure I'd fall apart any minute. Would I burst into a fit of tears? Would my wolf take over and rip these people to shreds? I didn't know. But at that moment, I didn't care.

"All right. So it's just you now. Do you know what that means?" Alverna clasped her hands together excitedly. "It means, unless you want to die, you will do what we tell you. Understand?"

I suddenly remembered why I was there in the first place. My eyes darted around for any sign of the missing boy. "Where is Rylan?" I asked, and wiped my eyes.

Theo frowned. "Who?"

"The kid you took from the woods." I clenched my jaw. "Where is he?"

"Oh, him," Theo said casually. "He's dead."

Something didn't feel right. I could feel Rylan there with me, though I wasn't sure how. "You're lying," I said firmly. I knew he was still alive. "Where is he?"

Alverna squinted at me. "Are you sure you want to see him?"

I nodded silently.

Theo made his way toward a long wooden box I hadn't noticed earlier, and I hoped he wasn't about to bring out a dead body. Please let Rylan still be alive, I thought. My gut told me he was alive, but I was starting to have doubts.

Theo brushed some dirt off the box, and it creaked as he opened it. "Oh, no," I said under my breath.

Rylan had been buried alive.

He dragged Rylan's limp body over to me, and threw him on the floor. Splinters were embedded in his blood-stained fingers. His nails were bent, tore up, and dirty, probably from clawing at the wooden ceiling of the coffin. His face was covered with scratches, as were his arms and neck. I wondered why he'd do that to himself, but then I saw. Bugs crawled out of the pine box Rylan had been trapped in. He opened his mouth to speak, but I couldn't make out what he said. His voice was hoarse, probably from screaming so much, begging and pleading to be let out.

I shuddered at the thought of Rylan being trapped in a small dark coffin with insects crawling all over him, not knowing if he would ever see the light of day again. He finally opened his eyes, but they didn't look right. They were cloudy. Rylan was looking in my direction, but I knew he couldn't see me. He was blind.

With a jolt I realized his right arm had been severed off, and my entire body instantly filled with rage.

"You bastard!" I shouted, no longer able to control myself. I ran toward Theo, knowing the others wouldn't let me kill him, but I had to try for Rylan. I shoved the man to the floor and jumped on top of him, punching his face as hard as I possibly could. Theo grabbed my shoulders and threw me off.

I ran toward the collapsible chairs. Theo ran after me, signaling the others not to intervene. I snatched up a chair and swung it at his face.

He spat blood onto the floor and leapt toward me, kicking the chair out of my hands. The man slammed his foot into my stomach, and I fell to my knees. Theo bashed my head into the wall and for a minute, I saw tiny stars circling my head.

I thought that only happened in cartoons?

Theo grabbed my shoulder, and I bit down on his arm, not stopping until I knew he was bleeding. "Damn it!" he yelled, and jerked back. "He fucking bit me!"

I hopped up and ran for the stairs, hoping to run outside and see Pierce.

But Alverna stepped in, following close behind. "This little shit belongs to me," she said through gritted teeth.

When Alverna caught up to me, she grabbed my wrist and twisted it behind my back until it snapped. I cried out and she threw her other hand over my mouth. "You're gonna have it so much worse than your friend over there." She nodded her head toward Rylan. "You think what he went through was torture? Just wait until you see what we've got in store for you."

I knocked my foot back into her knee and she screamed when it bent the wrong way, letting go of my broken wrist. I grabbed her head and chucked us over the edge of the stairs. The others gathered around at the top as Alverna and I tumbled down the entire flight.

My arm cracked against the edge of a stair, and a sharp pain shot through my body. With so many broken bones and no time to heal, I knew it was hopeless.

Alverna reached for a rusty screwdriver that was only a few steps below. I lunged for it, but in my weakened state, she was too fast. Laughing maniacally, she slammed it into my shoulder.

"Aaaaaaggh!" Blood gushed out from around the tool as I screamed at the top of my lungs. I felt nauseated and feverish. When I tried to pull it out of my shoulder, it wouldn't budge. The pain spread throughout my entire body, and my thoughts began to jumble in my head.

Too many wounds…

Alverna yanked the screwdriver out of my shoulder, and I forced myself to conjure my inner wolf. I thought about everything the SFT did to poor Rylan, and images of Eden crashing through the window flashed before my eyes.

My wolf's strength surged through my body, though I had to fight to remain in control. Snatching the screwdriver from Alverna's hand, I plunged it into her throat and dashed up the stairs, attacking the first person I saw.

He was a heavy man who moved slowly, but I didn't care. I was out for blood.

With my wolf's claws, I slit his throat and pounced on the two people behind him as he collapsed and bled out. I knocked them into a metal shelf, which toppled over and landed on someone on the other side.

WEREWOLVES OF BRISTOL MANOR

The more violent I became, the stronger, and more powerful I became.

I felt invincible.

Theo and another person ran up to me, guns aimed at my chest. Did they really think that was going to stop me? I almost laughed.

With an evil grin, I leapt over them, landing behind, and slashed my claws across their backs. They turned, and I clunked their heads together before kicking their legs out from under them. I grabbed one of their daggers. Right as I was about to plunge it into Theo's heart, Pierce pulled me back.

He and his pack thundered up the stairs and onto the tenth floor. His wolves quickly began tearing apart everyone who put up a fight. Those who surrendered were rounded up on the other side of the room, though most chose not to go down without a fight.

Pierce knelt by my side as he looked me over. "Are you all right?"

"Yeah," I said, my eyes still glowing red. I blinked a few times, and my eyes returned to normal. All my werewolf strength instantly left my body, and a wave of pain crashed over me. "Rylan," I gestured toward my unmoving friend. "He needs—"

"Can you move?" Pierce asked.

"Yeah," I murmured.

"Get Rylan. Take him downstairs as fast as you can. My car is parked in front." Pierce rose to his feet and ran after Theo, who scurried away. "Go, Crispin," he shouted. "Now!"

I stumbled toward Rylan, who was groaning softly. I tried to lift him, but I just couldn't do it. My broken bones hadn't healed yet, and I had no strength left in my body. Sweat glued my hair to my forehead and trickled down my back, sending a shiver down my spine. I tried again, hoping I could muster up enough energy to get him to safety.

As I lifted him, my broken wrist snapped, and I couldn't stop myself form crying out. I nearly dropped Rylan, and could feel myself losing hope.

"Need a hand?" asked a familiar voice.

I looked up as Eden knelt down beside me. He was covered in blood and stray shards of glass, but had a smile on his face. "Eden!" I pulled him into a hug, and my body began to tremble. I couldn't believe he was alive. I squeezed him tightly, never wanting to let go. "You saved me."

"I had to do something," he said softly. "I couldn't let her hurt you."

We eventually pulled apart, though I really didn't want to. "We need to get Rylan to the car," I shouted over the chaos.

When I looked at the fighting members of the pack, I couldn't help but notice Kaiden wasn't there. He should've been with them. Did Pierce tell him not to fight because he was new?

"Cris," Eden said, snapping me out of my thoughts. "Come on. We need to go."

I helped him carry Rylan down the many flights of stairs. By the time we got to the fourth floor, we could no longer hear the fighting. But I was panting and needed a break.

"Can we stop for a second?" I asked breathlessly.

Eden looked up at the ceiling, a worried expression on his face. "Sure," he said, anxiously. We gently placed Rylan on the floor, and I leaned back against the wall. My wrist was finally starting to heal, but when I touched it, I winced.

"You okay?" Eden asked.

I nodded silently. I was mentally and physically exhausted and felt as if I needed a week or two to recuperate. But when I heard a scream, I shot to my feet, knowing it was Kaiden.

I looked over my shoulder at Eden, who nodded. "Go on," he said. "I'll get Rylan to the car."

I took the stairs two at a time and paused on the first floor. Where is he? But I heard nothing. I saw nothing. At first, I wondered if I could have imagined the scream. Eden heard it too, though. Right?

I rushed outside and stared up at the broken window on the fifth floor. The one Eden had fallen out. My eyes fell to the lifeless body of the woman who fell with him, and I silently thanked the universe for allowing Eden to survive.

"Crispin!" Kaiden shouted.

I paused, trying hard to concentrate on my

surroundings. Where could he be?

The door to the building creaked open. I expected to see Eden stumbling out with Rylan. Instead I saw Wes, and Pierce was standing in front of him. I groaned and narrowed my eyes at the hunter. What's he doing here?

CHAPTER THIRTY-TWO

Through the windows on the upper floor, I could see the fight was over. Pierce's pack waited patiently by one of the giant windows, looking down at us. Pierce and Wes strode out into the parking lot, and a funny feeling crept into my stomach. The hunter had a gun to Pierce's back, but he lowered it when they came to a stop in front of me. "Can we talk?" Wes asked me.

Pierce's arms appeared to be broken, and his face contorted in pain.

"I have nothing to say to you," I muttered.

"That's fine," Wes replied. "I'll do the talking."

Eden then came staggering out of the building, Rylan's limp body in his arms. When they made it safely to the car, I returned my attention to Wes.

The hunter grinned. "Thanks to you almost completely

347

wiping out this area's SFT singlehandedly, you are now our highest priority."

"Leave him alone," Pierce said, and Wes whacked him on the side of the head with the gun.

"Don't worry, pup. I'm not coming after you today. As you can see," he gestured around the empty parking lot, "I'm alone today."

"If you're not going to kill me," I said, "then what exactly do you want?" I wasn't sure I believed him, and kept my guard up. Wes could not be trusted.

A gentle breeze blew an empty plastic bag across the parking lot, and the grey clouds rumbled overhead. It was getting dark, and I was anxious to get back to Bristol Manor.

"All I want is to pass along some information."

"Not interested," I said, and shoved my hands into my pockets. "You can be on your way now."

Wes eyed me. "Even if it's about your mother?"

There was a long pause where I didn't know what to say. What could Wes, a werewolf hunter, know about my mom that I didn't know? And why would he want to tell me now? Could whatever information he claimed to have be true?

Curious, I asked, "What about her?"

"Wes, don't tell him this," Pierce pleaded. "Not now. Not here."

"Tell me," I insisted.

"This man," Wes gestured toward his brother, "killed your mother." He dropped his gun and shoved Pierce forward, an ugly grin plastered on his face.

I looked up at the man I'd come to trust, heart pounding in my chest. "What?" I asked, shaking my head. "Is that true?" Tell me it's not true.

Pierce stepped closer. "No!" He ran a hand down over his face, and glared at Wes before meeting my gaze. "I didn't kill her, Crispin. She asked for the bite and I gave it to her, that's all. The hunters killed your mother."

"But—but—she was hit by a car. Wasn't she?" I found it hard to breathe. None of this could be true. They must've been lying to me. I desperately wanted them to be lying to me.

"The hunters arranged the accident," Pierce continued. "When my brother found out about her, I offered her protection. I asked her if the two of you would move in with me, but she refused, saying she'd moved on. But she said if anything ever happened, she wanted me to look out for you." He took another step closer, and I shoved him back. "I wanted to protect the two of you. But I didn't kill her."

"I had no choice," Wes said, and narrowed his eyes at Pierce. "If you cared for her at all, you would have refused her request to become like you."

I looked up at him, unshed tears burning my eyes. "Why didn't you say no?" I asked. "If you had, my mom would still be alive right now."

He sighed and shook his head. "No, buddy. She wouldn't be."

"What are you talking about? If you hadn't turned her—"

"The cancer would have killed her by now," he said, and I felt my heart drop. Cancer? My mom? No…she would have told me. How could this be true? "I'm so sorry, buddy. I wouldn't have done it otherwise. I—I just wanted to help."

Tears spilled from my eyes. The only thing my mom wanted was a chance to live, and it was taken from her. How could Wes do that? How could he think it was okay?

I turned my attention to the hunter, whose smile immediately faded.

Without hesitating, I darted forward, grabbing the gun that lay by Wes's feet. I had no werewolf strength left in me, but I was determined to make this asshole pay.

Eden ran after me, trying to pull the gun from my hand, but I jerked away.

"What are you doing?" he shouted.

"He's going to kill an unarmed man," Wes said casually. The smug grin returned to his face, which infuriated me even more.

"Cris, killing him won't bring your mom back." Eden grabbed hold of my arm, but I wouldn't release the gun.

"It'll make me feel better." I aimed at Wes's heart, ready to pull the trigger.

"No, it won't," Eden said. "Don't do this, Cris. Please don't do it."

"Go ahead, pup," Wes said. "If you think you have it in you."

"You killed my mom when all she wanted was a second chance at life!" I screamed, blinded by rage.

"Pierce doomed your mother the day he bit her," he spat.

"YOU killed her!"

"Come on, then." He waved me over. "Kill me, an unarmed man. Be the monster I know you are." I stormed closer until I stood only a couple feet away. The gun wobbled in my hand. "Do it, you worthless mutt!"

"NO!" Eden shouted.

Blood boiled in my veins. I wanted nothing more than to see this man pay for what he did to my mother. I was about to pull the trigger, but then I looked at Eden. His big blue eyes were full of despair, urging me not to do it. When I looked back at the hunter, I couldn't bring myself to kill him. So I emptied the bullets into my hand and threw the gun as far as I could. I tossed the bullets in the opposite direction and stormed toward the car.

Should I have killed him? If Eden hadn't stopped me, would I have gone through with it?

"I knew it," Wes said with a sneer. "Looks like we moved you to number one for no reason."

Pierce approached his brother, and his arms appeared to have healed. He whispered something to Wes, though I didn't care to eavesdrop. All I could think about was my mom. If she could see me right now, would she be proud? Would she be disappointed because I wasn't strong enough to avenge her?

Pierce's pack trudged out of the building as the hunter disappeared into the distance. Pierce let him go...again. "Come on," the man said quietly. "I'll take you kids back to Bristol Manor."

Before getting into the car, I looked around one last time. Kaiden was here, I just knew it. But where could he be? I sniffed the air until finally catching his scent, and took off toward the side of the building. Pierce ran after me, calling my name, but I made no attempt to answer.

Something was wrong with Kaiden.

I rounded the corner and saw him sitting with his back against the brick wall at the other end, hunched over and clutching his stomach. "Kaiden!" My friend looked up at me and I ran to him as fast as I could. I knew what was happening.

"Crispin..." His voice was quiet, barely audible. "It's okay," he said breathlessly, his eyes fluttering closed. "I knew this was gonna happen."

I shook my head, tears burning my eyes. "Why didn't you say anything? Why didn't you tell me?"

"What could you have done?" Kaiden lowered his body to the ground so he could lie on his side, facing me.

I couldn't understand how this was happening. Kaiden was strong, I knew he was. So why was this happening to him? Why was the bite killing him? "There has got to be something I can do." I turned to Pierce, who placed his hand on my shoulder. "What can I do? I have to help him!"

Pierce shook his head. "Nothing can be done, buddy.

I'm so sorry."

"No! There has to be something I can do. Anything!" Kaiden screamed as he gripped his sides, the pain becoming unbearable. His face paled and his body trembled. I knew he didn't have much time. "Please, Pierce. I'll do whatever it takes to save him. He's like my brother." I choked back a sob, my voice but a whisper. "I can't lose him."

Kaiden looked at me, a small smile on his face. "You're my brother, too," he said softly. His eyes glossed over, and his body stiffened. I screamed until my throat was raw.

"He's gone, Crispin," Pierce said.

"Nooooo!" I grabbed Kaiden and pressed my ear against his chest, begging to hear a heartbeat. But there wasn't one. Kaiden was really dead.

Pierce tried to pull me away, but I refused to leave his side. "Get off me!" I shouted as I struggled to breathe. But Pierce wouldn't leave me alone and didn't stop until he finally pulled me away. I turned to him, a look of hatred on my face, and shoved him away. "It's your fault! *You* killed him!"

"I had no way of knowing he would—"

"You had no right to bite him!" My face reddened as tears fell from my eyes. I balled my fists, blood roaring in my ears.

"Kaiden was more than willing, and he knew the risks." He lowered his head, unable to look at me. "I told him the bite could kill him, but he still chose it. Just be grateful that it was the bite that killed him, and not the transformation. That would have been much more painful."

"*Grateful?*" I yelled at the top of my lungs. "If you hadn't bitten him, he would still be alive right now! My mom's death may not be your fault, but Kaiden's is! Everything was fine until you showed up."

Pierce glared hard at me when I went to hit him. He pushed me against the wall and held his arm over my chest to keep me from getting away. I tried to knock his hand away, but I was too weak. "Don't lose your fucking temper with me," he growled. For a split-second, his eyes flashed red, but he remained calm. "I understand why you think this is my fault. But if someone else bit him, he still would have died. Don't tell me you haven't thought about turning him yourself..."

I stared sightlessly at the ground and wiped the tears from my face. "I thought about it," I admitted, and my shoulders slumped.

"Kaiden wanted this so he could be closer to you. His death isn't your fault, and it isn't mine." He removed his arm from my chest and pushed my hair back as I sniffled. "Are you gonna be okay?" Pierce's tone was softer now.

I sucked in a deep breath, unable to speak, and knelt down beside Kaiden. I closed his eyes, my hand shaking uncontrollably, and wished I could say something. But when I opened my mouth, nothing came out. I wiped my eyes as my bottom lip quivered.

I trudged back to the car, and Eden looked at me

with sympathetic eyes. "I'm so sorry," he said quietly, and wrapped his arms around me in a hug, squeezing me tightly. "Come on. Let's go home."

CHAPTER THIRTY-THREE

When we pulled into the Bristol Manor driveway, I shifted uncomfortably in my seat. I didn't know what to do. Since Kaiden died, I couldn't look at Pierce the same way. In my eyes, he was responsible for my best friend's death. But the Elders were heartless, and Eden was terrified of them. If Pierce accepted Eden, would he leave the Wolf House with me?

Eden was the first one out of the car. He helped Rylan out of the backseat and up the stairs to the front door.

I looked over my shoulder at Shiloh, Fitzgerald, and Zorya, and wished Kaiden was with them. I couldn't stop thinking about my dead friend. Well, *friends*. Summer and Aleksandr. Their deaths would also haunt me for the rest of my life, their images burned into my brain.

I slammed the car door behind me, wondering if I

should even bother asking Pierce about Eden. Could I live with the man who inadvertently killed my friend?

"Crispin," Pierce said, as he climbed out of the car. "I'll come back in a bit for your decision." He spoke in a low voice so the others couldn't hear. "I hope you're still thinking about joining us."

But I didn't respond, and he returned to his car as I joined my friends at the front door. Eden and I watched Pierce drive away. When he was out of sight, we hurried inside the Wolf House, and Ian instructed someone to help Rylan up to the nurse's office. The first floor was full of excited kids shouting about our return.

I wasn't sure how it felt to be back. Bristol Manor hadn't been my home for very long, but I climbed the stairs to my room and sat on the bed, grateful to have one of my own.

"Hey," Eden said, standing in the doorway. "Can I come in?" He was still wearing the clothes Pierce bought us and was covered with dirt and blood.

I nodded, and he closed the door before joining me on the bed. "I figured you'd try to get some sleep," I said. "It's been a rough week." That was quite an understatement.

He brushed the hair out of his eyes. "Do you remember when you said I don't take risks when I should?"

My face turned red, and I averted my eyes. "I shouldn't have said that. You risked your life to save me in that building."

He smiled and fidgeted nervously with his bracelet.

"Well, what you said got me thinking. There's another risk I want to take."

I blushed. "What is it?" I asked, already knowing the answer.

He leaned closer and planted his lips on mine. I kissed him back and gently placed my hand on his cheek as he wrapped his arms around my waist. When we parted, he bit his lip. "I've wanted to do that for so long."

I pulled him into another kiss, my heart beating faster and faster. But when a knock came at the door, my heart dropped, wishing that moment could've lasted longer.

The door swung open, and I turned to see Lydia standing in the doorway. She looked a little happier than she had the last time we saw her. But she just lost her brother, her only family, so how happy could she be?

Lydia held up her wrist, showing off the crescent moon tattoo. "I was accepted."

"That's great, Lydia," I said, and pulled her into a hug.

"Yeah," she said, and tucked her long hair behind her ear. "I didn't want to be alone, and you guys are the only real friends I have. So I thought, why not?"

When she stepped back, I noticed the whites of her eyes were red. She'd obviously been crying a lot.

Out of the corner of my eye, I saw a figure standing in the doorway. "Crispin," Pierce said. "Can we talk outside for a sec?" The hood of his jacket was up over his head, probably to avoid being recognized.

Lydia kissed my cheek. "I'll see you later," she said.

"I'm going to unpack."

I turned to Eden, who was already heading for the door. "It's okay. We'll talk later."

Pierce had terrible timing. I watched as Eden left the room, and turned my attention to the man in my doorway. Then I wondered if he'd accept Lydia too. She came to Bristol Manor to be with friends. How could we leave her behind?

I wasn't sure he'd take Eden, but I knew there was no way I'd leave without the two of them, no matter how bad things were at the Wolf House. If Pierce wanted me in his pack badly enough, he'd have no choice but to accept them.

"All right," I said with a sigh. "Let's get this over with."

CHAPTER THIRTY-FOUR

Pierce led me down the driveway, and I shivered as the temperature dropped. His car was parked at the side of the road, and we stood next to it. "Have you thought about it?" he asked. "Have you come to a decision?"

I lowered my head. "Not yet," I admitted. "I mean, kind of."

He furrowed his brow. "Well, which is it?"

I sighed, suddenly wishing I had a few more days to think things over. "Would you let anyone else into your pack?"

"Crispin—"

"Even though I'm still upset about Kaiden, I think I'd go with you if you accepted Eden and Lydia as well."

Pierce tilted his head in confusion. "Who is Lydia?"

I shifted uncomfortably on my feet. "She's just a friend."

He raised his eyebrows. "I see."

"It's not like that," I said. I brought my hands up to my face and groaned. "I'm not leaving Bristol Manor without them." I tried to keep my voice calm and steady. "If you want me, you have to take them too."

Pierce shook his head and crossed his arms. "Buddy, you're more powerful than they are. You think I let just anyone join my pack? I don't. I want only the best. The strongest, the fastest, the smartest."

I was getting annoyed now and stomped my foot in frustration. "You had no idea if Kaiden was going to survive, and you let him join."

"Crispin—"

"How do you even know I'm so powerful?" I asked, looking him up and down. "We barely know each other, and you don't know anything about me."

He stared blankly at me. "I saw what you did to the SFT," he said. "A normal newly-bitten werewolf wouldn't have been able to do that. And I knew you'd be powerful because lycanthropy is in your blood."

"What do you mean?"

Pierce paced in front of me, his hand under his chin as he spoke. "If you were to have children, by the time they turned eighteen, they would change naturally without the bite. And the same goes for you. Without the bite, you would have turned by eighteen, but I couldn't wait that long. I needed to turn you now."

"I don't understand," I said, knitting my eyebrows.

"Why do you need me right now?"

Pierce's eyes grew dark and serious. "There is a war coming," he said slowly and stopped in front of me. "We need the best on our side if we—"

"You want me to fight in a war? I'm fifteen!"

"Crispin," he said, his tone a bit softer. "I can't talk about this now, especially not here. I've already told you more than I should have." He ran a hand through his hair. "I'll answer all of your questions another time, but not when we're this close to the Elders."

I stared at him, unsure how to respond. What was he talking about? "How do I have lycanthropy in my blood? And how could you know?"

He took a deep breath. "You have it in your blood because I have it in mine."

My mind was racing, and Pierce wasn't making any sense. "Was it transferred through the bite?"

He shook his head and looked into my eyes. "You're my son, Crispin."

I swallowed hard, his last sentence repeating in my mind. My limbs went numb as I turned and walked away, anger pulsating throughout my body. I didn't look back when he called after me.

ACKNOWLEDGEMENTS

I would like to thank Chloe for supporting me in her own special way, my dad for always believing in me, and the fur babies who have helped me write and edit this book over the years: Fluffy, Sid, Loki, and Ashes.

Also Tiffany, Karen, and Ray, who read the story first, Megan, for being an enthusiastic editing buddy, and everyone at Fractured Mirror for all the amazing work they've done: Emily, Alex, and Allison.

And the rest of my friends and family.

ADAM ZAYNE WHITENER lives in Louisville, Kentucky with his daughter, their rescue cat, a loveable pit bull, and a toy poodle. He's been writing stories since the age of seven, and has dreamed of being an author since he was twelve. In high school, he played clarinet in marching

 band, was a member of the French, club, and winter guard. When he isn't writing or reading, he loves to travel and explore new places, especially caves. WEREWOLVES OF BRISTOL MANOR is his first novel.

CPSIA information can be obtained
at www.ICGtesting.com
Printed in the USA
BVHW090852140621
609525BV00010B/334/J